MELISSA ADDEY

THE FLIGHT OF BIRDS

· THE COLOSSEUM SERIES ·

For my Mamma, an extraordinary storyteller,
who left her life in Rome for a farm with strawberry grapes.

Have you read the Moroccan Empire series? Pick up the first in the series FREE from my website www.MelissaAddey.com and join my Readers' Group, so you will be notified about new releases.

A gifted healer. An impossible vow. An empire's destiny.

11th century North Africa. Hela has powers too strong for a child – both to feel the pain of those around her and to heal them. But when she is given a mysterious cup by a slave woman, its powers overtake her life, forcing her into a vow she cannot hope to keep.

Trapped by her vow, Hela loses one chance after another to love and be loved. Meanwhile, in her household, a child is born. Zaynab will one day become Morocco's queen and Hela's actions are already shaping her destiny.

Can a great healer ever heal her own wounds? Will Hela turn her back on her vow or follow it through to the bitter end? And will her choices forever warp the character of Morocco's greatest queen, and so shape the destiny of a future empire?

The Cup **is the magical prequel novella to the Moroccan Empire historical fiction series. If you enjoy exploring forgotten histories, the interwoven stories of women and emotional destinies then you will be gripped by this dramatic novella.**

Travel back to the beginnings of a legendary empire. Download your free copy of *The Cup* **today.**

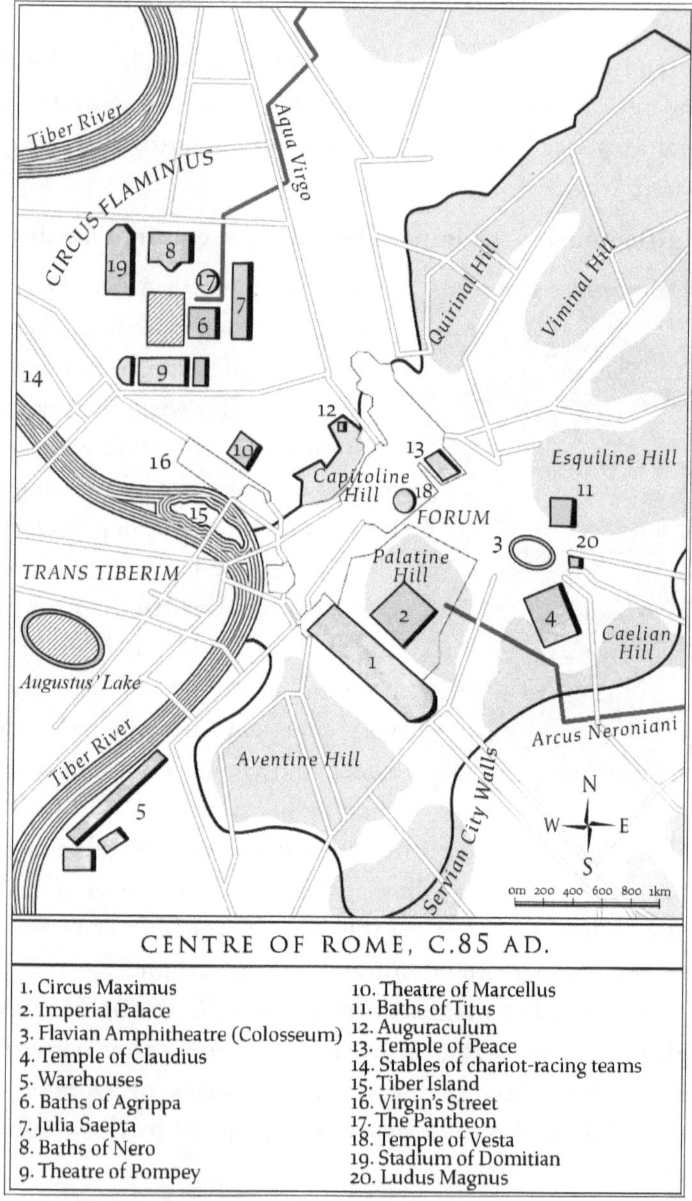

CENTRE OF ROME, C.85 AD.

*This map shows the locations of some of the places Domitian began building at this time, such as the Imperial Palace and the Stadium of Domitian, as well as the Ludus Magnus. The Ludus Matutinus would have been close to the Ludus Magnus.

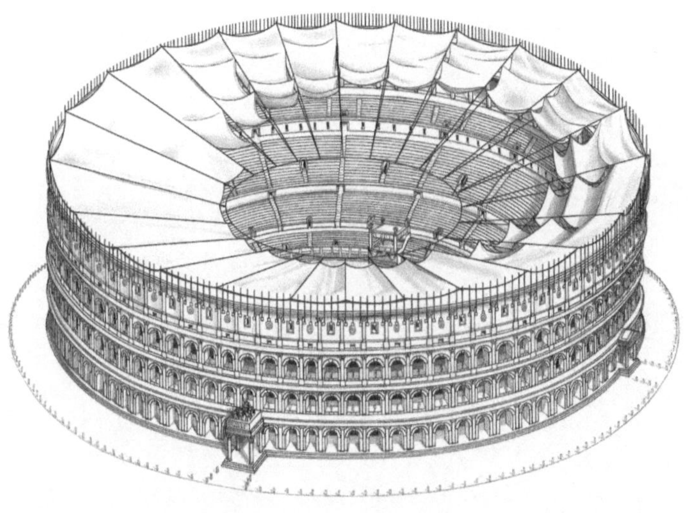

The Flavian Amphitheatre

HISTORICAL BACKGROUND TO 82AD

IN 66AD THE ROMAN PROVINCE of Judea rebelled against Roman rule and drove the Romans out. Fearful that this might spark further rebellions in other provinces of the Empire, Emperor Nero recalled General Vespasian from exile (punishment for falling asleep during a poetry reading by Nero) and sent Vespasian and his son Titus to quell the rebellion. This took four years, one quarter of the entire Roman army and ended in Titus' troops looting and burning the Temple of Jerusalem in 70AD. Hundreds of thousands of Jews were killed or enslaved during this period.

Emperor Nero died in 68AD, the last emperor of the Julian-Claudian dynasty. His reign started well but his later years were tainted by extravagance and cruelty, which mainly affected the aristocracy. He remained popular among the lower classes who made up the majority of the population. Nero had a large area of central Rome cleared to create his Golden House, a vast palace complex with a lake. There were rumours that the Great Fire of 64AD had been deliberately started by him to enable this project.

The Year of the Four Emperors followed Nero's death, culminating in Vespasian taking power in 69AD and founding the Flavian dynasty, which lasted twenty-seven years. He was the first emperor to come from the Equestrian rather than Senatorial rank and he set in motion a large number of building works, including the Flavian Amphitheatre, known to us as the Colosseum, which was located on Nero's now drained lake and largely paid for with loot from the Temple and the sale of Jewish slaves. Vespasian died in June 79AD and was succeeded by his son Titus.

In October 79AD, Mount Vesuvius erupted, destroying multiple cities including Pompeii. In spring and summer of 80AD, Rome suffered first a "pestilence" (possibly malaria) in which 10,000 people died, and then a three-day fire. The Flavian Amphitheatre was inaugurated that summer, with 100 days of consecutive Games including water-based spectacles, for which they flooded the arena. Titus ruled for only two years before he died, possibly of a brain tumour. He was succeeded by his younger brother Domitian in September 81AD.

ROME, OCTOBER 82AD

THE FLIGHT OF BIRDS

"Come on, then," says Marcus. "Let's get it over with."

"Will he be angry, do you think?" I ask. I try to rearrange Marcus' toga, which is sitting poorly on his shoulder, the heavy fabric in a scruffy bunch instead of neat folds. He makes an irritable face. He hates wearing a toga, but it's appropriate for a meeting with Domitian. I'm dressed well too, my best headwrap and tunic, my shoes shined.

"Probably," he says with a weary sigh. "He thinks we're fixtures, that we'll never leave. He won't be pleased. But the contract's up, we're free to go."

"What if he refuses?"

"We'll have to try and persuade him. Otherwise we'll be stuck in Rome managing the Games forever and neither of us wants that."

I try to cheer him up. "Maybe he'll be glad to see the back of us and we can leave as soon as we like."

Marcus smiles at the thought, pulls me close to him for a kiss. "Yes," he says. "Let's hope so. We can spend the winter getting ourselves ready, then head to the farm in the springtime. I can't wait to reclaim it."

We set off, making our way down the wooden staircase into

the courtyard below, then pause at Cassia's for breakfast. Marcus has his usual bread and cheese, while I ask for pancakes with date syrup. We're joined by sleepy-eyed Karbo, our adopted son, who wolfs three pancakes in the time it takes me to eat one.

"Stables?" asks Marcus.

"New horse," he mumbles through a mouthful of pancake.

"You helping to train him?"

He nods and swallows, his eyes opening wider. "He's so beautiful. But you can hardly get a harness on him before he's off and running."

"Sounds suited to the races," comments Cassia's husband Quintus, who is helping out at the counter, serving wine and platters of fresh bread and fruit rolls, still warm from the bakery next door.

Karbo shakes his head, earnest. "You can't just let him run. He's got to be more aware of the drivers, or he'll miss their cues."

The racing drivers wrap the long reins round their waists, then steer with their bodies, which means the horses have to be responsive to small movements, not just run wildly down the long track of the Circus Maximus.

Marcus pats him on the back. "Spoken like a true racing expert," he says. "I'm sure you'll be an excellent trainer as you grow to manhood."

"The best trainers were drivers in their youth," says Karbo in a hopeful tone.

"And most of the drivers never made old age," says Marcus. "Come on, Althea."

I gulp the last piece of my pancake and drink some fresh grape juice, hug Karbo and follow Marcus, waving to Cassia.

"Good luck," she calls. "May Janus be with you!"

I wave again and trot after Marcus. "You walk too fast," I say.

"You have to slow down when you have a bride-to-be walking with you."

"You managed to keep up when you were my humble scribe."

"A humble scribe is not allowed to question the length of her master's stride."

He slows, grinning. "I'm not sure you were ever humble. But I will do anything for your happiness. Even taking tiny steps."

All too soon the imperial palace looms over us, white and forbidding. The guards make an uninterested gesture to usher us in and we wait on the cold marble benches in the atrium to be summoned.

"Marcus Aquillius Scaurus."

"That'll be us then," whispers Marcus. "Janus, watch over us."

Domitian is seated at a small elegant wooden desk with two scribes in attendance, as well as three guards stationed around the room. He seems engrossed in reading a scroll. The Aedile, the senator supposedly in charge of the Games, is also present, already looking more anxious than usual. My eyes dart to the corner of the room where, as expected, is Gaius Petronius Stephanus, still and quiet in the shadows, as ever. I have never been informed as to what exactly his role is, but he seems to be one of the only people who can manage Domitian's sometimes odd behaviour. His head gives a tiny inclination when my gaze meets his. The other person in the room is an augur, one of the priests who can read the flights of birds and divine from them whether the gods are pleased or displeased with the plans of mere mortals. The augur is dressed in a white senatorial tunic, over which is the vivid toga of his office, in saffron yellow with purple stripes. In one hand he holds an augural wand, a carved piece of wood which starts straight but then curls in a spiral at the end.

He has pulled the toga up so it covers his head, which, combined with his self-satisfied air, is making him look somewhat like a male bird about to engage in a mating dance. I look away from him in case I get a fit of the giggles.

"Yes?" says Domitian to Marcus without looking up from the scroll. He is not one for niceties, rarely bothering with even basic greetings.

Marcus is on his best behaviour. "Imperator, as the Aedile will have already informed you, I am to be married and wish to return to my family's farm in the countryside outside Puteoli. My contract as Manager of the Games at the Flavian Amphitheatre has expired. I have been honoured by the opportunity to create Games for the imperial amphitheatre and your illustrious family, but I humbly beg leave to hand in my notice and pass on the role to a worthy replacement of your choosing."

"No," says Domitian.

"Imperator?"

Domitian finally looks up and raises his voice as though Marcus is deaf. "No. I am happy with you as the Manager and your –" he glances at me "– wife-to-be as your assistant. I have been pleased with your work. I do not wish you to leave. You will remain."

Marcus looks towards the Aedile for help, but the Aedile only twists his hands and avoids making eye contact. "Imperator, my contract is complete and I –"

"NO!" screams Domitian.

The guards, startled, pull out their swords, ready to attack, then realise Domitian is only angry and put them back in their scabbards, looking confused.

The Aedile takes a tiny step forwards, his body tight with

fear. "Imperator, I can assure you that I will procure the services of another, equally excellent Manager for the Games and that –"

But Domitian is on his feet, his usually ruddy face scarlet with rage. He grabs at the desk and hurls it to one side with enormous force, so that it skids across the polished marble floor and smashes into a wall, one leg breaking off in splinters. "THERE WILL BE NO CHANGE TO THE STAFF OF THE AMPHITHEATRE!" he screams, his voice echoing around the room. He comes closer to Marcus, stands a hand's breadth from his face and speaks so fast it is hard to understand him. "The augurs have spoken and they are certain, there must be no change of management of the amphitheatre or the gods will be displeased, furthermore I do not wish any such changes to be made and as your emperor and master, there is nothing further to be said. You will sign this document." He grabs a scroll from one of the scribes, crumpling it as he does so and thrusts it into Marcus' face. "And you will continue to serve as Manager of the Games." He strides across the room, pulls a sword from the scabbard of the nearest guard and points it at Marcus' throat. "If you refuse to do this, make no mistake, you will find yourself *and* your wife in the arena and you will not leave it alive. I will have you both crucified for treason against Rome. I do not wish you to leave, so you WILL. NOT. LEAVE."

"Ahem." Stephanus has left his post in the corner and is standing to one side of Domitian, calm despite Domitian's scarlet face and heaving chest, the shaking tip of the sword resting in the hollow of Marcus' neck.

I wonder for a terrible moment if the Emperor of Rome is about to cry. Domitian is like a small child who does not get their way and has a tantrum. Marcus is keeping perfectly still, giving no cause for Domitian to be angrier than he already is.

"I feel that it would be best if we were to adjourn this meeting," says Stephanus smoothly. "There is a great deal to discuss, many minor administrative details to be covered and we do not want the meeting to grow over-long and tiring for all concerned. Would you all please excuse us, so that the Emperor may collect his thoughts? I will send someone to fetch you from the atrium as soon as we are ready to continue."

"Of-of course," stammers the Aedile, scurrying out of the room as fast as he can, swiftly followed by the scribes and the augur, who all look petrified.

I put my hand on Marcus' arm. "We will await your command, Imperator," I say, trying to keep my voice from shaking. Marcus steps slowly back, the wavering tip of the sword a hand's breadth from his throat, then another step, his eyes lowered so as not to meet Domitian's gaze. Domitian remains in the same position, sword outstretched, his eyes glittering with unshed tears, face flushed.

"You may also leave," says Stephanus to the guards. "Please take your weapon with you," he adds to the guard whose sword Domitian is holding, as though the guard had somehow chosen to leave it in the Emperor's hand as a useful resting place.

Marcus and I continue edging backwards to the door behind us as the terrified guard eases the sword from Domitian, who lets it go without a struggle. The guard replaces it in his scabbard, salutes and backs away, reaching us as we get to the door. My last glimpse of Domitian is of him standing very still in the room, one hand at his mouth as though biting his fist, Stephanus standing by him as though faintly interested in something they are both looking at in companionable silence.

We close the door and I lean against Marcus, shaking. He

wraps his arms around me, speaks over my head to the Aedile in a furious whisper.

"What in Hades was that about? I thought you warned him!"

"I did." The Aedile grovels, wringing his hands. "He was calm when I mentioned it. Nodded and sent me on my way."

The scribes and guards are huddled in a corner, all of them pale. The augur, however, is all but preening.

"It is as the birds foretold," he says. "A highly inauspicious moment."

"Fuck off," says Marcus. "You and your stupid birds. He nearly killed me!" Pressed up against his body, I can feel he, too, is shaking.

The augur looks put out but is not getting any support from the rest of us. "The birds show the will of the gods," he mutters.

"They show whatever you want them to show according to who briefed you," spits Marcus. I've rarely seen him this angry and I put my hand on his chest.

"Let's walk in the Forum."

"What if he calls for you?" asks the Aedile.

"He's not going to calm himself that fast," I point out. "Come," I add to Marcus.

I get water from a fountain, walk us around the busy Forum until Marcus has calmed down.

"He's never going to let us go, is he?" he says.

"Stephanus will do something," I say.

"Do you trust him?"

"I have to hope I can. No-one else has a chance of getting through to Domitian."

"What if we're stuck running the Games forever?"

"We'll find a way," I say. "And even if we are, we have each other and that matters more than anything."

He squeezes my hand. "It does. But I want to get out of here."

We spend more time in the sunshine to steady our nerves, then return to the atrium to wait. The scribes, guards and augur have all gone, only the Aedile remains, seated alone on a bench, his expression forlorn.

"How did he ever get the role of Aedile for the Games?" I whisper to Marcus as we rejoin him.

We wait. And wait. More than three hours pass. My stomach begins to rumble for food, made worse part way through by two slave girls passing us, one with a platter of fresh bread with olives and a dipping sauce, the other with delicately cut fruits laid out on an elegant silver tray and a jug of wine. They both head into the room where we saw Domitian.

At last the door opens and Stephanus appears. "Would you join us, please?"

There's a new table in the room; the smashed desk has been removed. On this new table is a large model of the Flavian Amphitheatre, the width of a man's outstretched arms. But this amphitheatre has a very different appearance to the one I am accustomed to. Around the top tier, vertical wooden poles are set at regular intervals, from which an intricate rigging system of thin cords spans out, holding in place a red awning made of strips of linen, covering the whole of the amphitheatre apart from an open circle in the centre which is held in place by a ring of metal, the size of a man's fist.

Domitian is leaning over the model, closely inspecting it.

"Marcus Aquilius Scaurus and Althea Aquilius," announces Stephanus, as though the whole meeting is beginning again. "And the Aedile of the Games."

"Imperator," we chorus together.

Domitian looks up. His face has returned to its usual complexion and he nods as though he has very little idea of who we are.

"I have suggested a solution to the Emperor which he has found acceptable," says Stephanus. "Marcus Aquillius Scaurus will complete one more season of the Games, during which time we will find someone to continue the role for the foreseeable future, thus avoiding any further changes in staff and releasing Scaurus from his service to the imperial amphitheatre at the end of the season."

Marcus' eyes don't even flicker. "As you command, Imperator," he says, looking at Domitian.

Domitian looks away, as though interested in a marble column on the far side of the room. "I have three additional tasks," he says. "You must carry them out also."

"Imperator?"

"I want a velarium to protect spectators from the sun and an extra tier of seating adding to the amphitheatre. I want you to manage a private event at my villa in the Alban Hills. And I want a naumachia." He pauses, then, like a child forced to apologise, adds in a rush, "And then you will be dismissed from imperial service and be free to go."

"I am honoured to be of service," says Marcus.

Domitian glances at him, then points to the striped awning on the model. "The first task will be to install the additional seating and the velarium in the Flavian Amphitheatre," he says.

We approach the table and look at the model. The strips of red cloth are stretched out across the cord structure, like sails laid horizontally rather than vertically, secured in the centre by the metal circlet, and held in place at the outer edges by the poles.

"Pull those." Domitian points at the ends of the cords. He grasps two himself and Marcus and I each copy his movements. Six sections of the cloth awning move back from the centre circle towards the poles, as though we were lowering sails, each section of cloth folding in on itself until half of the amphitheatre's roof awning is left, the other half open to the sky.

"You can pull back all of it or parts of it, depending where the sun is coming from," says Domitian. "And when the whole thing is fully open, it creates a pool of light in the centre of the arena which draws the crowd's attention to whatever you want them to look at."

Marcus nods, but he looks troubled. "And those are…?" he asks, pointing at the now-revealed interior of the top tier of the building. This is where the women and slaves sit but above the current stone terraces of seating, there is an additional wooden structure.

"Additional seating," says Domitian. "The amphitheatre is proving very popular, even among women. Tickets to the Games are also a good way of rewarding slaves for diligent work. The slaves can be packed in tightly in the new wooden seats allowing more space for women on the stone terraces. They're very steeply raked."

Marcus draws a deep breath. I can see he's holding back but I know what he's thinking.

"Is there a timescale for the works, Imperator?" I ask.

"The tiers and awning to be ready for the start of the season," says Domitian.

"Our current team are not accustomed to that kind of

rigging," says Marcus, choosing his words with care. "It may take time to –"

"You'll use sailors," says Domitian. "The amphitheatre will be assigned two hundred sailors from the barracks at Misenum. They will travel here just before the start of each season in March or April, stay in their own barracks at the docks and be dismissed back to Misenum at the end of the season in October or November. The carpenters for the poles and wooden seating tiers have already been commissioned. They start work next week. The rigging and awning will be delivered in mid-March, which gives you two weeks to put it in place and practise using it with the sailors. They are accustomed to putting up and taking down sails. It's the same principle. Any other questions?"

We both know better than to question him.

"No, Imperator," we chorus.

"Excellent," says Domitian. "Now I wish to talk about the private spectacle at my villa in the Alban Hills."

"What kind of spectacle, Imperator?" Marcus asks.

"Gladiatorial Games. I have a five-hundred-seater amphitheatre being built there by my architect Rabirius. It will be completed by June and I'd like it inaugurated in style."

"Absolutely," says Marcus. "We will devise something spectacular."

"So that being all in hand, let's discuss the naumachia," says Domitian, giving one of his odd smiles, teeth bared.

I can actually hear Marcus swallow. "The amphitheatre can no longer be flooded, Imperator, the new underfloor hypogeum does not allow for –"

"Not at the amphitheatre. In Augustus' lake."

"In what?"

Domitian waves us over to another table set at the back of

the room, on top of which is the model of Rome we saw last year. He points to a large circle painted blue and surrounded by a low wall, situated just over the river from our own insula. "Augustus' lake. He held a naumachia there to celebrate the victory of Actium. It will need digging out again, of course. Silt and earth will have built up. It will need a wall to surround it and seating. I want a naumachia held there this summer. Bigger and better." He flashes his odd smile again, teeth bared, eyes glinting.

For a moment I think Marcus is going to refuse, but no doubt he is thinking of how it felt to be held at sword point by an apoplectic Emperor of Rome. "As you command, Imperator," he manages. "Perhaps July would be a suitable month? For the best weather?"

"Yes," says Domitian. He looks at the circle. "I believe there are drainage systems and an aqueduct that supplies it. You'll need to bring ships in."

"We will look into everything, Imperator."

I can tell Marcus just wants to get out of here, before Domitian comes up with any other odd requests which will require months of planning to pull off. Perhaps Stephanus is thinking the same thing, because he intervenes.

"You will need to start planning at once," he says. "The Emperor will permit you to leave. It is excellent to have come to an understanding."

Marcus bows his head. "Imperator."

We get as far as the door when Domitian speaks again. "I will visit your animals soon."

"Certainly," says Marcus, hovering on the threshold, his expression growing ever more fixed. "Did you have any particular animal in mind?"

Domitian considers. "Zebras," he says at last.

Marcus takes a couple of steps backwards, desperate to leave. "We look forward to your visit, Imperator."

Domitian nods, losing interest in us. He turns back towards his model and we leave the room, then walk fast away from the palace until we reach a quietish street where we can talk. Our pace finally slows.

"Thank Jupiter we got out of there alive," I say.

"So much for Janus watching over us," mutters Marcus.

"Shh," I say. "Don't anger him."

"I'd have liked a better start to our plans to leave Rome than to be forced to stay another year. And three additional tasks? What does he think this is, some old legend where we have to set out on a quest to please the gods by proving our heroism?"

I can't help but giggle, the fear of the past few hours and the relief of no harm coming to Marcus bursting out. I squat down, face in my hands, and laugh until I'm spent.

"I'm glad you're taking it so well," says Marcus when I finally stop.

"I was terrified," I say. "He's so unpredictable."

"He's losing his mind," says Marcus. "Let's hope he keeps it for one more year so we can get out of here safely."

"He assumes we have animals all year round," I say as we begin walking again.

Marcus shakes his head. "Zebras," he sighs. "At this time of year. Couldn't wait till we're in full Games season and have most things ready to hand?"

I don't think emperors care about that sort of thing," I say. "They want things when they want them. They don't wait, like the rest of us. What will it be like putting on private Games at his villa?"

"I'm less worried about that. Games are Games. We do them

all the time. We just find a good theme, pack up everyone who has to perform and take them all to the Alban Hills. It's a day's travel out of Rome."

I nod. "At least one of the tasks is straightforward."

Marcus stops by a fountain to drink and sits on the edge of it. "And another naumachia. Have we offended Poseidon, that we're cursed to put on a water show again?"

"How big does the lake have to be?"

"Big," says Marcus grimacing. "We'll be using real boats, not show boats. Full size."

"We will have two hundred sailors at our command," I say.

"Unless they're busy messing with the velarium's rigging. And what will their commander say when he loses two hundred of his men to the Games for a whole spring and summer?"

"Not our problem."

Marcus laughs and puts an arm about my shoulders. "You're right," he says. "I have you and that's all that matters. Just promise me we're not doing Hero and Leander again for the naumachia. Also, no crocodiles."

"No crocodiles," I say. "A safe, sunny naumachia. Big boats, lots of sailors, impressive fight scenes and we can all go home happy."

"That sounds perfect. I've had enough for one day. Let's go to the baths."

Safely back at the insula, we find our landlady Julia passing the time of day with Maria and Adah, the three older women sitting in the autumn sunshine together.

"You're back soon," says Maria. "Good news? Are you free?"

"I'm afraid not," I say.

"Sit," says Julia, pouring us each a cup of wine and pushing it towards us.

Marcus regales them with a description of Domitian losing his mind over our possible departure.

"And afterwards he was all calm? Just like that? After threatening to kill you?" asks Julia.

"Yes, but it took Stephanus a few hours and some food and drink," I say.

"That family are all monsters underneath," says Adah darkly. She hated Domitian's brother Titus for destroying the Temple of Jerusalem, and is quite ready to believe that Domitian is not to be trusted either.

"Time to rest," says Marcus. "Come."

We take our bed mats out onto the rooftop and lie in the sun. The shakiness of the morning is still in my limbs. "He said he would crucify us in the arena," I say, shuddering.

"Crucifixion is dull," says Marcus. "It isn't suitable for spectacle in the Games. They faint from the pain and just hang there. Doesn't work in the arena."

He's right. Crucifixion is mostly used as a deterrent along the roads in and out of Rome, where the hanging half-dead bodies remind Rome's slaves, pirates and state enemies of the kind of death they will endure, should they challenge the empire's laws and might. It is one of the most humiliating and painful deaths imaginable but it's mainly used for treasonous offences against the empire. "It's hardly treason to want to resign."

"I do wonder about his sanity." Marcus shakes his head. "He was so angry he could have killed me, I could see it in his eyes. And a few hours later, completely calm, as though nothing had happened."

"You really think he consulted the augur about who should

run the amphitheatre?" I turn onto my side to look at him. "I didn't think he'd consult them for things like that. Weddings and wars and appointing important officials, yes, but can't he just decide for himself when it comes to people like us?"

Marcus rolls his eyes.

"You don't believe the augur?" I ask. Marcus sacrifices at temples on appropriate occasions and has to my knowledge attended at least two augury sessions to bear witness that the omens were right for a wedding.

He shrugs. "In the army there's a pullarius, who looks after the sacred chickens. Before a battle, he'll open their cage and throw bread at them. If they refuse to eat, the omens are unfavourable."

"And?"

Marcus grins. "You can't have an unfavourable omen just before you send men into battle, it takes the spirit out of them. When I served in the army our pullarius once told me if he needed a favourable omen, he'd starve the chickens for a couple of days before the battle. They'd come rushing out, eager to eat everything in sight. They'd get a big cheer from the men. Made them feel invincible."

"And if the battle didn't go well?"

He raises his eyebrows. "Imagine how much worse it would have been, if the sacred chickens had decided it was unfavourable."

"Surely the priests of Rome are better augurs than some drunken soldier on a tour of duty? They can't control the flight of wild birds in the way your pullarius controlled chickens."

Marcus grimaces. "Wouldn't put it past them. They'll do anything to give the answer that's desired."

"But it depends on high or low the birds fly, which direction they come from, all sorts of things."

"You put on a show at the amphitheatre every day," says Marcus. "Are you telling me you couldn't arrange for birds to behave how you wanted them to, if you had to? Remember the coloured doves?"

I think back to the opening ceremony of the amphitheatre years ago, when we dyed five hundred white doves every possible bright colour and set them free just as the ceremony completed, the crowd murmuring approval at what they saw as a good omen. "I suppose you're right," I say.

"And how did we get them to fly high?"

"Released them low," I say.

"Exactly. Release them low with nowhere to go but up if they want to leave the amphitheatre. And if I'd wanted it to look unfavourable, I'd have trained them beforehand, released them high and had their feeding spot and nests down low."

"Don't let a priest hear you or we'll get hired to run the augury instead of the amphitheatre," I say.

"Oh, I'm sure they already have a team like ours, doing just that." He sighs. "We have no choice. One more season and Domitian's three ridiculous tasks. I'm sorry, my love, I know you are tired of the amphitheatre. Shall I run it alone this year? You can stay clear of it."

"What would I do all day?"

"Spend time with Cassia. Plan for the farm. Enjoy some freedom. I've worked you hard all these years. Now that you're about to be my wife I'd like you to enjoy yourself. You'll be working hard enough when we finally do get back to the farm. At least with the amphitheatre there's an off season and you come home at night. On a farm there is no off season and all sorts happen at night."

"Such as?"

"Animals being born. Storms so you have to rush out and clear ditches to avoid floods, lost livestock you have to go searching for before the wolves get to them..."

I nod. "It would be nice to rest, I suppose, but..."

"But?"

"I'd miss you," I say. "I'm used to seeing you every day and the times when – when things have not been well between us and we didn't see or speak much to one another I hated being distant from you."

He pulls me close to him. "I wish you'd told me sooner. The time we've wasted."

I rest my head on his chest, wrap my arms around him. "The gods chose their moment."

He tightens his hold. "Thanks be to Venus and Juno for bringing you to me."

SONGBIRDS

I WAKE EARLY BUT MARCUS HAS already gone somewhere. He doesn't appear until well after breakfast, carrying something by a metal loop. The package is covered in a large cloth, swaying gently from his hand. Karbo and I follow him across the rooftop.

"What is it?"

"Open it," he says, setting it on the ground. "A gift for my bride-to-be."

I pull away the cloth, unveiling a large birdcage which is divided into two halves. On one side are two nightingales. In the other part, crushed together, are six doves.

"Doves for Venus that she may bless our marriage," says Marcus. "Nightingales so they can sing to you. I'll build larger cages for them, now I've got them home."

Karbo pokes his finger through the slats, touching the doves' delicate feathers. They huddle together, resisting his curiosity.

"They're lovely. Thank you." I wrap my arms around his neck.

"Not more *kissing*," groans Karbo.

I laugh and come to coo at the doves, while Marcus goes to get his tools. He builds a large cage for the nightingales, so that they can hop about and sing, and a pen for the doves. They submit to having their wings clipped, which does not hurt them.

"When they're tame enough you can set them free and they'll always come home," says Marcus. "We'll need to clip their wings for a few months until they are certain of where to come back to. Then they can grow back their feathers and fly again."

The doves flutter but cannot take off. Karbo and I feed them grain, which they are greedy for.

"I'm sorry their wings must be clipped," I say.

"It is only for a while," says Marcus.

"The doves and I are both held here for a while," I say.

"And one day soon you will all be free to fly wherever you wish," he promises me.

The nightingales do not sing at once. They chirp and hop about but keep their songs to themselves, timid of their new home. I will cover their cage at night to keep their little bodies warm in the cooler nights of winter.

Marcus plans to travel south to Puteoli before the cold days of November arrive.

"Domitian may insist on us staying in Rome for one more year," he says, "but I can't wait any longer to secure our farm. I have the money. It would be foolish to risk losing it at the last moment if someone else buys it before us."

"How long will you be gone?"

"Perhaps ten days. Plenty of time for you to fuss about with wedding plans," he adds grinning.

"*I* don't want to hear about wedding plans for ten days." Karbo grimaces. "Can I come to Puteoli too?"

"You're staying here to look after Althea," says Marcus. "You are the man of the house while I'm gone. Can I rely on you?"

Karbo grows a hand's breadth as he stands at his full height. "Of course," he says with pride.

"Good lad. Look at the height of you. You'll be a man soon." Marcus shakes his head and strokes Karbo's soft locks.

It's odd to see Marcus riding away down Sand Street; we have not been apart for ten days since we first met three years ago, that strange day when I was gifted to him as a slave. So much has changed. I wave him off, then, determined to keep busy in his absence, talk to Cassia about food for the wedding.

"Cream pudding," says Karbo more than once.

"I heard you first time," I say. "What else?"

"Cream pudding."

"For every course?"

"Yes, please."

I poke his belly. "Never mind your height, you'll be round like an amphora if you eat as much cream pudding as you're planning to."

"What else are weddings good for?"

"The blessings of the gods?"

"Not as good as cream pudding," says Karbo in a stage whisper.

"Be careful or they'll hear you."

The food left in Cassia's capable hands, I spend the first day sewing my white wedding tunic by Maria's side at her established watching spot on the balcony overlooking the courtyard. We observe the usual comings and goings below us, pass the time of day with our neighbours and by the end of the day my tunic is ready. There is another task I need to complete before the wedding, but I'm uncertain of how to proceed. I make my way to Julia's apartment and she welcomes me.

"Excited about the wedding?"

"Yes," I say, "but before that I have to complete the ceremony of childhood toys and I don't have any toys from my childhood."

"Quintus could carve you something," suggests Julia.

"But it won't really be mine."

She smiles. "It's symbolic," she says. "It is about your intention to leave behind your childhood and become a grown woman, not about what you take to the temple."

I'm reassured. If even a Vestal can see no harm in it, then it must be satisfactory. "Thank you, Julia. I'll ask him."

I get as far as the doorway when she calls me back. "Althea."

"Yes?"

"I will dress you on your wedding day."

I'm touched and a little honoured. "Thank you, I'm grateful."

She waves me away. "Go and find Quintus."

I make my way to Cassia's popina for breakfast and find Fabia amongst the other customers. Standing at the counter like most people do would mean her head would barely be level with her food, so she's sitting at one of the few inside tables, a better fit for her tiny frame. I greet Quintus, who is looking after Emilia. He's carving a small wooden horse, and she is imitating him, holding a little stick as a knife, pretending to whittle away at another piece of wood. I praise her imaginary creation and sit next to Fabia.

"Will you come with me to the temple before the wedding?" I ask her. "I have to give up my childhood toys."

She nods, busy munching on a fruit roll.

"You're always hungry," I say.

"Never get to eat when I'm working," she says her mouth full. "Too much going on."

"You're the head physician," I say. "Don't you get to make the rules about the work?"

"There's always something," she says. "If it isn't a gladiator getting hurt it's one of their women giving birth or Paternus wanting to borrow me for one of his gladiators."

"He'll poach you from Labeo if you're not careful," I say.

She grins and sips from her wine cup. "That might not be a bad thing. A step up in the world. Though I owe Labeo a lot and also, I'm happy to be treating women and dwarfs like myself, I understand them better than most physicians. No-one else cares much about them, they see them as second-class gladiators. You should see the kind of care Paternus' top gladiators get. They're practically nobility. Their own villas and slaves and daily massages, special training regimes developed just for them, making sure they're in tip-top condition for the big fights. I wouldn't want Labeo's gladiators to be forgotten if a new physician took my place."

"At least their status has been elevated by being part of Rome's second biggest school," I say.

Fabia takes another bite of her fruit roll. "So, the ceremony of childhood toys?"

"Yes. Quintus, I came to ask you if you could make me something. I don't have any toys from my childhood. Julia said it would be acceptable."

He looks up from his carving. "What toys did you have as a child, before you were taken as a slave? Can you remember any?"

I try to think. So little of my childhood stays in my memory. I remember hardly anything from before I was taken. "My father gave me quills to write with," I say. "But they weren't toys, he wanted me to be a scribe, knowing that would give me the chance of a better life."

Quintus nods. "I'll make something," he promises me. "When are you going?"

"I wanted to go the day after tomorrow," I say. "Is that too soon?"

He shakes his head. "I'll have something ready."

I'm curious as to what Quintus will come up with. He is already doing well in his apprenticeship for Balbus, carving beautiful toys and learning new skills in toymaking from Balbus and his wife Floriana, who is skilled at weaving and sewing and makes hair and clothes for dolls, manes for horses and tiny colourful woollen trims for everything from soft balls for babies to play with to elaborate feathered strings to amuse the pampered cats of the rich. Quintus already runs the shop by himself one day a week, giving the older couple a much-needed rest, and has even been on visits to the fancy villas on the hill to display the wares to the rich children of senators.

When I come down two days later, Quintus is waiting for me.

"I made you this for the offering," he says. He holds out a wooden doll which looks like a small child, dressed in the Greek fashion with strands of brown wool for hair. In her clasped-together hands she holds a bundle of quills nearly as long as her body.

"Thank you," I say. "She's so lovely. I don't want to give her up."

He laughs. "Then she is a good offering."

Fabia and I walk together to the Temple of Juno, both of us washed and dressed in our best tunics and embroidered headwraps, with colourful woven belts. The temple looms over us, vast columns making us feel small, wafting incense perfuming the air as we enter through the great doors behind many other women come to pray to the goddess of wives. I carry the little doll with me and when it is our turn to reach the altar, I place her there along with a basket of gilded pomegranates and dates, with laurel leaves for decoration. If I had been a summer bride I could have left flowers, but the fruits and foliage will have to do. I hold my hands out, palms up and begin my prayer of offering.

"Lady Juno, hear me. In this place, at this time, in preparation for my wedding day, I lay before you the toys of my childhood and leave behind my childish ways, to become a married woman. Accept my offering of fruits and leaves, that my marriage hearth may be bountiful under your care. I will strive to be a good wife in your image, Lady Juno, and ask for your blessings. Watch over me as I change from girl to woman, from bride to wife, from daughter to mother."

I bow my head and Fabia bows hers alongside me.

"Another wedding," she says, as we leave the temple. "First Cassia, now you, married off."

"Your turn next," I say. "That handsome assistant of yours, Sadiki, is he going to propose to you one of these days?"

Fabia's cheeks go pink. "What nonsense you talk," she mutters.

"Why not? He worships you."

"He respects me," she corrects. "I'm his master."

"Bet he'd like you to be something e-else," I sing-song to her.

"Never mind about that," she says, her cheeks going a deeper shade of pink. "Have you got your veil?"

"I'm wearing Cassia's, as you know full well. Stop changing the subject."

Fabia shakes her head. "I want to marry and have children," she admits. "But I don't want to stop being a physician. I love what I do and a husband would want me to be a wife, to look after our children."

"If he were a physician too he might understand," I say.

"Perhaps," she says. "But I fear not many men would allow such a thing, for their wife to be a physician after the marriage. And until I am sure, I will not risk it. I would have to be a physician in a greater role than I am now to command such respect and not have to give it up after marriage."

"Isn't physician to Labeo's gladiatorial school an important enough role?"

She shrugs. "It's good, but we're the second school. If I were physician to Paternus' school it would be grander."

"Or physician to the Flavian Amphitheatre?" I ask, smiling.

"Father's nabbed that one," she says. "But I'm standing by to inherit it when he retires. Which will be never," she adds. "Father loves his work too much. He'll still be stitching up gladiators years from now. Anyway," she adds, "enough of all this. I have a gift for you. It's a wedding gift but you should have it before the wedding. You will be in need of it right away once you are married."

Back at the insula, she brings me a carefully folded blue cloth. I shake it out to find that it is a beautifully woven and trimmed palla, the wrap that married women wear. I stroke the soft wool, admiring the rich dark blue, the green braid trim. "It's so pretty. Thank you."

"Can't have a married woman going about without a palla," says Fabia, satisfied. "It's a good one for winter, though you'll also need something lighter or you'll burn up in the summer."

I make my way up the stairs, passing Adah on her way to market.

"Almost time," she says.

I grin. "I'm glad you will be giving me away on my wedding day."

She pats my arm and makes her way carefully down the stairs, one tremulous hand clinging to the bannisters.

I'm on the rooftop cooing to the doves and trying to coax the nightingales to sing when I hear the clattering of hooves in the courtyard below and look over the bannisters to see Marcus dismounting, a full day earlier than expected. I run down the steps and fling myself into his arms.

"You're back early!"

"I missed you too much to dawdle," he says.

"Ah, young lovers," says Maria from her usual balcony perch above us. "Welcome home, Marcus."

"It will not be our home for much longer," says Marcus, grinning up at her.

"Did you secure the farm?" I ask. I've fretted over the past nine days that another buyer would have snapped it up from under our noses. Although there are plenty of other places we could find to buy, Marcus has his heart set on reclaiming his family's property, gambled away by his grandfather, thereby restoring their family honour.

"I've made a down payment with the agreement that the rest of the money will follow when they've undertaken some basic repairs to the roof, the courtyard walls and gate. That way, the winter won't cause any more damage to the interior from leaks. When we get there we'll still have to clean the place up and repaint it inside, but at least it'll be dry and wild animals won't be able to get into the courtyard."

"The farm is ours?"

He beams, tightens his arms about me. "It's ours," he says. "I hardly dared to believe it would still be there waiting for me. I didn't even dare say it out loud till just now. It's ours!"

"It rightly belongs to your family," I say. "The gods kept it for you."

"Bona Dea bless you both," says Maria.

Marcus nods, serious again. "I will give thanks at the temple," he says.

Celer appears from his room, nods towards the horse. "Welcome back. You must be tired from the ride, Marcus, shall I take him up to the stables for you?"

"I'd be grateful, thank you," says Marcus, giving Celer a quick embrace. The two of them go outside for a moment, then Marcus returns carrying his saddlebags slung over one shoulder.

"It will be a new start," I say. "We will have everything the way it used to be when you were a boy."

Marcus smiles, his eyes dreamy. "It was such a busy place. Always something happening. We'll have pigs and sheep, horses, chickens and doves. Bees. The old vineyard and the olive and fruit trees will need pruning to bring them back to fruitfulness, but we will have our own wine, our own oil. You can plant vegetables." He starts to lead the way up the stairs.

I laugh, following him. "I'll try. I know nothing about farming."

"You'll learn," he says. "You and Karbo managed to grow beans and salad on a rooftop in Rome. You'll be fine."

We wave to Maria as we pass her and climb to the rooftop, where we settle ourselves to enjoy the pale sunshine, resting our backs on the hut's wall.

"We need a proper pergola with a table and chairs up here," says Marcus. "There was one at the farm with the strawberry grape vine climbing all over it, but it'll need rebuilding."

"I wish everyone could come with us," I say, a wave of sadness rising up. "I'm going to miss them."

"We'll have Karbo." He thinks, his head on one side. "I might ask Strabo. He's a good man, he's been loyal and a hard worker at the amphitheatre but he was brought up on a farm. You could ask Adah if she wants to come and live there with us, look after the bees, enjoy the countryside."

I smile at the thought. "She'll say no," I predict. "She doesn't like change. But I'll ask her. I'll ask everyone."

"Anyone who wants to come from our insula is welcome," he says. "But we will have to say some goodbyes."

"I just want there to be as few as possible."

"It's only a few days' travel. You can come back to visit."

"I won't miss all of it. I'll be glad to leave the Games behind."

"Me too," he says. "I've seen enough of them to last me a lifetime. All I want is a quiet happy life on the farm with you at my side."

"I've been thinking while you were away," I say. "I don't want to sit idle while you run the Games and carry out Domitian's tasks. We've always run the Games together. It's only one more year and we should do it side by side, like always. The velarium and the seating will be done before the Games season opens anyway, so that's one task complete. We've done a naumachia before and it can't be as bad as the one in the amphitheatre. And like you said, Games in his villa can't be as difficult as the ones we put on every day in the season." I hug him tighter to me. "This time next year we'll be on our farm."

A GOLDEN VEIL

The weather in December is not looking promising for a wedding. Most days there is a fine drizzle. Once or twice there have been thunderstorms, rain running through the courtyard as though our fountain had leaked, creating little brooks that make their way out into Virgin's Street and join larger rivers out in Sand Street. They all go down to join the Tiber as it swells to its winter height. The nightgales sit silent, unwilling to sing while the doves huddle together for warmth. Our wedding will take place a week before the official Saturnalia period begins and each day we wake to gloomy skies while Cassia speaks confidently of decorations and the feast she will be preparing for our celebrations.

"What if it rains?" asks Karbo.

"It won't," says Marcus with supreme confidence.

"It's been raining for weeks," says Karbo.

"Tomorrow is too important," says Marcus.

"We can set up tables in the storage rooms," says Cassia, ever practical.

It's hard to get to sleep that night. I try to lie in silence, but after a while Marcus speaks.

"Are you still awake?"

"Yes."

"Nervous?"

I take his hand. "Not about marrying you. But the ceremony…"

He squeezes my hand, rolls onto his side so that he can kiss me. "It will be fun. Weddings are fun."

"You haven't gone to sleep either," I point out.

He chuckles. "You've caught me out. I knew I'd chosen a clever woman."

I nestle closer to him, wondering whether Livia has been on his mind. He must remember his first wedding. Livia's family did not much approve of her marrying a penniless wounded ex-centurion, a man descended from a grandfather who had lost everything, even the family farm, to a gambling addiction. But they were happy together. I remember his tenderness with her and I'm glad we are in the dark, because my eyes fill with sudden tears. I don't doubt that Marcus loves me. I don't feel second best to Livia, but the thought of Marcus' grief in losing the woman he loved as well as his baby son to the searing wrath of Vesuvius, now that I know what it is to love someone, is painful.

Perhaps he feels what I am thinking. "You have brought happiness back to my life," he says softly. "I thought I was content, with friends about me. But having you by my side is different. I feel whole again and I did not even know I was still broken."

My nervous excitement about tomorrow drifts away at his words. I inhale the warm scent of him, feel his skin against mine and sleep comes while I am safe in his arms and heart.

When I wake Marcus has already gone to the augurs to get the blessings of the gods from the bird omens, as required for a wedding, whatever his own views on their accuracy. Anxious, I check the sky, but we have already been blessed. Although the air is cold, the sky is pale blue with the promise of a bright day of sunlight. I pull on my tunic, leaving it unbelted, for Julia will be dressing me soon in my bridal clothes, already prepared and taken to her own apartment. But first there is something I want to do alone.

I take out two beeswax candles I have been saving for today, place them carefully on the Lararium in my hut and light them in front of the two tiny dolls who symbolise my mother and father. I touch the hair of my mother's doll, dressed in the Greek style by Floriana, Balbus the toymaker's wife, stroke the little wax tablet of my father's doll. I clear my throat, raise my palms.

"Father and Mother, I am to be married today. I wish you were by my side, Father, to give me your blessing. Mother, I wish you were here to place my hands in Marcus' and see my happiness." I have to take a deep breath before continuing, tears falling down my face. "I have been blessed by Venus and Juno to have found Marcus as my husband, but I have been blessed in so many other ways. I have found so many friends here in Rome and even had a child, Karbo, come to me by the grace of Juno that I might adopt him as my own. I pray that your shades walk in peace, hand in hand through the flowery fields of Elysium, that one day I will see you again. I ask for your blessings to make my day complete and my marriage a happy one." I wipe one hand across my face so that I can see more clearly, touch the little dolls one more time, bow my head to them and step away, gather my comb and the ribbons that will be woven into my hair and step outside the roof hut. The nightingales are singing and I pause by their cage to listen to them, a happy omen on my wedding day. The doves potter around the rooftop, unable yet to fly but growing used to my presence after many days of being fed. I go downstairs to Julia.

It's an odd feeling to be dressed by someone who used to be a priestess. I might not notice it so much were she not treating it like a sacred duty. When I helped to dress Cassia for her wedding we chattered together, but Julia has me strip off, then washes me herself with a cloth and warm water, head to toe. She keeps an unnerving silence throughout, only coughing once or twice.

"Are you well?" I ask at last, hoping to break the silence.

"Just a cough," she says. "Maria has given me a syrup for it made with Adah's honey."

I try to think of something else to say, but her silence is forbidding, although I doubt she means it that way. I wonder whether this is something all Vestals learn, not to fill up a silent space while they go about their divine work.

Julia lifts up the white tunic and I lift my arms, am dressed like a small child. She spends time getting the Knot of Hercules just right with my belt and indicates a stool on which I can sit while she prepares my hair. The *seni crines* hairstyle is an ancient style that the first Roman women wore, now worn by Vestals and brides, so Julia of all people would be able to arrange it. It's made up of six braids and I can feel her sectioning my hair with a spear point.

"This is the spear of a gladiator who fought in the Flavian Amphitheatre itself, sent as a gift from Paternus," she says, fingers tugging as she begins plaiting the six plaits that will create the base of the hairstyle. "You can't ask for better luck on your marriage day. You will bring forth brave sons."

I don't much like the idea of a bloodied spear running through my hair, even if the blood did dry a long while back, but it's tradition and weddings are full of superstitions that must be adhered to. Besides, a spear is sacred to Juno and every bride wants Juno to watch over her. I follow Julia's instructions when it comes time to weave in the red ribbon which will bind the plaits together, placing my fingers on my forehead and just above my ears to keep the ribbon in place while Julia plaits it into my hair, so that there will be little flashes of red between my plaits.

It takes a while to braid my long hair, twist it at the nape of my neck followed by a final wrapping of the plaits around my head and a tiny bun to complete the wrapping on to the top of my head. Julia uses so many bone pins to hold everything in place that I wonder if I will look like a hedgehog rather than a bride, but finally she places a wreath of rosemary on my head and adds a few more pins to secure it.

"Your veil," she says at last, lifting up the flame-yellow fabric that Cassia has lent me. She drapes it with care over my elaborate hair and wreath, then indicates my saffron-yellow shoes, made by the cobbler of the insula for me. Not only will they be good omens, but when I wear them in public everyone will know that I am a newlywed. Some women keep the yellow upper leather when the soles wear out and have it turned into their first child's first pair of shoes. I step into them, hampered by the veil, which hangs down the sides of my face and over my forehead, obscuring my view.

"Perfect," announces Julia. "Are you ready for Adah?"

I nod very carefully, in case the whole elaborate headdress falls.

"That's what all the hairpins are for," Julia says. "You can dance as joyously as you wish, no harm will come to the hairstyle."

She holds her hands above my head for a moment. "The blessings of all the gods on you today and always, Althea," she says in her Vestal voice. "Be happy." She coughs as she lowers her hands.

"You need to take more of the syrup," I say.

"I will," she says. "Here is Adah."

Adah is hovering in the doorway, her wrinkled face anxious.

"I'm glad you are taking me to be wed," I say.

She gives a small smile. "Because you asked, child," she says. "Only because you asked. I hope my Lord will forgive that you worship elsewhere." Her own people are Jews and she was anxious about this point when I asked her to give me away.

"Your god will know you care about me," I say and Julia nods.

"Come," Adah says, holding out a hand.

I turn to Julia for an embrace, and she leaves the room ahead of us, making her way into the courtyard where the wedding party will be waiting.

I take Adah's hand and follow her out onto the landing.

"The bride! The bride!" come shouts from below.

I stop walking when I see the courtyard. Not only is it full of red ribbons and fruits laid over greenery, but it is packed with people. Everyone from our insula is here, as well as many from our team at the amphitheatre and others we work with. Strabo our stage manager, of course, but also Paternus, Labeo and his assistant, Fabia and Fabius, with Fabia's apprentice Sadiki and assistant Decima, and even some of the gladiators, such as Alyssa. Carpophorous has arrived, I'm touched to see, even though he is retired from his time as a gladiator. The whole of the baker's family. Maria. Julia. Celer. My eyes sting as tears well up. To see everyone who cares about me gathered together in one small space, their faces tilted up to me in the sunshine, fills me with happiness.

And at the centre of the crowd stands Marcus, with Karbo by his side, Cassia holding Emilia with Quintus and Cassius next to her. Marcus' eyes, full of love, hold my own and my smile is the widest it has ever been. I think of my mother, lost so long ago, and my father, who tried to save me from a life of slavery. I hope that their shades will see my happiness today, that I am a free woman marrying a man I love, with a ready-grown child who has become my own and a whole community of people who care about me. I blink back my tears and walk, following Adah along the landing and onto the stairs. She is murmuring something in her own tongue as we walk.

"What are you saying?" I whisper, bending my head closer to her.

Adah finishes her murmur and peers up at me. She speaks quietly, translating as she goes, so that the words come slowly. "Blessed art thou, O Lord, King of the universe, who hath created joy and gladness, bridegroom and bride, mirth and exultation, pleasure and delight, love and brotherhood, peace and friendship." She gives a little shrug, as though to excuse her words. "A blessing for a wedding among my own people, child," she explains. "You needn't believe in my Lord," she adds, as though I am about to object to her foreign prayers and deity. "But I would have His blessing on you today, child."

Tears prick my eyes and I let go of her hand, wrapping my arms around her fragile, hunched frame. "Thank you, Adah."

"Mustn't keep your groom waiting," she says, lightly pushing me away as I let go of her. But her eyes are wet too and our hands grip each other as we step down the last stairs and into the courtyard, through the beaming crowd and come to stand close to Marcus. I gaze up into his warm brown eyes, his joyful smile lighting up my heart.

The priest begins his declarations but I don't hear him. It is his task to assure the witnesses here that all the bird signs were good for this marriage, that the gods have given their consent and blessing for this union. I am barely aware of wine being poured for the gods, my eyes still fixed on Marcus and his on mine.

"Who gives this woman to be wed?"

Adah repeats her name and mine as she lifts my hands and places them in Marcus'. I smile at her as she lets go, her own eyes brimming with tears, but Marcus pulls me to him at once, holds me in a tight embrace that leaves me breathless, in part at his strong hold on me, in part at sharing his emotion in this moment, the deep breath he takes, his face buried in my neck.

"You must swear your oaths," says the priest, irritated at Marcus ignoring him and the formalities that must be completed.

Marcus loosens his grip, though instead of holding my hands as he should, he puts one arm about me, his remaining hand holding both mine, so that I am held tightly within his embrace. The priest looks as if he is about to intervene, so I begin my vows before he can tell Marcus to let me go.

"When and where you are Gaius, everyman, I then and there am Gaia, everywoman," I say, leaning my head on Marcus' chest.

"When and where you are Gaia, everywoman, I then and there am Gaius, everyman," says Marcus, his cheek pressed to mine. We should be gazing at each other as we repeat our oaths, but this embrace feels more intimate, our skin touching, breathing together as one.

He lets go of my waist only to slip the iron ring onto the third finger of my left hand, takes an unleavened loaf from Fabius and breaks it over my head.

The priest, only mollified by us both remembering our vows

unprompted, takes a chunk of the bread and places it on the altar, then looks back at me.

I twist to look up at Marcus. "I am part of your family," I say and he tightens his embrace.

These words, usually an acknowledgement of a bride joining a large family and the connections that will be required of her, today have greater meaning, for Marcus has no family left, a rarity. From today we can rebuild a family together, with me as his new wife and Karbo already adopted by both of us.

Cheers break out as Marcus and I are guided to stools by the altar and given pieces of the loaf with which to feed one another. Being unleavened, the bread is hard to chew, and Marcus shakes his head after the first piece.

"No more bread," he says, reaching out to push back my veil. "I am hungry for a kiss!"

We lean forward from our perches and kiss, the courtyard full of applause and laughter, before Marcus reaches out a hand and pulls me to my feet and back into his arms, where he proceeds to cover my whole face in kisses.

"Enough, enough!" calls Fabius. "We haven't yet feasted and already you're in need of the marriage chamber?"

We break apart for a moment, laughing, and at once we're swept into the crowd in different directions, moving from person to person as we're embraced and kissed by everyone. By the time I can see clearly again Cassia and Julia, Maria and Adah have made a vast long table appear and women are coming from every direction with platters and bowls of food. Fabia is helping the children with the table decorations, green laurel leaves and pine branches entwined with bright red ribbons, pomegranates and pinecones, one of which Cassia's toddler daughter Emilia is trying to eat.

"On the table," encourages Fabia and finding the pinecone too hard to bite into, Emilia adds hers to the centrepieces.

Cassia has outdone herself. There is the traditional wedding cake sweetened with grape juice, but it can barely be seen amongst the dozens of dishes heaped high with good foods. Endless platters of olives and pickles, roasted chickpeas, mushrooms fried with garlic and herbs. A whole deer is the centrepiece, surrounded by chunks of roasted pumpkin, turnips, carrots and parsnips. There are big pots of Cassia's barley grits, known for their aromatic flavouring of cumin, onions and dill and, of course, her saltfish fritters, without which no feast from her hands is complete. Fresh walnut rolls from the bakers are piled high, as well as oil-rich flatbreads studded with olives. We drink warm wine flavoured with spices and sweetened with honey, suitable for the time of year, although the bright winter sun has done its best to warm the sheltered courtyard and most people have discarded their cloaks.

"More people should get married in winter," says Fabia, who is sitting by me. "I thought a winter wedding feast would be odd, but look at all this, it's delicious."

"Here's to the cook!" calls out Marcus, raising his cup to Cassia and everyone applauds.

We eat till we are more than full and then realise we should have saved space for the sweet treats Cassia and the bakery have come up with, all of them irresistible. Tiny hard almond biscuits to be dipped into a strong sweet raisin wine, damson-topped pastries served with a cinnamon custard, as well as nut tarts with a layer of quince preserves.

"And cream pudding!" says Karbo enthusiastically, holding his bowl aloft to secure the largest possible portion of his favourite dish.

"I did promise," I say. I spoon a triple helping into his bowl and embrace him.

"Your veil is in my cream pudding," he remonstrates, but he gives me something approximating a hug back, then hurries to immerse himself in indulgent sweetness.

"Happy?" asks Cassia, pausing at my side as she circles the table, making sure everyone is stuffed to bursting and beyond.

"So happy," I say. I wave my hand at the table, the dozens of friends enjoying the feast and the occasion, laughing and joking with one another, "I never dreamt this could be possible when I was a motherless slave girl."

Cassia leans to hug me, her black curls soft against my cheek. "We've done alright, we motherless ones, haven't we? I think our mothers would be proud of us."

Fabia smiles at the two of us, reaches out to place her hand over ours. "Our mothers are smiling today," she says and although her voice cracks, her smile is wide.

"You're next," says Cassia pointing at her. "Can't have two of us married and not the third. Got your eye on anyone?"

"Her assistant has his eye on her," I say, tilting my head towards where Sadiki is sitting near Fabius, Fabia's father.

"Oh, got ideas above his station, has he? Making friends with your father, I see."

Fabia laughs, but her cheeks have gone pink. "I want to achieve other things before I get married," she says.

"So it's you that's the ambitious one, as if we hadn't noticed," says Cassia. "Imperial physician? Fancy looking after Domitian, perhaps? Cushy job if you can get it."

"No thanks," says Fabia. "Emperors are not always healthy and who gets blamed?"

"Their enemies," says Cassia, refilling Marcus' cup of wine

and offering Emilia a spoon of cream pudding, which the child opens her mouth very wide for. "Look at the size of this one, she's grown so fast."

"More," says Emilia through a mouthful of cream.

"Walking and talking," says Fabia, stroking Emilia's hair. "Running soon."

"And climbing everywhere," says Cassia. "And taking all my best pots to play with. Can't find a thing in the popina these days with her on the loose." She bends to kiss Emilia and offers her another spoonful of pudding.

"Sit," says Fabia, moving up the bench. "You've done all the cooking, no need to serve everyone as well, they can help themselves."

"I prefer wandering," says Cassia. "Can't help it. After all the years in the popina, it's a habit. And I like to be sure everyone's been well fed."

Fabia looks over her shoulder. "Time to kidnap the bride," she says to Quintus, who has appeared behind her.

"What?" I say but Quintus, Celer and Fabius have already laid hands on me and lifted me out of my seat.

"We're kidnapping you, Althea!" they say, pulling me away from Marcus, who is laughing and beseechingly holding out his hands to me.

"Kidnapping!" yells everyone, jumping to their feet.

Marcus reaches out and takes my hand. "A bride needs kidnapping," he says, "even if she does live in the same insula as her groom. And besides, I want everyone to see you on your wedding day and know how lucky I am."

He heads towards the courtyard gate with Quintus, Celer and Fabius pushing and pulling at me as though I am being forced to go and everyone follows us out of the gate and into Virgin's Street.

"Oh no!" I call out. "I'm being kidnapped. Help, help!" I can't help laughing though, and Marcus shakes his head at me.

"You're an awful actor," he says. "You have to try harder than that."

"HELP!" I scream and heads appear from all the neighbouring doors and windows of insulas and shops nearby. "I'm being kidnapped!" I shriek.

Marcus pretends to cover his ears as everyone shouts obscenities to drive away any lurking evil spirits while I try to shield myself from handfuls of nuts which are being thrown everywhere.

We wind our way round the block, down the tiny streets, accompanied by ribaldry and applause from all the neighbouring homes, till we come back round the insula, past the cobbler's and Balbus' toy shop and finally Cassia's popina which today has its shutters closed. Outside the courtyard gate we pause. The men let go of me and Marcus turns me to face the crowd.

"When and where you are everyman, Gaius, I then and there am everywoman, Gaia," I say, looking up at Marcus. "I am part of your family."

Everyone cheers and Marcus lifts me into his arms and carries me into the courtyard as they stream in behind us. I cling on to him, giggling, then stroke his face, a tiny moment of intimacy in all the noise and rush around us.

He puts me gently down in front of Julia, who is holding a bowl of water in one hand, a burning brazier in the other, welcoming me back into the insula as a bride into her new home. Smiling, she sets both items aside and takes my hand, leading me up the stairs with Marcus following us, all the way to the rooftop where we turn to wave at everyone gathered in the courtyard below us. Julia leads the way to our roof hut and opens the door. Someone has been busy here. New lamps have been lit, a bright new golden-yellow blanket which echoes my bridal veil has been laid on the bed and bunches of leaves bound with red ribbons have been nailed to the walls.

"It's beautiful," I say. "Thank you, Julia."

Julia turns to us and reaches out, places one hand on each of our heads in a silent blessing, then leaves us alone together.

Marcus takes a deep breath and pulls me towards him. "You have lain in my arms already," he says. "But now you are my bride, I feel nervous."

I lean my head against his chest. "I don't," I say. "I have never felt so safe and loved."

"In that case," says Marcus, "you are about to be loved a great deal more." He sweeps me back up into his arms and I wrap my arms about his neck as he carries me across our threshold and into bed.

I'm woken the next morning by hammering.

"Come in," I mumble, but the hammering keeps going. I roll to my side and put out a hand to Marcus, but he isn't there. "Come in," I say, a little louder. The hammering doesn't stop. I reluctantly climb out of bed, pulling my green tunic over my head.

I open the door and squint in the sunlight. It's later than I thought, I'm used to rising at dawn, when the light is still a pale imitation of daylight. The sky is already blue and the hammering is not stopping.

"The gods," I mutter to myself. I step further out onto the

rooftop, grimacing at the brightness, see the source of the noise and smile.

Marcus is surrounded by wooden posts and the hammering stops for a moment as he, Celer and Karbo lift up a long wooden plank and place it across two others. Marcus bends to pick up his hammer again and notices me. He tries to smile, which is hard with nails in his mouth, but his eyes are warm. He pulls first one nail and then the other two out and hammers them in, the plank held neatly in place.

"Morning, my love," he says. "We are making you a pergola for the heat of the summer days. You might as well enjoy your last year in Rome."

I smile and nod, go back into the roof hut where I pull a comb through my hair before pinning it up into a bun, tying a blue and green braided belt round my tunic and putting on my shoes. I don't really need the palla Fabia gave me if it's going to be a sunny day, but it is a novelty to me to wear a married woman's item of clothing, so I wrap it about my head and shoulders.

"Very matronly," says Marcus when I come back out again, a mischievous smirk on his face at the sight of my palla. "Very much the married lady, isn't she?" he adds to Celer.

"Very," agrees Celer with a smile. "Good morning, Althea." He passes Marcus some more nails and picks up another post, ready to hold it in place while Marcus fastens it to the growing structure. "Sorry about the noise," Celer adds. "I said Marcus should let you sleep in."

"Why would she want to sleep late on a glorious day like today?" says Marcus, sorting through a pot of nails to find the ones he wants. "Go have breakfast, we've already eaten," he adds to me.

"I want another breakfast," says Karbo. "The first one was *hours* ago."

"It was an hour, if that," says Marcus laughing.

"It was dark."

"Go with her, you poor famished boy."

I make soothing noises to the doves and nightingales, who are cowering in corners, scared by all the noise. "Come on, Karbo."

I start towards the stairs, Karbo at my heels.

"You're forgetting something," says Marcus.

"What?"

"A kiss," he says. "You don't get to go anywhere without a kiss. I'm your husband now, you have to do whatever I say. No arguing."

"I'm a very obedient wife," I say. I walk to him and place my head on his chest, wrap my arms about him. He puts one arm about me, hugs me to him, then kisses me.

"*Breakfast*," moans Karbo. "Honestly, you two have been cursed by Venus. You can't do anything without kissing first."

I giggle and hug Marcus one last time before following Karbo down the stairs, singing an old dancing song under my breath.

"Morning, Maria," I sing out when I spot her on the walkway.

"Ah, a cheerful bride," she says with a lascivious wink. "Not so sad to stay in Rome after all?"

I shrug. "I have Marcus and Karbo," I say. "And all my friends. It's only one more year, it can't be that bad."

"The gods willing," says Maria.

"The gods willing," I echo. "Would you like me to bring you something up from Cassia's?"

She shakes her head. "Already eaten. But if you spot grapes in the market any time, bring me some back. I've a hankering for them and they should be ripe any day. And if you're a good boy," she says to Karbo, "I'll press you some and you can drink your fill of grape juice."

"That's a rash promise," I say. "Filling Karbo is a difficult thing to accomplish."

Maria smiles, indulgent. "He's a growing boy," she says with fondness. "Got to feed him up so he'll grow up tall and strong."

I watch him clatter down the stairs ahead of me. "He's already grown so much," I say. "He might even be ready for the Liberalia next March."

"Do you think so?"

"We're not sure of his age," I say. "But he's so tall. He might well be."

When we first found Karbo we thought he must be about nine or ten, but perhaps he was older; he could have been an undernourished twelve-year-old. He has grown a good deal since being fed properly, perhaps we misjudged his age. Boys between fourteen and seventeen take part in March's Liberalia festival, when boys become men. I watch Karbo as he crosses the courtyard, wondering if he is already fourteen. He might be. He has the height for it and he is filling out more now, no longer all legs and arms. His shoulders are broader, he feels more solid when I hug him or when he barrels into me at the end of the day, pleased to see me like an enthusiastic puppy that does not understand it is now a large dog and can knock you over with one bound. I think of his local friends and their ages; most of them are over thirteen and some will be heading for the Liberalia in the spring. I decide to speak to Marcus about it. It would be fun to celebrate Karbo's coming of age in Rome, surrounded by all the inhabitants of the insula, for country life will be quieter. And if he is a year younger than he should be, that is no great matter, most families choose when to celebrate the coming of age of their young men and Karbo has been through more than most boys his age. Fausta comes to my mind, how proud she would be if she could see him, so different from the small, frightened boy who curled up in a corner of her room, adopting her as his mother, not caring about her dubious background, only needing the certainty and comfort her fierce demeanour gave him.

In the market I find grapes for Maria and buy some to leave at a local temple to Venus in Fausta's memory. I wish she could have seen what became of Marcus and me, how we have ended up as husband and wife. I grin at the thought of what kind of pre-wedding night advice an old she-wolf like her might have delivered to me, though knowing her she'd have left me to find out such things for myself and made a few choice comments the next morning to watch me blush.

Back at Cassia's I find Marcus drinking wine.

"You're stuck with the Games again?" says Quintus with sympathy. "Still, we'll be glad to have you here for another year, Cassia will miss you when you're gone, Althea. You're like a sister to her."

"We haven't even got a theme for a new season of the Games," I say, sighing. "I didn't think we'd need one, thought we'd have escaped already."

Cassia nods, one hand pouring batter for pancakes, the other gently pushing Emilia away from the hot fire. She turns to speak to a customer and I pass Marcus some grapes, which he accepts, picking morosely at the bunch. He offers a couple of grapes to Emilia, who reaches up with her chubby little hand to take them and chews, dribbling juice down her chin.

"We could have done without the augur poking his nose in. Cursed birds," says Marcus.

"Your theme is birds?" says Cassia, turning back to hear the last word. "Like what? Leda and the Swan leading to the Trojan war? Or the Dwarfs and the Cranes? I always liked that story when I was little. Father says I used to get two bits of cloth and tie them to my arms and swoop about the place pretending to be a crane, attacking all my friends who were supposed to be the Dwarfs."

Marcus frowns at her while popping more grapes into Emilia's waiting mouth. "What? No, I was saying the augury birds were the cause of us having to do another season, I wasn't –"

"Or," says Cassia, warming to her theme and ignoring a customer who is waving his cup at her for more wine, "Prometheus being punished by an eagle eating his liver, didn't they do that one time in the Games?"

"Yes," I say, grimacing.

Marcus pauses with a grape halfway to Emilia, who glares at him and points to her mouth. "There are a lot of myths about birds," he says. "We could use the velarium to create illusions of light and air. We can have gods and goddesses and people turning into birds or heroes battling them. We can have some lighter touches, the actors can do comedy. And Cassia's right, the battle between the Dwarfs and the Cranes is a good story. We can do elements of it throughout the season and the big battle as the finale."

"Labeo will love you," I say. "You'll clear out his whole gladiatorial school of dwarfs."

Marcus' eyes light up. "Better and better," he says. "We'll dress the gladiatrices up as the Cranes, white tunics and big white wings. Labeo can take care of the whole thing for us, he'll be delighted and it'll be a job off our hands. I'm liking it already."

"You're welcome," says Cassia grinning at our growing enthusiasm and giving a mock bow. "Just remember I want a proper Crane costume in payment for my excellent ideas after all those years making do with strips of cloth."

Marcus lifts Emilia onto his knee and offers her more grapes but now that she is at the right height, she lunges for his fresh bread roll, stuffing it into her mouth with a gleeful smile.

"Your daughter is eating up all my food," says Marcus to Quintus in mock outrage. "Cassia, I'm going to need more bread."

"What do you mean by illusions of light and air?" I ask, trying to work out what will be involved.

"We can use coloured awnings so the arena floor changes colours or use fire if we do a night show. I have some ideas but I need to find the right person to help us. Let me make some plans and I'll show you what I mean."

THE VELARIUM

SATURNALIA SEEMS TO RUSH PAST after the wedding. A flurry of cold winds and, "Io, Saturnalia!" greetings in the streets, gifts to and from our loved ones and acquaintances. We hold a meal for the amphitheatre slaves, where we wait on them for once, and there is plenty of teasing of Marcus and me for being newlyweds. And somehow it is January and we have three months to get the new season of Games planned, as well as Domitian's first task: the additional seating and the velarium.

"Oh good," says Marcus. "I look forward to installing a velarium in the wind and rain of winter. Lots of wet flapping canvas."

"Let's get the seating underway," I suggest.

Marcus agrees. The first crew to start work will be the carpenters and orders are made for the wood they will need for the seating tiers. The weather is not on our side though. Almost a month of rain and high winds goes by, which makes our plans difficult, the work postponed several times, leaving us hanging around the insula with nothing to do.

"I'm sure it will all come good in the end," smiles Julia when she hears me complaining. "Come and sit with us."

Julia, Maria and Adah have taken to sitting together on rainy and cold days, sometimes sewing or spinning, sometimes telling stories or preparing food, Julia's apartment being one of the few in our insula with cooking facilities.

"You're still coughing," I say to Julia. "Was the syrup no good?"

She shrugs my concern away. "It's fading," she says. "When the sun comes back and the days warm it'll clear up."

While we're stuck waiting, Domitian takes to visiting us most weeks, wanting to see animals. Marcus grinds his teeth each time a message is delivered listing what kind of animal Domitian would like to see next.

"This is a total waste of everyone's time and money, having a beast hunter provide animals out of season so they can be a petting zoo for one man. You deal with this, I don't even want to see him."

Our new beast hunter, brought in to replace Funis after his tragic death, is a taciturn man who does what we tell him to and doesn't ask questions. When I ask for the first two zebras, followed by a lion, and later on a crocodile, he is happy to oblige.

"I'm sorry about it being out of season," I say.

"You pays for it, you gets it whenever you want it," he says.

"The imperial purse is bountiful," I say, grimacing.

"Then you gets whatever you asks for."

I have to stand by while Domitian feeds various animals, from the zebras, who it turns out are like horses and are fond of stored apples, to a tiger which turns up its nose at the ready-prepared meat offered until Domitian demands a live goat be brought in, at which point the tiger suddenly comes to life, ripping the poor beast's throat open in a matter of moments, while Domitian watches the bloody spectacle with calm interest.

"It must have been bored," he says.

"Yes, Imperator," I say.

"Next time I would like to see a bear."

I suppress a sigh. "Of course, Imperator."

I watch him leave, still unsure how I should feel about him. He has undertaken a vast building programme to benefit Rome, he has stamped down on bribery and corruption within the administrative and legal system, he ought to be an exemplary model of a good emperor and yet I cannot erase my memory of his shaking hand holding Marcus at sword point, about to weep with rage at the very idea of his amphitheatre team being changed. Such inconsistent behaviour is unsettling.

Finally in February we get a few dry days, allowing us to start. I stand with Marcus in the arena, squinting up at the very top of the amphitheatre.

Above us, behind the top tier of stone seating, a space which until now was empty will have a tightly raked set of wooden seating built into it, as per Domitian's orders. It will allow for more women and slaves to attend. The Games have proved very popular amongst women and tokens to attend have been a way to reward slaves for good service, as well as having them conveniently to hand if their masters wish to be served in any way. I suspect the ladies of Rome will be taking the stone seating tier originally designed for this purpose and sending the slaves to the wooden rows, because the stone pillars at the very top will obscure the view of the arena from certain angles, but a seat at the Games is still a seat at the Games.

"Back to hammering," says Marcus, noticing my pained expression as the team of carpenters get to work.

We've been here since dawn, as cartloads of planks were unloaded and carried, with much sweating and muttered oaths, up the steep stairs to the very top of the building. It's taken a few hours to start assembling the pieces, even though they were all sawn to size before they got here. But now that the right elements are in place, the hammering is going to be continuous for days.

"It never stops," I say. "Every year there's something else being built." I crane my neck to look up at the carpenters. "The materials they've got will barely cover an eighth of the way round so far."

"We have daily deliveries planned for eight days," says Marcus. "The carpenters have to keep up with them. We just need the weather to hold. And that's the easy part of this task. Wait till we try to install the velarium. I'm glad I wasn't in charge of getting that quantity of fabric dyed red."

The sections of the velarium canvas must be cut to an exact set of measurements, wider at the top, narrower at the base, to fit the oval shape of the amphitheatre. They will be sent to us numbered so that we will be able to put them in the right places.

"The extra seating is going to slow the exits at the top," says Marcus. "Wasn't designed to have a few extra thousand people leaving from the top tier."

"That's not something Domitian would worry about though, is it?"

"Exactly."

The hammering continues for the eight days, then, much to my despair, an additional two as the works slip behind due to a few wet days which slow deliveries. But finally the wooden tiers of seating are in place and the hammering stops.

Now the awning poles can be put into the two-hundred-and-forty post brackets that have been waiting for this moment. Made of stone, the brackets were built into the amphitheatre during its construction, since the awning was planned from the start. They sit on the outside of the building at its very top, adding strength to the structure. Most amphitheatres and theatres have retractable awnings, often in bright colours such as red, yellow and purple, sometimes just in the plain cream canvas used for sails on ships. I've seen very elaborate ones, where the cloth has been painted with scenes from mythology or with impressive animals, such as dolphins or elephants, but one colour is sufficient decoration for an audience who is not looking up, but rather down at the arena.

The posts are vast and have to be winched into place from the ground as it would be impossible to carry them up the tight stairs. A team on the ground lines up each pole, fastens ropes to it which are pulled by another team to the top of the amphitheatre and mounted into each bracket. I feel ill watching them, the men who must guide each pole into place standing one step away from a certain death should they fall to the ground far below.

My fear is not shared by the crowd of small children who come to inspect the works every day, fascinated to see the awning progress. They are sent on errands by the builders, to buy food at the local markets or popinas, sometimes sent to another site or home to fetch and carry messages. It's worth coming every day, for the quick and willing can earn food or even a small coin if they make themselves useful. They perch like little sparrows around the site, chattering to each other, enjoying the constant stream of interesting cursing from the builders and the chance to volunteer for a task, before fluttering away to wherever they come from as twilight falls.

On a wet day I visit Labeo's gladiatorial school.

"Dwarfs? My dear, I have all the dwarfs Rome's empire can bring me! And the best gladiatrices. The Battle of the Dwarfs and the Cranes will be glorious. You are too good to me, what will I do without you?"

"I'm sure the Games will continue without us," I say.

"Ah, but you and Marcus understand *spectacle*. Most Games managers just put on round after round of gladiators. They don't mix it up enough. Gets boring. You have to have *variety*, that's what makes for the best Games."

"I'm leaving the Cranes and Dwarfs in your hands," I tell him. "Costumes can be stored in the amphitheatre. I'll send the dancing girls over to teach the gladiatrices some moves. We'll need to have a dance sequence that turns into a battle, so we'll have to mix them together. Your gladiatrices can start the fights and the dancing girls can make themselves scarce."

"It'll be perfect," enthuses Labeo.

"I need to speak with Fabia," I say.

"Busy in her medical rooms," says Labeo.

I go to the physician's bay, where I find Fabia surrounded by scrolls and tablets.

"Fabia, will you visit Julia? She keeps coughing and she just shrugs me away when I mention it. She's taken a few remedies, but nothing seems to be working."

Fabia looks up from her scrolls and frowns. "Bad coughing?"

"Not terrible. But often."

"I'll ask to look her over, see what I can offer."

"Thank you. What's all the scribing for?"

She sighs. "Training and feeding plans for each gladiator. It takes up so much time, making sure they're all accounted for and records are kept. My assistant Decima can't write, though I'm teaching her. Sadiki can, but it takes up hours of both our time. So boring. Father never has to do this nonsense," she adds. "He just patches up gladiators at the amphitheatre and sends them back to their own schools to the physicians there. Too much writing and record-keeping for my liking."

"You just like wounds, don't you?" I say, "Which is what you used to say about your father."

She grins. "Wounds don't require all this nonsense. You stitch them up and move on."

"I don't even believe you," I say. "I never met a woman who liked reading as much as you. All that research you did to find out about that bronze hand you made for Alyssa."

"Reading's one thing," she says. "Who am I doing all this writing for? The cooks know what to feed the gladiators, their trainers know what each one needs in the way of training. It's all for show. Labeo wants to be taken more seriously now that he's one of Rome's two largest gladiatorial schools, so he's insisted everything be recorded."

I pat her on the back. "Get a scribe," I say. "You're wasted in here."

The next day Marcus and I set off early, as the sailors from Misenum are due to arrive, ready to install the velarium. We feed the birds and set free the doves for the day. Most of their feathers have now grown back, they take little flights to test their strength, perching on the rooftop wall or going as far as another rooftop before returning.

"They're getting confident," says Marcus with satisfaction. "But they know this is their home now."

Early though we are, when we arrive there are two hundred men in blue-grey tunics standing on the arena floor in military formation, with one commander at the front, who salutes Marcus. He is very young and tall, with a nose dotted with freckles and green eyes, something of a rarity.

"Servius Gratius Celsus, sir. At your command."

Marcus nods. "You're in command of these men?"

"Yes, sir."

"You don't need to 'sir' me. Marcus will do."

"They are good men. Hardworking."

"Ever done awnings like this before?"

"No. Only sails."

Marcus sighs. "We'll go to a theatre later today and try out their awnings. They're a lot smaller but it's the same concept. It's the size of the things that's the problem. There's a light metal ring in the centre, two hundred and forty poles around the amphitheatre, with ropes that connect the poles to the circle. Forty-eight strips of cloth, a heavy canvas. Five poles per strip. The cloth itself is only attached to two of the ropes, and has additional finer ropes which control letting it out to open up the velarium, covering the audience, or pulling it in to close it when it's not needed or not safe. We can leave it open for some days when the weather settles but if we get a lot of rain, it'll be too heavy and the whole thing could collapse. The poles might break and if one of those falls into the audience it could kill someone. And if there's too much wind, the whole thing will rip right off and we'll have to start all over again."

"Yes, sir."

I bite back a smile. The young commander Servius is not going to call Marcus by his name, no matter how much he's encouraged to.

Marcus continues. "So there's two parts to opening the velarium. One is to pull on all the ropes together. This will lift the metal circle off the arena floor and, as the ropes tighten, it will be lifted high over the audience's heads, just below the top of the whole amphitheatre's height. Then we lock those ropes in place unless we wish to lower the whole structure again for repairs, change the cloth strips, or if it's too windy to risk keeping it elevated."

"Yes, sir."

"Once the whole structure is elevated, there are the additional finer ropes which control the canvas strips, and those allow us to open and close the awning at will. They will need to be opened every morning and closed every night, for fear of wind or rain. The canvas needs to be opened and closed with care, especially in regard to balance. It will not be safe to open just one half, for instance, because there will be far greater weight on the other side and it will put too great a strain on the structure as a whole. So if we wish to open part of the strips only, according to where the sun is, we need to be mindful of that."

"Yes, sir."

Marcus finishes his lecture and leaves Servius to pass on the information to his men.

"He keeps calling me sir," he says to me, rolling his eyes.

"He's very young," I say. "It's his first command and he's not used to working with people like us. He's trained to speak to his superior officers."

"I feel like I'm back in the army. Or old."

"If you're back in the army you must be young," I say.

At the theatre we go to that afternoon, the sailors swarm all over the building watching the awnings being opened and closed by the regular team of stagehands, who are used to the process.

I wince at the sailors walking on the very top of the high walls, without any kind of safety measures.

"I don't want any of them to fall," I say.

Servius, standing next to me, looks surprised. "That will

not happen. They are accustomed to keeping their balance on a moving ship. The walls will feel stable by comparison."

I smile at his earnestness, he looks very young to be in charge of such a large team of men. "Is this your first command?"

"Yes," he says, his chest expanding. "My commander said that it was a chance to prove myself, to show that I could be called on for more than sailing, that I could be relied upon to serve the Emperor in a different capacity."

"We're grateful to have you," I say. "It's not an easy task, I would not have liked to have trained our slaves to carry it out."

He looks affronted at the very idea. "No," he agrees. "It is a very skilled task."

"You're stationed at Misenum, is that where you're from?"

He nods. "My father was a sailor too, I follow in the family tradition."

"He must be proud of you."

"He was killed by pirates," he says. "But my mother is very proud that I have been given this posting."

I imagine his mother is grateful that he is safe in Rome's Flavian Amphitheatre opening and closing our awning on demand, rather than chasing pirates round the seas, risking his life as his father did before him.

"My mother was also killed by pirates," I say. "My father and I were taken as slaves."

"I am sorry Rome's navy failed you," he says, his young face fierce.

"I am sure you have dispatched many of them," I say. "It's good that our seas are being patrolled."

The next day sees the arrival of the giant metal ring, which again is far too large to enter through any of the arches and has to be winched over the top of the amphitheatre and then brought from the top tier to the arena floor. Thankfully the sailors see this as their job and wrestle the awkward burden to the wooden arena floor. It's fitted with two hundred and forty metal rings, each of which has to be threaded with a rope and tied securely, then the ropes need to be taken up to their equivalent post and secured in place with additional knots and a wooden locking mechanism. There's a lot of swearing, as well as confusion with ropes getting mixed up here and there, but as the hours pass the task begins to near completion, although it takes all day. Marcus, less afraid of heights than I am, goes up at the end with Servius to inspect the work, checking that each rope is locked in place on its post and that it runs smoothly down to the metal circle with no mistaken crossed ropes. I look away from the sight of him, as he makes his way round the top of the amphitheatre on the narrow walkway where the sailors will stand to manage the ropes.

The next day comes the moment of truth: will the structure, the largest ever made, hold up? Or is it too heavy? Marcus wants us to try it without the canvas first. One hundred and twenty men pull their rope on Servius' command and slowly, slowly, the ropes grow taut and the metal circle begins to rise up. When it is dangling half-way up, the men lock the ropes in position and pull in the other hundred and twenty. Once those are locked, they pull the first ones again, bringing the circle to its final place, level with the top of the amphitheatre. Once all the ropes have been tightened and locked, we stand to admire it.

"I keep thinking it will come crashing down," I say.

Marcus and Servius shake their heads. "The circle is heavy but there's a lot of good ropes holding it there and the poles are robust," says Marcus. "What we do need to do is mark the ropes, blue and red alternating, so that we can always be sure we're pulling the right ones. You can't have it all lopsided."

"And the awning fabric?" I say.

"It's coming up from the docks tomorrow morning," says Marcus. "I need a bath after all that."

In the morning four large cartloads of fabric arrive. Forty-eight strips of red canvas, broader at one end, narrower at the point where they will meet the metal circle. Each one has been ready prepared with metal loops sewn along the sides where they will be attached to thin cords. The strips are unloaded into our corridor and the metal circle slowly lowered back to the arena floor.

"Not looking forward to today," mutters Marcus.

He's right. Attaching the vast strips onto the correct ropes using additional cords takes hours. By the end of the day we've only managed ten, although the work is beginning to speed up as we learn from our mistakes. My eyes hurt from squinting upwards all day and everyone has blisters from running ropes and cords through our hands. The rest of the heavy fabric has to be stored downstairs overnight for fear that it will be stolen if we leave it in the corridors.

It takes three more days till every strip of canvas is correctly in place.

"Baths," says Marcus when we reach the last one and the men cheer. There's still a couple of hours of daylight. We could have tested it's all working, but everyone's patience and energy is running low and even Servius, keen as he is, nods gratefully and leads the men off to the Baths of Titus over the road for a well-earned soak.

"Aquilo, Favonius, Auster and Vulturnus, look on us with

kindness and rest your strength," says Marcus the next morning, calling on the four winds as he stands on the arena floor.

"They've heard you," I say. It's a sunny day with hardly a breeze, unusual for March.

Each strip requires two cords to be pulled in order to open or close, so ninety-six men are required for this part.

The men start singing a sea shanty, bellowing out the words to try and keep a steady rhythm.

"Sailors who race over deep waves,

along Triton's salty swells,

Nile-runners who make their sweet way,

sailing over the waters' smile,

friends, tell us your judgment

between the sea and the fertile Nile."

"I'm surprised they have breath enough for singing as well as hauling," I say.

"Helps them keep in time," says Servius, watching them and grimacing. "It doesn't look very smooth. It's getting caught up there on the left." He sighs. "We'll have to start again."

"At least the shanty's clean," grins Marcus. "I've heard a lot worse from sailors. We'll leave you for a while. Althea and I have someone to visit."

"Who are we visiting?" I ask as we leave the amphitheatre, the chorus behind us sounding much bawdier, with reference to sailors having to choose between mermaids and Egyptian beauties.

"A maker of flames," says Marcus. "You'll see."

We thread our way through a confusing jumble of small streets south of the amphitheatre, until we turn into a crumbling insula which reminds me of Julia's before it was repaired. The courtyard is very odd, there is a strong smell in the air and there are patches of pitch and soot everywhere, as though fires have been lit at random points across the cobbles. A little girl stares at us from a balcony.

"I'm looking for Appius Vibius Corda," calls up Marcus.

The little girl stares.

"The flame-maker?"

The little girl disappears but we can hear her calling. "Ignis! Ignis!"

"Looks like he's known by another name," I tell Marcus.

The man who appears from the doorway below the balcony is short, with black curls and dark eyes. His skin would be pale, except that a lot of what's visible is smeared with soot. He comes towards us, then stands, waiting, silent.

"I sent a messenger," says Marcus. "I am Marcus Aquillius Scaurus, manager of the Flavian Amphitheatre. This is my wife Althea, who serves as my scribe and right hand. I need to talk to you about a fire spectacle for the closing night of this Games season. You sent me word back that you could demonstrate what is possible."

The man nods and points towards a decrepit wooden bench nearby, onto which we lower ourselves with care, anxious it will collapse if either of us moves too much. The man goes into a storeroom door at the end of the courtyard.

"Not very talkative, is he?" I murmur to Marcus.

"His tongue was cut out," Marcus says.

I look at him in horror. "By whom?"

He shrugs. "Perhaps someone who didn't want him to reveal his secrets. Or perhaps he revealed the secrets of his trade and was punished for it. He can create sea fire, like the Greeks did. It can be used in battles and not many know how it is done."

I'm about to ask more questions but Ignis emerges with a long reed and two torches, ready prepared with pitch to be lit. He sets the torches up in heavy stone stands made for the purpose, setting the reed aside on another rickety bench.

He goes indoors and returns with a burning lamp, which he uses to ignite the two torches. When they are burning strongly he returns to his storerooms and returns with a series of little metal containers with spouts, which he sets on the bench.

Taking the hollow reed he uses the first little spouted container to pour a grey powder into it. Directing the reed at the first torch, he puts it to his lips and blows quickly. The grey powder hits the torch and the pale flame turns a bright orange.

He repeats the demonstration several times, the flames turning red, green, violet and blue as the different powders hit them.

Marcus is beaming. "Magnificent," he says. "What are the powders?"

Ignis' dark eyes crease into an amused smile and he shakes his head.

"Fair enough," says Marcus. "Have you seen the amphitheatre's new velarium?"

He nods.

"I want to set fire to it."

Ignis' eyes widen.

Marcus smiles. "The ropes will need to be replaced yearly. They will get wet, frayed, weakened by the sun and rain. So at the end of the season, I wish to set fire to the whole structure. I will need it to burn in a myriad of colours and for the fire to spread slowly, so that as the crowds leave with it burning above them none of it falls into the audience."

Ignis considers for a moment. He points to my tablet and I

hold it out to him along with my stylus. He scratches onto it, hands it over to me. I read it out.

"Risky."

"No risk, no reward."

He writes again. "Reward?"

"The imperial purse is ample," says Marcus. He looks about the soot-stained courtyard. "Enough for a new workshop away from your own home. I am sure your wife and neighbours would appreciate not having flammable materials so close to home."

Ignis nods and hands back my tablet without further communication.

"You'll test what is possible," says Marcus.

Ignis nods again.

"I'll bid you farewell," says Marcus. "I look forward to seeing what is possible."

The next day is rainy, there can be no more practice with the velarium. The canopy cannot hold wet cloth, it would be far too heavy, so the velarium will be left entirely pulled back today and the sailors will have to spend a day in barracks.

But there is always work to do. It's a late start, as there is no rush, but I make my way round the whole of the hypogeum, noting on my tablet the works needed before we re-open. There is always cleaning and mending to be done. When I come to the room where we usually keep the dancers' clothing, I pause on the threshold. The last time I was here I was cradling Funis' dead body, my hands covered in his blood. I have a sudden memory of pressing my bloody palms against the senator's white toga and his look of horror and anger, his bodyguards stepping forwards. It would have gone badly with me if it hadn't been for Stephanus' silent appearance and intervention.

The room is empty, the bright dancing tunics put away over winter and the floor washed; there is no trace of blood. I say a silent thank you to Strabo and our cleaning crew, who never asked what to do. They have erased the violence of that moment from the room, if not from my memories.

Still on the threshold, I write a note about the carpenters needing to build a longer hanging rack so that the clothes can be better organised when fast changes are required. Having fifty-odd dancers rapidly changing in a small space is bad enough without items of clothing being scattered across the floor. I try to be practical, think only of the work to be done, but sadness is pulling at me, along with a welling-up of the terror of that moment.

"Althea."

I nearly scream, whirl about to find Stephanus standing behind me in the gloom, as though I have conjured him up from my memories.

"Apologies, I did not mean to startle you." He speaks calmly as ever, his toga's folds immaculate. I wonder for a moment whether he ever loses his temper or shows any emotion, or whether all his calm is needed to deal with Domitian's sudden outbursts.

"I was…" I wave my hand at the room beyond me.

"Perhaps you would walk with me through the hallways?"

I follow him through the dim hypogeum and up the stairs to the ground floor, wondering whether he's here with some other obscure task that Domitian wants completing. I can't imagine Marcus being willing to accept any more requests, although with Domitian, we don't have any choice.

The vast curved hallway which runs round the amphitheatre allows us to stay dry while the grey drizzle falls outside, as well as letting us see out of each of the great arches we pass to the Forum beyond. The unpleasant weather means that the corridor is fairly quiet. We meet the odd person scurrying along, using the amphitheatre as a break from the rain, but on a day like this much of Rome stays at home or enjoys the comfort of hot baths.

We've walked halfway round the amphitheatre. I stay silent. Whatever he wants, he will reveal it when he's ready.

At last he speaks. "You came from a Greek island? Kefalonia?"

I nod. Barely anyone has ever heard of my home island, tiny as it is, but I'm sure he knows everything about all of us.

"And were enslaved along with your father?"

"Yes."

"How did you end up at the amphitheatre?"

I'm sure he knows this too, but I continue the pretence. "I was slave to a merchant who spent time in Pompeii. He was tasked with finding a manager for the Flavian Amphitheatre. When he found Marcus, he gifted me to him as a scribe, to sweeten the deal."

"Scaurus lost family during the disaster, I believe?"

"His wife and baby son," I say. I try not to think of the endless grey of Pompeii, how Marcus dug through the ashes for hours while I prayed for him, knowing there was no possibility that his loved ones were alive.

Stephanus nods, grave. "I had family in Herculaneum who were fortunate enough to move to Britannia two years before Vesuvius erupted. At the time they left, they felt the loss of their homeland keenly but it seems the gods knew best after all."

"Are they still in Britannia?"

"Yes."

"Not homesick after all these years?"

"For the sunshine, no doubt," he says. "It does not sound like a kind climate."

"I hear it rains a lot," I say. "Like today."

"So it seems."

I'm beginning to wonder where this conversation is headed. Stephanus has never struck me as a person who enjoys small talk, he barely bothers with greetings, and now we are conversing on the weather and everyone's family histories. It's very odd.

"The Emperor is pleased with the progress of the velarium," he says.

"I'm glad to hear it," I say. "It's difficult but we can see signs of progress. The crowds will be delighted. The ladies of Rome don't care for being sunburnt."

"And after this is complete," says Stephanus, "I believe your second task for Domitian was to put on a private spectacle at his villa in the Alban Hills."

"Yes," I say. "We haven't yet planned the themes, but I can assure you it will be spectacular."

"I don't doubt that," he says. "The place is very beautiful and the amphitheatre has been well-designed, I am sure you will find everything you need."

"Is he there often?" I ask.

"He goes whenever possible in the hotter months. Rome's summers can be taxing and the Emperor feels the heat."

This chitchat about weather is beginning to strike me as ridiculous. "Did you want something particular from me today?" I ask, trying to sound polite.

He is silent for the space of three arches. "Can you include a lion in the spectacle?"

"A lion?"

"Yes."

I look at him but he seems to be looking through the arches, to the golden legs of the Colossoss statue which we can see from where we've reached.

"Is there a reason why you want a lion?"

"Yes."

I wait for further information but he doesn't say anything else. "May I know why?"

"No."

I open my mouth again but Stephanus stops and turns to me. His face is serious, and it strikes me that he is sad. "I have not forgotten your friend's untimely death," he says.

"Funis."

"Yes."

"Has the lion something to do with Funis?"

He gazes at me for a moment. "I would like the Games held in the Alban Hills to include a lion," he says. "Can you arrange that?"

"Yes," I say.

"Excellent. I must leave you."

And he's gone, disappearing into the busy Forum and leaving me wondering what is going on. Why would he want a lion? Is he going to throw some poor criminal to it? What would that have to do with Funis' death? I hope that he will not have the man who killed him put to death: much as I despise him, whoever held the knife was only a blade for hire, the real murderer was Funis' own father, who ordered his death, ashamed of having a gladiator and beast hunter for a bastard son by a slave woman, his own strange fixation with being high status leading him to obsessively hunt down and kill his own son, when any other senator or man of high rank would have shrugged and ignored him. I spit at the thought of him, hope that the gods will see what he did and punish him for it, one way or another. In my rage at Funis' death I had even thought of curse tablets, of finding a curse-maker and having my curse engraved in a lead sheet, calling on the gods to find the man and have him die as he had his own son die. Half of Rome has used curse tablets at one time or another, from the most absurd reasons such as their favourite pair of sandals being stolen at the baths to those seeking vengeance for greater misdeeds, but I have never done so myself. They frighten me, for what if they were to turn against the person laying the curse? Instead I have mourned Funis, taken fruits and flowers to temples in his memory, visited his friends in the gladiatorial barracks. I am not sure revenge or retribution could ever be brought down on a senator by plebians.

Later that day, I tell Marcus what has been asked of us.

"Why a lion?"

"He didn't say."

He frowns, turning it over in his mind. "I don't like requests I don't know the reason for," he says.

"I don't think Stephanus is going to share any further information with us."

Marcus shrugs. "Domitian likes wild beasts. If he wants a lion, we'll include a lion. I'm not looking forward to transporting one, mind. It'll be angry after hours of rattling along roads to the Alban Hills in a cart." He thinks. "We'll send it ahead, so that it has a day or so to become calm. Else it may not perform. It can eat before it leaves, so that a few days later it feels frisky again."

"We don't know what he wants it to do."

Marcus laughs. "Sing and dance? It'll be nothing. He'll have taken a fancy to having a lion as part of his Games. Our job is to keep him happy."

I nod as though I agree, but Stephanus' careful request for a lion comes back to me from time to time and I wonder what it may lead to.

Adah makes her way up to the rooftop to check on her bees. Now that spring has come, they are busy again, coming and going at a steady pace, setting out on their quests to find flowers across Rome, from the gardens of the wealthy up on the Palatine to the smallest patch of scrubby ground with early dandelions showing their bright flowers. The doves cluster around her feet, hopeful for corn.

"Thankfully they don't much care for eating bees," I say, throwing a few handfuls of corn away from her so the doves will get out from under her feet.

She nods. "They make good companions."

"I could have both at the farm. You could teach me how to care for the bees."

She nods but doesn't answer, she has begun a song she sings to them which she claims calms them, a song in her own Jewish tongue.

The time has come for the opening Games of the season. We reach the amphitheatre, where the usual ropes have been put up and our staff are manning the entrances to avoid people sneaking in without tokens. We show our own red tokens and make our usual checks of the hypogeum and seating areas. The velarium is folded up.

"You don't want it opened?"

Marcus shakes his head. "We need to open it when everyone's here. It'll get a round of applause which will please Domitian."

Servius is pacing back and forth in one of the corridors.

"What are you doing?" I ask.

"What if it doesn't open smoothly?" he asks. "In front of the Emperor, no less? Will he be very angry?"

I think of Domitian, scarlet with rage, eyes filled with furious tears, a sword in one shaking hand pointed at Marcus' throat. "I'm sure it'll be fine," I say. "Your men have practised a lot. It all seemed to be working well, didn't it? You've fixed any small niggles?"

He nods, miserable. "Could we try it one more time?"

"No," I say. "It takes at least half an hour to open and close it without any problems. I'm not risking it. If we hurry, something will go wrong. The crowds will start to gather in the next hour, I don't want last minute worries."

His shoulders slump.

It's like having a disappointed Karbo in front of me. I pat his arm. "You've done all you can. Now we have to focus on the show."

All too soon the crowds are allowed entrance. The wooden tiers fill up with slaves, as expected, leaving more room for the fine ladies of Rome to see and be seen on this, the opening day, when the most prestigious tickets are issued. They put up their parasols, which have always caused us trouble, since they block the view of those behind them, but I can see some of them peering upwards at the folded up velarium and the rope and metal structures towering over them. They are sitting close to where the velarium will be operated from, I notice quite a few of them casting admiring glances at the young sailors, smart in their blue-grey tunics which show off plenty of arm and thigh muscles ready to be used, unlike the portly toga-clad husbands of the ladies, who may be rich and high status but are perhaps no longer well-endowed with youth and strength.

I go to the corridor where Domitian and the imperial party will soon be arriving. There I meet Marcus and the Aedile, the three of us converging just as trumpets sound, followed by the tramp of heavy feet as his Praetorian bodyguards appear, all dressed in their crisp white togas. Despite their superficial appearance as ordinary citizens, their military haircuts, soldiers' boots and the menacing presence of sword hilts sticking out from their waistbands makes their purpose clear. They surround a small group made up of Domitian and Domitia with a few friends and relatives, invited to the opening day as a special sign of favour. We bow our heads as they swish past us and into the silken enclosure of the imperial box. Domitia's perfume trailing behind her, a heady mix of roses and sweet spices, no doubt the expensive work of Cosmus, Rome's most accomplished perfumier.

Domitian installed, Marcus gives the signal and, to the sound of rippling music, the velarium begins to open. The endless practice has paid off: it opens smoothly, gently, without noise or impediments and the audience breaks into applause as a deep and satisfying rosy-tinged shade covers them, leaving the arena itself shining in the bright sunlight. Servius sighs with relief next to me and I catch Marcus' pleased nod as a flock of white doves is released and heads straight through the open circle above us, a perfectly timed omen of good luck for the season ahead.

The venatores begin the day with a display of hunting ostriches and flamingos, which get the crowd's attention. We have never shown off such large birds and the ostriches are not only fast but violent, turning on their attackers, striking out with their clawed feet and large beaks.

We have a display of what appear to be painted statues of gods and heroes, which come to life and carry out some of the great myths beloved of the people; Zeus transforming into a swan and seducing Leda, who gives birth to a golden egg which becomes Helen, later stolen by Paris and starting the great war of Troy, which allows us to stage a range of battle scenes with our gladiators.

We have our rippling blue cloth sea across which sails Odysseus, who must close his ears to the song of the sirens, who are half-bird, half-woman. They should just be singing but these are the Games, after all, so the chorus provides the singing and a band of gladiatrices attacks a ship full of gladiators for a satisfying battle.

We re-enact Perseus and the Gorgon Medusa, where the gladiatrix playing Medusa first kills five criminals due for execution that day and then battles with Perseus. When she is overcome, from her blood springs forth Pegasus, a white horse whom we have provided with magnificent white wings, which are extended as it gallops around the arena.

Using tightrope walkers, Icarus spreads his wide wings and flies with his father, but comes too close to the sun, melting the wax holding his feathers in place and plummets to the ground, dying as his father grieves over him.

There are a few intervals during the day, where we continue our theme. Peacocks are brought into the arena and coaxed to put on a display for the peahens we have provided, the crowd murmuring at the beauty of their astonishing blue and green feathers trembling in the sunlight. A comedic routine is provided by a man and his wilful geese, who peck at his behind and attack him when he brings out a bucket of grain, having been kept hungry for a few days, leaving him lying flat on his back, disappearing under a pile of feathers. The crowd enjoys these lighter sections, they laugh and jeer while buying and eating snacks purchased from vendors who walk between the tiers with trays of food and drink. Chickpeas that have been salted and spiced, then roasted so that they are crunchy, cups of wine, warm bread and garum sauce to dip it in, fritters including those made with broad beans.

It is time to conclude the day with something special. The audience leaps to their feet, especially those in the cheaper stands, when instead of wooden balls with the names of gifts inscribed on them, we release hundreds of birds with ribbons tied to their feet, which flutter above the crowd, who grab at them and catch many, from the common doves to expensive parrots who have the gift of speech and many songbirds. The amphitheatre is a riot of colours and squawks, shouts and flapping birds. Some make their way to freedom, others think they have found freedom before they are suddenly caught and returned to captivity, either to be eaten or kept as pets.

"An excellent first day," says Domitian as he passes us in the corridor. He pauses and his entourage come to an abrupt halt. "The opening of the velarium was very smooth. How are the sailors doing?"

"They have been most professional," says Marcus. He pushes Servius forward. "This is Servius Gratius Celsus, Imperator, he is on his first command and has been a credit to the navy."

Servius gives a smart salute, standing to attention.

Domitian gives one of his rare smiles. "Excellent," he says. "Keep up the good work, you may make a name for yourself." He sweeps along the corridor, his entourage hurrying to keep up.

Servius is still standing to attention.

"You can relax," I say, laughing. "He's gone and he's happy with you."

He turns to Marcus, eyes wide, cheeks flushed. "You presented me to him."

Marcus grins. "I wanted you to have some credit too. You and your men have done a good job."

"Yes, sir. Thank you, sir. It was a great honour to meet the Emperor himself. My mother will be…" He takes a deep breath and for a brief moment his eyes shine as though he is about to cry. "She will be very proud, sir," he finishes.

Marcus pats his shoulder. "As she should be. Are you ever going to stop calling me sir?"

"No, sir."

"Perhaps a few drinks will loosen your tongue and you'll start calling me Marcus. Let's go. We all deserve a celebration."

Marcus has arranged for cakes and wine to be served when the crowds have gone and we gather in the swept arena, over a thousand of us, slaves, sailors, our staff, a few of the gladiators and Paternus and Labeo. There is a happy atmosphere, toasts are made and drunk to, a few people dance when the musicians strike up. I cannot remember such a celebration since we started. Marcus is full of cheer. The Games are underway, Domitian's first task has been accomplished in style, there are only two more to go and we will be free. The long winter is gone and our spirits are high.

IMPERIAL COLOURS

WE SETTLE INTO OUR ROUTINES, with Games every few days, allowing us the odd rest day when there is little to do, as well as time to prepare for the more elaborate shows. Some elements are repeated, others are one-off spectacles, but the theme of birds is popular. Girls who follow the Games wear feather trims on their best tunics and graffiti appears with various bird mythologies, in particular the battle of the Dwarfs and the Cranes, which we have as a running story. There are fewer arguments in the ladies' stands now that they no longer need their parasols. With things running smoothly we can turn our attention to Karbo's Liberalia festival, when he will become a man.

Two days before, Quintus arrives on the rooftop where I'm listening to the nightingales, who have grown bolder and now sing often. He has a parcel which he hands to me with excessive care. "I had mother put her best slave on the job," he says.

When he's gone I open the parcel and find inside Fausta's toga, which I kept all these years in my chest. The fullery have cleaned it perfectly. I walk down into the courtyard where I find Julia caring for her plants.

"I wanted to put scent on Karbo's adult toga," I tell her.

She helps me pick rosemary, sage and mint from her collection of herbs.

"You have a whole garden in a courtyard," I say.

She straightens, puts a hand to her back. "I started with a tiny rosemary plant, I barely thought it would survive. Now look at it."

It's a huge bush, the children sometimes hide behind it when they play their games. "I'll have to take a cutting with me to the farm," I say.

She smiles. "I would like to think your plants on the farm were kin to mine here in Rome."

I rub the herbs across the creamy folds of the toga to give the scent Fausta always had about her, fold it with care and put it out of sight. At the ceremony, Karbo will give up the purple-bordered toga praetexta of childhood, not that he has ever worn it much, for the plain white toga which will mark him as an adult. I've decided to give him Fausta's to wear. It might seem odd to give him a she-wolf's toga, but she was like a mother to him. This way, he will have a lasting memory of her; Fausta will be wrapped about him every time he goes out into the world as a well-dressed man.

Some of Karbo's friends and their parents are making preparations as well, the fathers booking barbers for their son's first ritual shave, the mothers sewing new tunics and ordering togas. We exchange congratulations and also worries: is it too soon? Should we have waited another year? This fear is in part allayed when we see the boys together, almost the height of men, seriously discussing the merits of one racing team or another, but their excitement gets the better of them and they end up playing their old games of catch, rushing about the courtyard and up and down the stairs, making a huge amount of noise and laughing till they almost cry. On these occasions they look like little children again and we feel like fools for believing they are grown up enough to have a coming-of-age ceremony. But we are committed, the seventeenth day of March is only a few days away and with it will come Liberalia, the festival celebrating Liber Pata, an ancient god of fertility similar to Bacchus for his love of wine and merriment, as well as his consort Libera. Masks are hung in trees all over Rome the day before in preparation and Marcus takes Karbo to the baths, where he will be shaved, so that a little stubble can be placed in his protective bulla necklace.

"Stubble? What stubble?" teases Marcus as they go down the stairs, to applause. Everyone in our insula is leaning from their balconies, doors and windows. "I think we will put it off till next year after all."

"I do have stubble," protests Karbo, rubbing his hand over his chin.

"Ah well, I suppose you are a man." Marcus sighs dramatically. "A man already, in my own household. Who would have thought it, when you first came to us? A pup, that's all you were. And now look at you, you vast hound!" He winks at me as they stride off together down Sand Street.

"He's so grown up," I say to the baker's wife. "A man already."

"Ah, they stay your child for many years to come," she tells me. "Come to think of it, I'm not sure they ever really grow up. You'll see him come running back to you with his worries even when you thought you had him safely married off. Your mother is always your mother."

Karbo returns, glowing from being rubbed down with oil and bathed, as well as from receiving his first shave. He shows me the tiny dots of stubble they have collected and we carefully place them inside his bulla, ready to be offered up at our Lararium, the shrine of our household gods. I take his purple-bordered toga praetexta and lay it on the ground below the shrine.

As head of our household, it falls to Marcus to present Karbo to the household gods. We stand in front of the Lararium, where two candles have been lit, and Marcus raises his palms, speaking with formality.

"Gods of this household and of the world beyond our doors, it is I, Marcus Aquillius Scaurus, master of this home, who asks for your blessings today for the Liberalia ceremony. I present to you my son Karbo, grown to be a man. Accept the toga of his childhood, the bulla which protected him as a boy and the stubble of his first shave. Watch over him now that he is no longer a child. Let him be a good man, honourable and brave, and let him always come home safe to his family. May he live a long and peaceful life, may he find love one day and may he sire many sons."

He lifts the bulla away from Karbo's neck and places it on the small ledge in front of the shrine. I pass him the folded adult toga and he shakes it out, the vast folds of cream cloth taking up most of the room.

"It was Fausta's," I whisper to Karbo and his eyes shine with tears for a moment at the thought of her, but he is beaming as Marcus dresses him with care. The endless quantity of heavy fabric swamps even Karbo's long frame, but I can see that he is delighted and that Marcus, for all his teasing, is bursting with pride.

Dressed in our best clothes, we reach the Forum, where a huge procession has developed. At the centre is the wooden and painted structure of a large phallus, set onto a bier and carried by a multitude of young men celebrating their coming of age. As it moves unsteadily through the crowd, different boys step forward to shoulder the heavy statue and then step back into the crowd, beaming. Karbo wriggles to the front of the crowd and takes his turn, returning to us further down the street.

"It's really heavy!"

Marcus laughs. "The burden of being a good man is a heavy load," he says. "Better learn that quickly. Come, we must sacrifice."

We find one of many roadside altars surrounded by the Sacerdos Liberi, the older women who serve as priestesses to Liber. Today they are crowned with ivy and have baked cakes made with honey and oil. These we place on the altar and pray for Karbo to be granted a long and happy life. There is dancing and the singing of increasingly ribald songs, cakes and wine to eat and drink. As the day comes to a close a respected matron is chosen to place a wreath of foliage and flowers over the phallus and we return home, tired and happy. We both embrace Karbo before he goes off to sleep.

"A good day," says Marcus with satisfaction.

"It was," I agree. I take the little bulla from the altar and tuck it away in my chest of clothes.

"Superstitious?" asks Marcus watching me with a smile.

I shrug. "Everyone does it," I say. If a son should ever receive a public triumph or be otherwise successful, the bulla of his childhood, if kept by his mother, is said to protect him against envy.

"He's going to be a farmer," says Marcus.

"People can be envious for many reasons," I say.

"I envy people who are asleep," says Marcus, holding out his arms to me. "Come here."

Formal announcements are made, but they're not needed;

word has already spread all over Rome that Domitian is going to introduce two new racing teams to the existing four. The Whites, Reds, Greens and Blues will be joined by the imperial Purple and Gold teams. There's excitement about what this will mean for race days: more teams competing, more combinations of different teams to race each other. There will be opportunities for promising young drivers to be considered for new roles as older, more experienced, drivers receive promotions or leave one team to join another. The team owners and trainers will have more chances of poaching the best and bravest, luring those who are free away from their existing teams with promises of greater riches and glory, those who are enslaved with their freedom.

The fans are unsure what this will mean. Each fan has been loyal to their own team for years, perhaps even generations, father to son passing down a deep and abiding love for the Reds, or the Blues, sneering at the Greens or the Whites, jeering at their drivers, scornfully assessing their lack of prowess, even to the point of ending up in a scuffle. It would be unthinkable for them to support another team. But what if a favourite driver is poached? Should they follow him to the new colours, or deride him for leaving the team behind? If the new teams have been chosen by Domitian, will they have the very best of everything, making them more likely to win? Will they even, the gods forbid, be given privileges on the track, a tiny headstart? The officials looking the other way when teams or drivers misbehave, try to rig the races? It's all anyone talks about while the drivers preen and pose, hoping for their biggest chance yet to make a name for themselves.

"They'll be recruiting soon," says Celer as I pass him in the courtyard on the way back from the bakery. Karbo is sitting next to him, the two of them engrossed in conversation.

I pause by them, pass each of them a fruit roll. "Who?"

"The Purple and Gold racing teams," says Celer, his shrug making it clear this is the only possible topic he could have been referring to.

"The stables must be in a frenzy," I say.

"They are. They're being expanded to accommodate the two new teams. Building works everywhere. The horses don't like all the noise, it's making them skittish."

"Be careful when you're working, Karbo," I say.

He nods without answering, mouth full of bun.

"They need everything from stable cleaners to drivers," says Celer.

"You sticking with the Blues or hoping to switch to a new team?" I ask Karbo, a teasing smile on my face. I expect an outraged answer complete with all the reasons why it would be unthinkable to leave the Blues, his favourite team.

But he looks thoughtful. "Might be better opportunities on a new team," he says.

"Opportunities? Are the Purple and Gold horses more likely to need their stables cleaning?" I smile, pat his arm and am halfway up the stairs before a sudden thought strikes me and I lean over the bannister. "As long as you have no intentions of going for a driving position, Karbo, you know how I feel about that."

"I know," he says.

"You know as well, Celer," I say, pointing at him. "Don't go putting ideas in his head, if you please. Or you'll have me to answer to."

He raises his hands in a placatory gesture. "Never said a word. Just discussing what they're doing. How things may change. Who's tipped for new drivers, all of that. Only gossip, Althea."

"It had better be all you're discussing," I say. "I want Karbo with me on the farm, where I know he is safe."

Adah is passing and she nods at my warning. "That place is cursed," she says, referring to the Flavian Amphitheatre. "The sooner you leave the better. A farm is a good place for a growing boy."

"See?" I tell Karbo. "Adah agrees with me too."

The Games keep us busy. Most mornings I head to the amphitheatre to ensure everything is prepared for each show and on the days when the Games are on I am always in attendance.

The criminal in today's Games is going to fight blind. He's been given a real sword, but the helmet that has been forced onto his head, which he cannot remove, only leaves space for his mouth, so he can breathe. Where a face should be, where the eyeholes should be, there is nothing, just smooth metal, making him faceless, blind. He will fight in terrifying darkness, flailing about him with the sword, hoping for death to come quickly, not to suffer too long. I lower my eyes as he is loaded into the lift, shaking and begging for mercy. It's not a kind fate and I hope the professional gladiator he'll be fighting will finish him off as soon as possible.

The fight begins. A young gladiator has been chosen to engage with the blind criminal. He's a promising fighter and may have a good career ahead of him, so it's a good opportunity for him to get attention but not be in much danger; the criminal cannot fight well, being neither a fighter by trade nor even able to see. When the criminal staggers out of the lift he turns this way and that, unsure of where his opponent is, until a fast cut on the arm draws immediate blood. In terrified desperation, the criminal slashes all around him, wielding the heavy sword poorly, at one moment almost dropping it. The gladiator, light on his feet, dances around him, his sword quick and sharp, the criminal crying out when he is cut on his torso and again on one thigh. Frantic, he lunges forwards and by some stroke of luck manages to slice into the gladiator's leg, who steps back in shock, then, angered, rushes forwards and stabs the criminal in the neck, so that a sudden gush of blood spills out. But as the criminal falls, he manages to grab at his opponent's tunic hem and in his dying moments, gives one last swing of his sword and cuts the gladiator's arm open. The referee steps forwards to intervene but it's too late anyway, the criminal sinks to the sand and takes his last breath, while the young gladiator, shocked and wounded, is hurried away to our physician Fabius.

In the medical bay, Fabius is irritable as he patches him up. "Bloody fool, getting your arm cut by a blinded criminal, what will happen to you when you're in a real gladiatorial bout?" he snaps to the crestfallen young man, then gestures for his assistant. "Clean up the leg wound so I can stitch it. Not there, *there*, have you learnt nothing at all in your time with me? Idiot."

It's unlike calm Fabius to be so grumpy, but the young gladiator could do with a telling off for taking stupid chances. A blind man with a sword still has a sword, he should not have risked being injured. If the cuts had been deeper, he could have been limping for the rest of his life and that would have put an end to his career in the arena.

"Are you alright, Fabius?" I ask.

"Yes, yes," he snaps, then sighs. "Sorry, Althea. Can't be doing with this nonsense anymore. Stupid boy. Put your leg there so I can see what I'm doing."

I nod to the beleaguered assistant and slumped gladiator and go home for the day. Fabius does not lose his temper when he's working. Perhaps he, too, is tiring of the Games, or is sorry to be losing Marcus as the manager of the amphitheatre, not knowing who they will choose as a replacement. I should ask Marcus to persuade Fabius to retire to the countryside near the farm so that he can have a peaceful life and Marcus will have his old friend nearby.

There are a few updates from the racing stables over the next few weeks. The head trainer from the Blues has been poached for the Purples, three skilled drivers have shifted from one team to another for the chance of being one of their top drivers. It's all promotions and poaching for a while, along with endless gossip and speculation. I get bored of it soon enough and stop listening. So when Karbo comes home one afternoon and sits slumped in the courtyard while I am washing our tunics, unusually silent, I think of things any mother thinks of.

"Are you well? You're very quiet," I say.

"I'm fine."

"None of your friends here to play today?"

"We don't *play*," he says, huffing. "We talk and things. We're men now," he reminds me.

I think of the yelling and running games that still appeal, Liberalia or no Liberalia. "Of course. But they're not here today? Did you fall out?"

"No."

"Is there anything you need to talk about?"

"No."

I carry on washing my two linen tunics, which have spent the winter in storage and are in need of fresh water and air. My woollen clothes are beginning to get too hot as the days grow ever warmer. I dunk the tunics in the cold fountain water, then immerse them a few more times. They're clean enough but hanging in the fresh warm spring air, followed by a light rubbing of fresh herbs, will make them fragrant again. Karbo's summer tunics, I realise when I hold them up, will barely reach his knees.

"Looks like you need some new clothes," I say, hoping to raise a smile, for Karbo is fond of looking smart, excited by the prospect of a new belt or shoes and always by new tunics.

There's no reply. I glance at him again and see him sitting with his chin on his knees, staring at me.

"Thought of something you want to say to me after all?"

"The Purple team held try outs today."

"Held what?"

"Try outs."

"Which are what?"

"Boys who want to be drivers get a chance to take a chariot and two horses round the arena. Three laps. They start in the morning and the slowest driver in each round gets eliminated. The fastest one at the end of the day gets hired as a driver in the lowest tier, but they can work their way up to be top drivers one day."

Perhaps he has seen one of the horrible accidents that happen on the track involving young drivers or those desperate to prove themselves and it has upset him. "Was there an accident?"

"What? No. Well, yes, but nothing bad. The boy was one of the early ones in the morning, he couldn't control the horses well enough and they crashed into a wall. The left horse was hurt but it can be saved. He was just embarrassed."

"Lucky to only be embarrassed," I say.

Karbo mumbles something but I can't hear him as I pull out a dripping tunic and start squeezing the water out of it.

"What?"

"I tried out."

I drop the tunic into the water. "You tried out as a driver?"

"Yes." He won't meet my eyes.

I sigh, try to manage my emotions. "And it didn't go well? Karbo, I didn't want you to try out. But perhaps it's just as well you did and realised it's harder than it looks. Stick with what you do. You could be a trainer one day, it's a lot safer."

"I won."

"What?"

He lifts his chin, defiant, though his eyes flicker away under my aghast gaze. "I was the fastest. All day. I finished half a lap ahead of the second fastest. They made me race one more time against their top driver. I was one chariot length behind him and he's won everything, he has the finest horses in the stable. They said I'm the best they've ever seen at try outs." He swallows and his newly deep voice wavers with resentment and frustration; I can hear the child he was until not very long ago. "I'm the best they've seen – and you and Marcus won't let me race."

It's my turn to swallow. "Karbo, I –"

He's up and running up the stairs, face screwed up in a crying grimace, a little boy again. I start after him, before sinking back down in despair. I've known this day was coming, I tell myself, it was always coming even though I tried to ward it off. Karbo is truly gifted with horses. They listen to him, they calm at his approach. He begged to work for the Blues, was ecstatic when told he could clean stables and polish leather tack for them. He has watched races with a gleam in his eye which told me there was trouble ahead. And yes, there are racing drivers who are the toast of Rome, who have screaming fans and lavish lifestyles, earning more than most people can dream of making; even the best gladiators struggle to match their money. But the cold hard truth is that the drivers are young, there are no old drivers. It's a young man's game, because the older drivers lose their nerve when they have wives and children and because far too many promising young drivers meet horrible ends, losing limbs and lives to the dizzying speed and lethal corners of the Circus. I've seen such accidents for myself. Celer, who escaped with his life, has terrifying scars down his body and a drinking habit that left him all alone before Julia took him in and kept him more or less in this world. My shoulders sag. It's not what I want for Karbo, nor what Marcus wants. Marcus, as his father, can forbid it of course, can oblige him to come to the farm, to the safe life we have planned in the country, but is that cruel to Karbo, to drag him away from what he so desperately wants, from what he seems born for? I don't know what to do.

I find Marcus and the same conversation plays out between us, this time out loud instead of in my head. It makes it less lonely I suppose, but both of us sigh often, grimace at either option available to us, shake our heads, then start the circular logic all over again. Karbo stays out of sight until Marcus goes to talk to him, but the talk does not last long and Marcus returns looking defeated.

"I feel I'm taking his dreams away," he says. "But I can't bear to think of losing him when I've already…" He trails off, but I complete the thought in my mind. Marcus has already lost one child, his baby son Amantius, only just walking when Vesuvius erupted and crushed Pompeii, taking Marcus' wife and child. To find another child and adopt him, to open up his wounded heart only to have it broken again…

We lie in our bed in gloomy silence. There is nothing we have not already said and when we meet for breakfast Karbo's eyes are red-rimmed and he is silent, poking at his food at Cassia's counter before morosely heading to the stables, where no doubt the team are waiting to praise him and yet he cannot revel in it because he does not have our consent.

"We need to go to the stables," says Marcus at last. "I can't think about anything else with this hanging over us. We have to make a decision."

We trail down the streets hand in hand, neither of us saying anything, until the stables come into view. There's building work everywhere, as Celer told us; making room for two whole new teams is a substantial undertaking and everyone seems to be in a hurry.

"Scaurus!"

Marcus nods at the trainer for the Blues. "Good to see you, my friend."

"Ah but you've raised a star, Marcus! Never seen anything like it. The boy's going to be crowned with golden laurels, I swear it. We should have spotted him sooner and kept him for ourselves. There's no chance now the Purples have seen him, they've got the imperial purse on their side and they know a hero when they see one. Half a lap ahead! And he was one chariot length, perhaps not even that, behind our top driver and that didn't half humiliate him, I can tell you. Neck and neck with a nobody? He'll not hear the end of that soon, I tell you, everyone was calling him 'new boy' and referring to Karbo as 'champion.'"

Marcus nods. "I need a word, though."

"Don't say you won't allow it, Scaurus, the boy is under Neptune's protection, anyone can see it."

"Will Neptune be protecting him when someone comes up too close and there's an accident? They happen all the time, you can't tell me they don't. I can't stand by and let him take the risk."

"We all walk into danger every day that we wake up and get out of bed, Scaurus. The boy has a gift. And he's well liked here, the little boys look up to him and the older ones hang about with him. The trainers always have time for his questions."

"None of that will help on the racetrack."

"It helps if you know what you're doing. I have drivers who have nothing but wool for brains. They're young. They like the speed, they like the thrill. They like the applause and the women afterwards. They take stupid risks and get themselves hurt or killed."

"That's what we're afraid of," says Marcus.

"But Karbo, he's different. He spent weeks with the wheelwrights, learning everything about their trade that he could, he spends hours checking how the tack fits, whether adjustments can be made to better suit each horse, he pays attention to each beast's temperament, whether it would be better suited to the left or the right in training. Everything. Every little detail. He didn't keep pace with the top driver because he whipped on the horses, he kept pace because he chose the right beasts and spent over an hour readying them before he took them out. Every round we put them through he was adjusting tiny things, things no-one else would even bother with. His own stance, the horse's bit, the condition of the track."

Marcus nods, though he doesn't look comforted at hearing Karbo's skills and attention extolled. The trainer is still gushing.

"He walked the track before every single round, did you know that? And when the time came to race Museus, he asked for an extra half hour so the horses could rest, he made sure they had warm water to drink, not cold and he walked the track again even though the other lads were laughing at him and asking how much could it have changed in half an hour? But he was right to do it. Scorpus of the Greens was watching and he said that's a boy he'd like to race in a few years' time. Scorpus said that!"

"I'd like to see him on the track," says Marcus. "Can that be arranged?"

"Of course. The Purples are training today and they'll let him take a chariot out for you to see. He has to have your permission or they'll not be able to have him."

We follow him in silence to the training track, a less ostentatious version of the Circus Maximus. It's shorter on the lengths, but the ends are a similar size, so that the charioteers can grow used to the cornering. Twelve chariots are ready for use, with teams varying from one horse for the beginners to the most used twos and fours, as well as one team of six and one of twelve, used for the impressive effect they give when driven, a test of the driver's skills, not for true racing.

"Karbo is preparing them, as you can see."

Karbo is inspecting a horse's hooves, running one hand down each leg and gently lifting it. The horse is allowing this, although as soon as he has finished it snorts and tosses its head, eager to be let loose on the track. These horses have been born and bred for speed; the racetrack is their home and the place where they are eager to perform. They are restless, stamping feet and sniffing the air, waiting for the moment when they will take flight, their hooves pounding down the track, the screams of the crowd, their driver's voice urging them on.

I tighten my grip on Marcus' hand as the trainer walks down to Karbo and speaks with him. Karbo's head turns quickly in our direction, a guilty look on his face as though we have caught him doing something wrong, even though he is only doing what is expected of a senior stableboy. Marcus raises his hand in salutation and after a moment's hesitation Karbo waves back.

The trainer speaks with him again and Karbo's face changes, he frowns and shakes his head.

"He doesn't want to race in front of us," I say.

"We need to see him," says Marcus. "I can't make a decision without seeing him for myself."

"Are you thinking of allowing it? It would mean him not coming to the farm. He would live all alone in Rome."

Marcus looks down at me. "I don't know," he says honestly. "I'm afraid for him, just as you are, that's the truth. But I can't trample on his dreams without being fair to him and the only fair thing I can think of is to see him race for myself. I've seen him with horses before and what they say is true, he does have a gift for them. Is it right for me to take away what he is good at? It would mean him staying here when we go, but our insula would take every care of him."

"He could be a trainer," I mutter, but I have a horrible feeling I am about to lose my case.

"He could," agrees Marcus. "But most of the trainers were once drivers."

"They're the ones who survived," I say.

"Yes," agrees Marcus. He lets go of my hand, puts his arm about me and pulls me closer. "I'm not going against you, Althea. I would not worry you for nothing. But Karbo has a right to be successful, if he has talent."

"I don't care about him being successful," I say. "I'm scared for him."

"Let's see him drive," says Marcus.

It seems Karbo has been persuaded. He is walking the track, looking on the ground as well as all around him as he progresses round the elongated oval.

"What is he looking for?" I ask the trainer, who has made his way back to us.

"Any bumps, dips. The track's kept smooth but even a pebble can throw your chariot off course if you put a wheel on it the wrong way. And he's feeling it, thinking about what he can do at each part, what happens if another driver forces him to take a different part of the track."

"Is he going to drive against someone now?" I ask, anxiety rising.

"Yes, but that proves what I was telling you," says the trainer. "It's just an informal trial and he's still doing all the work."

"Don't the other drivers do this?" I protest.

"They don't," says the trainer with a grimace. "They rely on their trainer, or they do it once in the morning and call it done. They don't do it before every time trial or practice, that's for sure. They don't even bother doing it more than once on race day. They're told it will make them better drivers, but they don't listen. Young men think they're gods, that it's all about talent, no hard work required. They think they're immortal."

"That's what I'm afraid of," I say.

"But that's not Karbo," insists the trainer. "Look at him, he's walked half the track and when he gets back, he won't leap in the chariot and be off. He'll check the harness and the wheels, he'll talk to the horses, he'll check his reins and he'll check his knife."

I shudder at the thought of the knife that every charioteer keeps on their person, the knife that will cut them free of the reins wrapped round their waist, should the worst happen and the chariot be turned over. A driver can be dragged behind the horses, ripping their flesh open, even killing them, if they cannot get free of the reins. Marcus' tightening arm reminds me of the moment when Karbo took Celer's knife and slipped into the dark waters of the flooded amphitheatre to save Marcus' life, while I sat next to the Emperor Titus and believed I was watching them both die. I swallow.

At last Karbo steps into the chariot, which is drawn by two horses. The more senior drivers use four, but two, with a light chariot, can get to astonishing speeds. A stablehand helps to wrap the reins round Karbo's waist, allowing him to steer with his body as well as his hands. Meanwhile a second chariot is being prepared, with a tall young man having reins wrapped about him. He has an arrogant look to him, smirking over his shoulder at Karbo.

"That's Museus," says the trainer. "He's still a slave, but he's going to be rich one day, no doubt about it. He's been the best driver for the Whites since that accident last year when two of their team died. Now he's transferred to the Purples there'll be no stopping him. Except your boy, of course."

I shudder and the trainer catches it. "I know. But did you see Museus walk the track? No, you didn't, because he's an arrogant young pup. He's got his eye on girls and money. Karbo's got his eye on the horses because he cares. He loves being with them. Museus sees them as the means to an end. There's a difference and it shows in their results."

The two chariots are lined up, the horses tossing their heads and sidestepping, the stable hands holding them back so that they won't suddenly take off.

"Three laps," says the trainer. "Enough to see how they do against each other. Museus isn't best pleased about this," he adds. "He thought he'd be the shining star on this team, but Karbo made him look a fool. A stable hand who cleans the tack and shovels the shit, almost beating him? And a freedman, of course, that will rile him too. Museus wants to earn his freedom, but no stables will grant that too soon. It's what makes him a good driver, the need to do well so that he might be free."

I'm sorry for Museus. Still a slave, earning his masters large amounts of money and desperate for his freedom, desperate enough to go that little bit faster, to take the corner that little more recklessly… I give a silent prayer of gratitude that Karbo is already free. If he must race, he can race because he loves it, not out of desperation.

"They're ready," says the trainer. I grip Marcus' hand.

The white handkerchief falls and the horses leap forward, the chariots in full motion where they were stationary only a breath ago. They head away from us, speeding down the track, dust rising under the hooves and wheels. Museus is using his whip, lashing the backs of the horses, while Karbo is swaying in his chariot.

"He's moving them round every little imperfection of the track," murmurs the trainer. "I told you."

Karbo's chariot edges ahead, but it is not enough, Museus manages to take the inside track on the first corner, Karbo just behind, but as they come down the track towards us, he begins to gain.

"Not enough for the corner," says the trainer.

He's right. Again, Museus takes the corner and Karbo is forced to go wider.

"But he's catching up every time," says the trainer in admiration. "Can you see? Even though he's had to go wide twice, he's catching up. If he was in the Circus Maximus, he'd be winning, no contest."

The third corner and the fourth, Karbo is edged out but as he heads out for the final lap he leans forwards more and, incredibly, the horses go faster, even though the reins are looser.

"Letting them feel freedom," says the trainer. "It's risky, because some horses lose focus when you do that. You have to know the team, you have to let them feel the excitement and let them loose at the right moment."

They come down the final straight neck and neck and then Karbo edges ahead, his chariot in line with Museus' horses and Museus' face contorts in a grimace of rage as they finish with Karbo the winner. The stable hands run out to hold the sweating horses, a junior trainer unwinds the reins. Museus turns and stamps away without a word, face dark with anger and humiliation. Karbo watches him go, awaiting his own assistance with patience. At last the reins are unwound and he steps out of the chariot and walks round to the horses, nuzzles each of them, patting their necks, speaks to a stable hand, giving instructions, before heading up towards us.

He stands in front of us, face flushed, eyes pleading.

"Well raced, Karbo," says the trainer.

"Thank you, Dominus," says Karbo respectfully. He looks at Marcus. "You saw me?" he says, knowing full well we have both seen the race.

Marcus nods, his face serious. "We saw you."

"I'm not saying it because you're his parents," says the trainer. "He's the best I've ever seen and I've seen boys and men come and go in the racing game. Poor ones, good one, even the greats. I spotted Scorpus when he was a boy and I knew he had talent. But Karbo, he's even better than Scorpus was at his age. He feels the horses. And they feel him, you can see how they respond and he's a new driver. Wait till he has a team of horses who've raced with him a hundred times."

Marcus is looking at the ground. "I will give my permission," he starts, "but his mother must have her say. I cannot break her heart and I know she is fearful for him. Althea?"

I look down at Karbo's feet, now the size of Marcus', the twitching movement of his toes inside the leather as he waits, anxious, for my reply. I think of how he was the first time I saw him, a struggling scrawny boy held fast in Maria's grip, who told me his name under duress. A street rat, she called him, a runaway slave scraping a living on the street who had to be coaxed with the promise of food and a safe place to sleep at night to become our messenger boy. He had attached himself to Fausta and lost her to the fever, then slowly came to see me as his mother. I wonder where his real mother is, if she would let him become a driver because he wants it so much or whether she would allow her own fears for him to take hold of her and refuse, keep him safe but unhappy at her side. I wish it could be her choosing, but it falls to me.

Swallowing, I bow my head in assent and am almost knocked over by Karbo flinging his arms around me.

"Thank you! Thank you! I'll be safe, I'll be careful, I promise, I promise. Thank you!"

I put my arms around him and try to smile at Marcus, although it's more of a grimace. He pats Karbo's shoulder and nods at me.

"Do your best to keep that promise, Karbo, Althea would be heartbroken should any harm come to you. As would I."

I let Karbo chatter and show us round the half-built Purple stables, look in at the Blues, whom he is still fond of, accepting the praises and well wishes of everyone who knows him. I can see for myself that he is well liked and trusted, that he has built his own community here and that gives me some comfort.

"We should be going," says Marcus at last. "We will see you back at the insula, Karbo."

We walk back together in silence until we reach the rooftop and sit down under the pergola.

"Was I right?" asks Marcus at last.

"Yes," I say. "But I am so afraid." And my tears come. I held them back all this time and now they pour out of me, the fear and worry released. Marcus holds me, allows me to cry without trying to falsely comfort me.

"I want him to be happy and safe," I say at last when the tears have slowed, trying to wipe my face.

"I fear for him as you do," says Marcus. "But I cannot bring myself to forbid him."

I nod, shaky. "I never thought we'd have to make such choices."

"I hoped he'd want to be safe in the countryside with us. But there are few paths in life without some danger attached to them."

"I suppose."

"If Neptune has smiled on him thus far, he will keep him safe."

I allow myself to be comforted, but when Marcus has fallen asleep I take out Karbo's bulla from my chest and say another small prayer to the gods, above all Neptune, to protect the boy they have set on this path. Then I hide it away again, for a driver touted to be as great as Scorpus will one day need protection from envy.

ILL OMENS

T HE LONGER DAYS OF MAY have fooled me into leaving the baths late, and twilight is coming. I walk faster, anxious to be back inside the safety of the insula before darkness falls. The streets of Rome are not safe for anyone when night comes. I join Sand Street, relieved to be just a few moments from home, but ahead of me a figure steps out, stands motionless, blocking my way to the welcoming lanterns inside Cassia's popina. I gasp before I realise it is a woman. A dark green palla covers her head and drapes down to her long brown tunic. Her face is hard to see. I could correct my course, move to the left or right of her and keep walking, but there is something about her that makes me think she is here for me, that she wants to address me.

"Can I help you?" I call out, still twenty paces from her, my steps slowing, growing anxious again because of her stillness in the darkening twilight.

"Althea," she says.

"Yes?" I say. "Do I know you?"

She pulls back her palla so I can see her face. The sorceress. The one who lives close to Quintus' family fullery, a few streets away. I have not seen her since the day Cassia's wedding to Rullus failed, when the sorceress threw strange words at us and I grew angry with her. Only afterwards did Cassia and I look back and think that her words had been wise, that she had changed our actions on that doomed day and set the Fates to weave a better story for Cassia – or perhaps she knew all along the story they were weaving and pushed us to take the right steps. Either way, that day her words and actions had saved Cassia from a terrible marriage and so I bow my head with respect, then look up with a smile.

"I never thanked you for what you did, what you said," I say. "Cassia brought you a thank you gift for herself, but I was grateful too." I give a laugh. "And really, I owe you a gift myself. You said that when I knew what my desire was, I should say it out loud. And I did and it took some time, but you were right, my desire did come to me." I gesture at my own palla, wrapped about my head and shoulders against the evening chill. "I am a married woman now."

The sorceress does not smile. She does not act as though she has ever seen me before, only stares into my eyes, her face devoid of expression. "There is a darkness coming," she says.

"What?"

"There is a darkness coming," she repeats. Her voice sounds cold and hard, echoing in the empty street. "A creeping black, seeping into your life. You must leave Rome."

I stare at her. The hairs across the back of my neck rise and a cold shiver ripples across me. "A creeping black? What do you mean? When is it coming? What is it?" My voice is too high, I sound like a child. I swallow and try to speak more normally. "Have you had a vision?" I ask. "Did you see something bad come into my life?" The decision we have made about Karbo's future, have we made a mistake, set something bad in motion?

"Leave Rome," she says again, and her voice has not changed, it is still too loud and cold and without feeling, as if a stone statue is speaking.

She pulls up her palla, so that her face is thrown back into deep shadow and turns away, walks down Sand Street, turns into Virgin's Street and onwards, disappearing into the growing gloom.

The words of the sorceress linger, I cannot dismiss them with ease. I wonder if perhaps she is angry. Her advice to me led, in a way, to knowing my true feelings for Marcus and telling him so, yet I have not offered her payment. Fabia and Cassia both made payments to her and so, the next day, I take some of my savings and go to a jeweller, where I ask for a little dove made in silver, a sign of love and marriage. He works a pretty thing, tiny and yet beautiful. It sits in my palm as I turn it to admire the dainty workmanship. I pay him and make my way towards home, but go further down Virgin's Street, past the welcoming insula gate and the bakery, onwards down a warren of little streets, the acrid stench of the fullery hitting my nostrils. I wave at one of Quintus' brothers as I pass. We know all of his family now, a friendly, noisy group, always cheerful and full of stories and songs to while away time when work is busy.

I turn down another little street. I have reached my destination, the house of the sorceress set in a tiny courtyard. The same silent slave girl I saw before appears and when she sees me she nods, as though I had made an appointment, and gestures to me to follow. I do so and she leaves me in the room I visited with Cassia and Fabia over two years ago. It is full of the smell of incense and dimly lit, tinted red from the scarlet cloth hanging over the single window. I sit down on the low bench that faces the sorceress' carved chair, wishing for the comfort of Cassia and Fabia on either side of me, huddled together for courage.

"I did not expect you."

I jump, even though I knew she would appear like this, all of a sudden from behind the high red screen. I half-rise, then sit again. "When I saw you – when you spoke to me in the street – I said I owed you a gift, and I do," I say.

She stays standing, looking down on me. "A gift?"

I take out the little package of cloth and pass it to her. She takes it, opens it with care, nods her head in acceptance at the silver dove.

"Did you think I was angry because you had not given me a gift in recognition of what I told you about finding your desires?" she asks.

"Yes," I confess.

She shakes her head. "I do not care if those I help acknowledge it or not," she says. "I thank you for this and am glad you are now a married woman. But I saw a darkness in your future and I needed to tell you of it."

"But what did you see?" I ask. "What exactly?"

"Black," she says.

"Black what?" I ask.

She shakes her head. "I don't know. Everything was black. You were dressed in black, all around you was black. Everything."

I swallow. When we first came to see the sorceress, on a whim of Cassia's, it seemed no more than something to laugh over between friends, for who could know if she really had any powers or was just a fraud? But her words came true for Fabia, followed by her much-needed intervention in Cassia's first doomed wedding plans, and more recently my own union with Marcus has been guided by her and so her words hold more sway with me. I struggle to think what she might mean. "You couldn't see anything around me but black?" I try again.

"Everything around you was black," she corrects me. "A black room, with black walls, black furniture. The light…" she hesitates, as though unwilling to add this detail. "The only light came from a funerary lamp."

I pull back from her, gesturing against evil. I think for a moment with horror at the fate of Cornelia last year, the Vestal Virgin entombed alive for violating her sacred duty by lying with a man. Darkness was all around her as she waited for death to come, buried under the earth while Rome watched in silent horror at what the law required. I am no Vestal, such a fate could not befall me no matter how much I might enrage Domitian, but why would the sorceress see such a thing when she looks at me?

"I do not mean to frighten you but to warn you," she says. She finally takes her own seat, though she leans forward towards me, eager to impart her knowledge. "I saw you in this vision and I came to tell you because I know who you are, it was not a vision of an unnamed woman, it was you I saw."

"And there was danger?" I ask, though how could there not be, with such a vision?

She nods. "It was all around you, but I did not see where you were. Can you think of such a place?"

"No."

She leans back in her seat, looking weary. "I cannot see more than that, I have tried," she says. "I can only warn you that the place is dangerous and that you should avoid it."

"How can I avoid it if I don't know where or what it is?"

"Be wary of anything that may come to resemble it."

I try to think of dark places in my life. Pompeii, lost under unending grey ash. The under-arena. It has already claimed its share of unexpected and unfair deaths, with Funis last year and those who were mistaken for him. The Vestal Virgin's last resting place, but that is sealed up. The Tullianum, the prison I once visited when we needed a condemned man to play the part of Leander and swim across the flooded amphitheatre, braving the dangerous creatures of the dark waters below him. But the Tullianum is reserved for important enemies of Rome, I cannot imagine why I should find myself there again. I shiver at the thought of it, its darkness and stone-cold damp air even at the height of summer.

"Did you think of a place?" she asks, watching my arms grow goosefleshed.

"The Tullianum," I say. "But I am not a threat to Rome."

She sighs. "Visions seldom come to me," she says. "Sometimes they are too strange to understand, other times they are clear. Often they contain symbols. Rarely do I have a vision where I know the person. That is why I came to you, I remembered who you were."

"Thank you for warning me," I say.

She frowns. "Be careful how you tread," she says. "For a common woman, your job takes you close to power, and power is always dangerous."

I shrug. "I – we intend to leave Rome anyway, all being well," I say. "My new husband and I, we will move to the countryside, to a farm, and live there."

"Soon?"

"As soon as we can," I say. "Dom – the Emperor wishes us to complete one more year of the Games."

"Leave as soon as you can," she says. "And should you recognise the place I saw, leave it immediately, no matter the risk."

I wait for her to say something more, but she only sits in silence staring down at the little silver dove. I get to my feet and still she does not stir.

"Thank you," I say.

She nods without looking up. I edge past her back out into the courtyard, where her slave girl escorts me to the entryway.

I return to the insula lost in thought. What can the sorceress have seen? I cannot imagine a place such as the one she has described. I wonder if I should tell Marcus what she said but decide not to, it is all too vague and may come to nothing. He frets enough already about not being able to go to the farm right away. If I start making him worry that we are in danger it will only be worse. I will tell him if I see something that I recognise from her description. No need for him to worry when there is nothing yet to worry about.

The season is going well. Our themes of birds, the illusions and changes, magic and gods that we have drawn on, is proving popular. This morning we have already had a demonstration of the flying skills of two eagles and an archery demonstration by the venatores, who have shot doves out of the air. Now we move on to some light relief before the execution later on of some criminals; the gladiatorial combats will come after lunch.

Fabius is displeased with his assistant, who is setting up the medical area for the day. "More lamps! I can't be expected to see what I'm doing in the dark."

As far as I can recall, the number of lamps has always been the same in Fabius' medical bay, but I suppose it depends on how complex the wounds brought to him are and what details he needs to take care of. Stitching wounds requires precision if the wound is to heal well. I nod to the beleaguered assistant and smile at Fabius, who half-waves a hand at me.

It's a hot day and the awning is fully open, meaning that only a circle of sunlight penetrates, illuminating the man standing at the centre of the arena. He has two assistants, dressed exotically in the Egyptian fashion. Each boy holds a collection of white doves on their outstretched arms, while the man talks about how doves, so white and delicate, are wonderful temple offerings to the gods.

"I sacrifice to the goddess Venus, bringer of love, that she may bring me a bride, a beautiful woman with whom I may share my life."

He takes one dove and puts his hand around its head, in one quick movement twists and pulls the head away, releasing a burst of scarlet blood and showing with his other hand the now-headless corpse of the dove. "Poor creature," he adds. "But its life is over and so it will fly to Venus and ask for her blessing in this matter." He moves his hand and the bird suddenly comes back to life, its head reappearing before it flutters up and through the centre of the velarium, white against the blue sky. The crowd gasps.

"Perhaps you did not see it clearly enough," says the man. "And if Venus is to send me a woman, one dove will not be enough. I do not want an ugly bride!"

The audience laughs.

The man dispatches the remaining birds one after another, each time with a crack of their necks and a spurt of blood, and yet each time, the bird miraculously comes back to life and flies away.

"I have faith that Venus will send me a beautiful bride," says the man. "I even have a palla ready for her, so that she will be clad as befits a virtuous matron of Rome."

He pulls out a delicate palla in fine woven dark red wool, drapes it over the head of one of the young male assistants, then swiftly removes it to reveal, in his place, a young Egyptian woman, with long hair and a shapely body. "Venus! You have outdone yourself. Here is my bride to be!"

The crowd applauds, impressed with the illusions. Standing inside the arena door to the hypogeum, I can hear the hum of voices as they chatter amongst themselves about how to create such an illusion. The illusionist and his assistants walk past me as they leave the arena. Close up, the beautiful and divinely sent bride is of course a boy, albeit now wearing a well-padded white dress, jewellery and a flattering wig. I am still impressed by how fast the assistant can change his costume underneath a palla without wriggling too much, which would give the trick away.

The Games are going well and the first task is completed, but we cannot yet rest on our laurels. I keep reminding Marcus that we need to begin planning both the naumachia and the event at Domitian's villa, neither of which will happen without careful preparation.

"Tomorrow we'll need to go and see the lake," Marcus says with a sigh one afternoon while we're sat in the courtyard. "I need some sense of the size of it."

"You can see the grove of trees surrounding it from the temple of Aesculapius on the Tiber Island," says Julia. She's busy tending to her flowers, but she sits down to rest beside us. "I've never seen the space within the grove, it must be quite wild by now."

The next day, we go down Sand Street to the river, cross it partway, onto the Tiber Island, passing the temple of Aesculapius, god of healing, being mindful of the sacred snakes which are plentiful here in his honour. Then up onto the next bridge, which takes us closer to the smell of the tanneries on this far side of the river. The road here is busy with carts trundling back and forth with raw skins for the tanneries. I wrinkle my nose at the stench. Marcus guides me towards a wide grove of trees beyond the busy road.

"Augustus wanted the lake to be surrounded by this grove," says Marcus. "As though it were set in the countryside."

"Wouldn't smell this bad in the countryside," I say.

"True."

The trees must have been saplings when they were planted, but more than fifty years have passed and their trunks are sturdy. The saplings were planted too close together so the grove would seem well-grown right away, so they stand tight-packed, reaching for sunlight amidst their too-close fellows. We walk through the dappled spaces left to us.

"We may have to cull some of these," mutters Marcus. "How are thousands of people supposed to get here quickly?"

The sunlight grows stronger and we come out of the trees and into a wide-open space, with a broken-down wall ahead of us.

"Here," says Marcus, offering his hand to me. I climb after him, stepping through the broken section of travertine wall and down onto the wide cobbled pavement.

We stand at the edge of the basin. Domitian was right. What was once a lake is now a large area of scrubby ground with a dip in it, a marshy look to the very centre of it. The pavement is in need of weeding and the wall surrounding the space is less of a proper structure and more of a suggestion that there ought to be a wall.

"It's big," says Marcus, stating the obvious. He sounds worried. "Too big to control well, not like the amphitheatre when we held the naumachia there."

"Though that was big enough," I say.

"It was." He lifts one hand to shade his eyes, squints at the other side.

"How big is it?"

"Over one-thousand-eight-hundred feet in length, one thousand two hundred feet in width. Digging it out again will be a huge task."

"And filling it?"

"That's less of a problem, we have the aqueduct to help us and this time we don't need to fill it and empty it so fast. It can be done over a few days and we'll keep the stream going to keep it topped up. And that wall needs rebuilding."

"No seating," I say.

"The carpenters who did the seating in the amphitheatre will be spending their next two months down here. As will hundreds of other people if this is to be made ready in time."

"Augustus had more than thirty full-sized ships taking part, with over three thousand men," I say, having read up on the event.

Marcus sighs. "I wish someone hadn't made a note of how many ships and how many men. Domitian will want more."

"Will he?"

"You think he wants to have a lesser show than Augustus?"

I shake my head.

The original basin was the work of Augustus, built to commemorate and celebrate the victory of Actium. Its walls used to be twice the height of a man, although most of them are wobbly and large stretches have collapsed altogether, no doubt encouraged along by local people scavenging building materials. There are eight gates, or gaps for them at least. Within the walls and close to the lapping waters is a wide pavement. Plants are growing through cracks in the mortar and cobbles.

The pavement and walls will allow for five tiers all around the lake, offering seating for about thirty thousand spectators.

"How do we empty it?

Marcus turns back to me. "The Aqua Alsietina aqueduct fills it, the water comes from Lake Alsietinus. To empty it there's a drainage channel that allows it to empty out into the Tiber. It's a bit silted up but we can clear it out. The good thing is that when it's full you can bring boats in via the aqueduct if you're careful."

I spend most of the rest of that day and the next drawing up the plans. We have two months to create a lake, as well as collect enough ships and men. The Games are progressing smoothly, so we decide to shift three hundred of our slaves to work on the basin. We plan to have a man-made island in the centre, which will mean less removal of earth and the creation of an elite viewing platform for Domitian and high-ranking guests. Shovels in huge numbers are the first item to appear on my list.

Within a week, work begins on the basin, with four separate teams attached to it full time. Our slaves will dig out the basin and create the central island. Builders from all over Rome are recruited to rebuild or fix the stone wall which surrounds the oval space. The carpenters plan a five-tier stand of wooden seating which will go all the way around the soon-to-be lake, as well as a wooden bridge which will take Domitian and his guests from the shoreline to the central island. They will also build eight sturdy wooden gates, so that we can lock up the site in the days before the event, to avoid anyone sneaking in without a token. Finally, we pay anyone who wants to earn a few coins, including children, to weed the cobbled pavement to return it to its previous neat appearance. Notifications are sent that we will require prisoners of war and criminals to take part. We will undertake only a few executions in the arena for the next two months, so as to have enough criminals at the naumachia. We send timings for sailors, soldiers and ships to join us one week beforehand for practice sessions.

One trireme ship, so named because they have three rows of oars, making them faster than the biremes which have but two rows of oars, takes one-hundred-and-eighty men to row, so over six thousand rowers will be required to move the ships. We will also have some quadriremes, which have shallow draughts making them suitable for the lake. They are very manoeuvrable, which will be important in the limited space we have available.

A normal ship would have fifty to sixty armed fighters on board, but Domitian will want to see more action, so each ship will have one hundred men, meaning we will need three-thousand-five-hundred men to fight. Of these, we decide that five hundred will be killed, so they must be made up of criminals and prisoners of war, along with any gladiators whom our gladiatorial schools are happy to be rid of. They will be marked on the forehead with a red dot, an indicator to everyone else taking part that they can be killed. Everyone else will fight, but not to kill.

I come home one day to find Adah and Julia sitting together among the flowers, heads close together, murmuring, but they stop as soon as I enter the courtyard.

"Keeping secrets?" I ask, laughing, as I pass by. "Here, I brought back new plums from the market."

They thank me but as I climb higher up the stairs and leave some plums with Maria I can hear them murmuring again.

"They really must have secrets," I say to Maria.

"They are old friends," she says, looking down at the two of them. "Thank you for the plums, the new season's fruits are always welcome."

A few weeks into our preparations, a scroll arrives at the amphitheatre from the imperial palace, which Marcus smiles over.

"Domitian says you are to be the commander of one of the ships in the naumachia," he tells Servius. "Your ship will lead the parade. We will have fifteen ships do an initial parade around the lake to music, then two bouts of fighting between pairs of twenty-six ships, then we'll bring in all thirty-five for a free for all: no-one will be able to manoeuvre of course, but it'll be spectacular."

"The Emperor remembered my name?" asks Servius, awestruck.

"He did. You will be in charge of the lead ship."

"I'm grateful to you, sir, for presenting me to him," says Servius earnestly.

Marcus tries to explain the concept of a naumachia to Servius. He knows what one is, of course, but due to the vast resources required, they are hardly ever put on and he has never witnessed one.

"It's not a real battle, not like you've been trained for. It's not play-fighting either, but only some people will get hurt or killed and they'll be criminals and prisoners of war. What's needed is spectacle. So the movements for fighting need to be bigger, broader, there needs to be lots of shouting and screaming. I'll put all your men on the same ship as you, so you'll all need to fight in the right style for the event. I'll probably send you and your men down to the gladiator barracks for some training."

Servius looks affronted. "Train with gladiators?"

"You need to know how to put on a show. You've been trained for real combat, it's not as interesting to watch, believe me."

Servius and his men acquiesce with reluctance, mostly because they want to take part in the biggest naumachia Rome has seen in decades, but when they arrive in the gladiator barracks at the Ludus Magnus they're stiff, holding themselves apart from the gladiators. The sailors are freeborn men who belong to the Roman army, they consider themselves a cut above gladiators, even though gladiators are known for being irresistible to the ladies. The start of the training does not go well. The men fight as they've been trained and drilled to do by the Roman army; efficient, focused moves. Paternus, who is doing us a favour by training them for a couple of days, looks weary beyond his advancing years.

"Give me a slave any day," he sighs. "Army recruits are the worst. They think they're superior to everyone else, think there's the army way to fight and the wrong way to fight. No flexibility."

But the men start to bond; sharing meals and round after round of training softens the distance between them. The gladiators, used as they are to suggesting ideas to create a more spectacular show, are open with their praise when they see a change in the sailors' fighting style, while the sailors enjoy getting to rub shoulders with some of Rome's top gladiatorial names. By the time the three days are up, they are putting on a better show, shouting with the best of them, their sword arcs wider, their responses more dramatic to everything from a thrust to a near miss.

"Thank you, Paternus," I say.

"Where are you getting three thousand fighters from?"

I shake my head. "Don't ask. The ships come with their own rowing teams. For the fighting crews we've emptied every gladiatorial school in Rome, the Misenum sailors, plus we've borrowed more sailors from Ostia and Misenum and more soldiers from the Praetorian Guards' barracks. We've got our slaves from the amphitheatre to bulk out the numbers, not that they're trained to fight."

"That'll be fun," comments Paternus. "Someone will get killed just because they're waving a sword about with too much vigour."

"I doubt you'll be able to tell with the numbers we've got," I say. "When all thirty-five ships are out there'll be hardly any space between one ship and the next, you could cross the whole lake stepping from ship to ship and never get wet."

"Rather you than me."

I sigh. "I'd willingly trade," I say. "But I'm stuck with it."

The lake is rapidly taking shape. The ground, having already been dug out and replaced but not much used since, is soft and easier to remove than hard compacted earth. The island is in place and I arrange for it to be planted with flowers and grass, making it seem natural. A wooden platform is added with seating for Domitian and his guests. The bridge is swiftly erected, the task made easier because the water has not yet been added, so supporting posts can be sunk into the ground. The cobbled pavement is looking neat again, many hands having removed the weeds and moss in a matter of weeks. The builders have reached the halfway point of the wall and the eight wooden gates are in their proper places.

"How fast will the water drain away?" I ask Marcus, looking over the vast expanse of bare earth, now reaching its full depth, at least the height of two men.

"It's a marshy area anyway, that's why the trees grow so well," he says with confidence. "We'll fill it up and keep the water flowing. The aqueduct is well-sourced and will keep pace with any drainage."

I look round at the scene. "It's shaping up well," I say. "Don't forget the other task, though."

"Domitian's villa," says Marcus with a sigh. "No chance of forgetting that."

THE VILLA OF DOMITIAN

THE WARMER DAYS OF JUNE mean the amphitheatre is full for every show, especially now that we have the velarium to keep the hot sun off the audience. The daily shows are proceeding well; our team are experienced after a few years of this life. Now Marcus and I have to put our heads together to develop a show worthy of Domitian's private villa and amphitheatre.

Based on a well-received show last season to inaugurate Paternus's Ludus Magnus, and partly because it allows us to incorporate a lion as requested by Stephanus, we have decided to reprise the story of Hercules and his twelve labours. This will involve several animals, including a lion, a boar, horses, a deer and a bull, as well as multiple gladiators dressed as animals. In short, we will be in need of a bestiarius, accustomed to fighting wild animals.

"Carpophorus would love it," I say. "How is he these days? Enjoying his retirement?"

"Bored," says Marcus. "He never really wanted to stop. I've heard he hangs around the barracks at the Ludus Magnus half the time, chatting to old friends and even taking part in the training though he doesn't need to. He could be at home in his villa enjoying the attention of his wife and any handy slave girls, eating fine dishes, but instead he's eating barley porridge and swinging a wooden sword at a pole."

"He does private events, doesn't he? Could we use him again?"

Marcus looks interested. "It's a good idea. No one takes down an animal like Carpophorus and since he's kept himself in trim, perhaps we can use him. Have a word."

I find Carpophorus, as promised, in the Ludus Magnus. He's showing a group of new young bestiarii exactly how to approach killing a bull, with a rickety wooden model which looks pathetically puny next to Carpophorus' rippling bulk.

"Don't let it keep its head up,' he explains. "You drop your left arm, see, nice big movement so it lowers its head to charge at you." He nods to an assistant who pushes the model's head downwards. "Now you can get at its shoulders, you need to drive your sword between the shoulder blades, see, and that kills it nice and quick. You step right and to the side, else it'll fall on top of you, and you'll be dead as well as the bull."

The new recruits look appalled at how casually Carpophorus is demonstrating a move which puts his life at risk and needs to be completed in the time it takes to breathe in, yet he acts as though he has all the time in the world.

"Carpophorus," I say. "How are you?"

"Althea! Move, you lot, that's the right-hand woman and wife of the manager of the Flavian Amphitheatre, that is. Mind your manners, she's a good friend of mine."

He embraces me and pats me on the back, which would knock me over, were he not holding me in place with his other arm. Winded, I emerge smiling.

"Drink?" he asks and when I nod he waves a slave over. "Wine," he instructs them and escorts me to a wooden bench.

"How's married life going?" he says.

"Very well."

"Marcus treating you right, I hope."

"He is."

"Ah, he's a good man, Marcus, honest. Honourable." His smile fades. "I still think of Funis," he says. "Haven't forgotten him."

I pat his hand. "We none of us will forget him."

"He was one of us," he says, his face solemn.

I nod. "He thought well of you," I say. "Said he'd never seen a finer bestiarius."

Carpophorus glows.

"Are you enjoying retirement?" I ask.

"Of course," he says heartily. "All those years I fought, got my fair share of scars but retired safe and sound, got my wooden sword from the Emperor himself, got a nice villa over in the smart area, good wife. I'm a lucky man."

"I'm speaking out of turn," I say. "I was going to ask if I could coax you out of retirement for one very special event, but I don't want to spoil your comfortable life, you've earnt it."

He narrows his eyes. "What sort of special event?"

I shrug. "At Domitian's villa. He has a five-hundred-seat amphitheatre in the Alban Hills, wants a spectacle putting on. Marcus and I, we thought of Hercules and his twelve labours, something showy. But we need a top bestiarius for that and we couldn't think of anyone good enough since you've retired. Perhaps you can point me to some young man who might do at a pinch? We can make it easier for him, there are ways…"

But as I hoped, Carpophorus' eyes have lit up. "You can't have some second-rate show for Domitian," he says, leaning towards me. "It wouldn't be right. I mean you got to kill the lion and the boar and the bull at the very least and I'm not sure who I'd recommend for that. I know a good lad who's handy with a boar, but he'll get worn out after that. Won't be able to carry off all three in one evening and you can't have Hercules being eaten by a lion, can you? Ruin the whole show."

"I'm a bit worried," I say. "We can't have something that isn't truly spectacular for the Emperor. I wish you'd consider coming out of retirement for me, but you've earnt the rest."

"I'd do it for you and Marcus," he says, "as a favour, I mean I wouldn't do it for anyone, but… Domitian's private villa…" His eyes are shining with enthusiasm.

"Would you?" I ask, one hand on his bulky arm. "We'd be so thrilled. Domitian would be delighted. Everyone would be. And you could take on all the animals and keep going."

He rolls his shoulders. "Might have to get back to my training," he says, looking down at his bulging biceps as though they are embarrassingly puny. "Lost a bit of my full physique. How long till the event?"

"End of the month," I say.

"I'll be in shape by then," he promises me.

"You're making Marcus and me very happy," I say and smile to myself as I watch him strut over to the training area with a new-found swagger in his step.

Our star secured, we hurry along with the rest of the preparations.

"So that's the main part of the show," says Marcus. "And what are we doing for the opening act, something lighter?"

"Acrobats? A tightrope walker?"

Marcus nods. "What's the story?"

"Arachne and Minerva?"

"Good. Have a structure built for them, something we can assemble and take apart easily."

When they do a simple tightrope walk from one place to another, acrobats use a structure of two triangular posts at each side, a rope between them, but having seen the velarium I talk to our carpenters and the acrobat who will perform and we create something more complex, a five-sided structure with a web of ropes passing between the poles, so that the acrobat can go not just back and forth but across to multiple points. Our costumiers create a costume for her according to my instructions and we are ready; the structure and costume are packed up ready for our departure.

Twenty carts set off three days before Marcus and I will follow. Their task is to settle in, calm the animals and prepare things like the acrobat's structure. We will arrive to put the finishing touches on the event and manage it as it plays out in front of Domitian and his guests.

We wave off the procession. The carts contain the acrobat and her structure, a giant from Labeo's school, a lion, musicians and singers, Carpophorus and a whole crew of gladiators and gladiatrices, piles of costumes and armour, as well as a comedian and various slaves who will take care of everyone while we are away. There are additional animals as well, a bull, a deer, snakes, horses and cattle who can walk by themselves which helps, over a hundred white ibis birds and a wild boar with ferocious tusks.

Marcus nods with satisfaction. "They'll take two days to get there, so they'll have a day to settle in before we arrive. Then the performance. We'll travel home the same way, but with fewer animals to transport."

Marcus and I plan to leave the insula well before dawn. When the day comes, Karbo has made ready the cart and horses. We remind him to keep the birds fed and wave to Maria, already in her watching spot. Julia and Adah as well as the rest of the inhabitants are not yet awake, though Cassia is lighting her fire and offers us a bowl of barley porridge if we want it, but we have packed food for the journey so as not to slow our progress. The Alban Hills are to the southeast of Rome, set high above the sea and will take most of the day to reach.

"Sleep," says Marcus, gesturing towards the back of the cart where he has laid out sleeping mats and blankets. I huddle under them, glad of the warmth. At first the jolting of the cart keeps me awake, but after a while tiredness overtakes me and when I open my eyes again it is broad daylight and we are in the countryside, Rome's walls well behind us.

"We can cover a lot of ground this morning," says Marcus when I join him to sit up front. "Once we get to the hills we'll have to go more slowly."

"I've never been there," I say.

"Seen them once," he says. "Lots of important rich people have villas up there, it's cooler in the summers to be in the green hills with a lake nearby and a sea breeze than being stuck in Rome when the heat and smell is unbearable."

"How close is it to the sea?"

"Not close enough to visit every day, but you can see it in the distance. Lake Alban is better for swimming. Much cooler."

It takes another few hours of slow travel but at last we spot the villa on the hilltop and come to a stop nearby. The location is extraordinary. Vibrant green surrounds us, thick woods and lush mountain pastures. Used to Rome's bustling streets, I find the green in every direction almost too much to take in. Marcus is right, even on a hot day, there is a refreshing breeze.

"Welcome to Albanum Domitiani," a voice calls out.

We turn to see Domitian's architect Rabirius standing among a small grove of trees, his large owl-like eyes observing us with interest. His ruffled hair is even more scruffy than the last time I saw him although on this occasion he is not holding armfuls of scrolls, just a tablet like my own.

"Good to see you again," says Marcus, jumping down from the cart and holding up his hand to help me down.

"I am not sure you were pleased to see me when we were building the hypogeum at the amphitheatre," says Rabirius.

Marcus shrugs. "It was not something we wanted while we tried to put on the Games," he says. "But it's done now."

"I hear congratulations are in order," says Rabirius, nodding at me. "May Juno bless your marriage."

"Thank you," I say. "Did you design the villa here?"

"Indeed. It is a very large project and still ongoing. Would you like to see the grounds?"

"Thank you," says Marcus, handing the reins to a slave boy who has appeared at his side.

"So there is the villa, built around three central courtyards, set on the second of three terraces, commanding views of both the sea and the lake. A bathing complex to one side. The lake has its own docks, for ease of use, as you can see." He points.

"They're having a boating party by the looks of it," says Marcus.

I look to where he is pointing and there are a dozen pleasure boats being rowed around the lake, even from here I can see the bright parasols of the ladies in the party.

"The Emperor is fond of taking his guests boating. There is

also an archery grove close to the lakeshore, he is very intent on practising his skills with a bow. If you follow me I will show you the stadium and the theatre."

"Stadium?" asks Marcus.

"Indeed," says Rabirius, as though the erection of a racing stadium were a common part of building a villa. "The Emperor is very fond of chariot races and now that we have undertaken so many construction projects related to the Games he is turning his attention to the races. We will be creating a stadium in Rome in the Ninth Region, as well as the one here for his own private entertainment."

"We live in the Ninth," I say.

He nods. "He is adding two new teams to the stables, Purple and Gold."

"Our son Karbo will be racing for the Purple team," I say, unable to stop a bubble of pride at being able to say this, even though the thought of him racing still frightens me.

"The path to the theatre," says Rabirius, waving ahead.

There is a vast avenue ahead, lined with still-young trees on one side, on the other with a high wall set into the hillside in which domed niches house statues of the gods painted in bright colours. I spot Minerva in a prominent position and nod to myself; we made a good choice by including her in the show.

"I'm surprised all of this has been done so fast," I say.

Rabirius nods. "The Emperor was keen to have his own residence made ready as soon as possible. He does not like the heat of the summers in Rome and is sensitive to extremes of temperature. The cooler air here suits him better, he says he can think better."

I wonder whether it helps him keep a cooler temper, but say nothing.

"The racing stadium is there." Rabirius indicates the site ahead.

It is still being built, but the shape of it has been marked out already. Seating is being constructed on one side, using the hillside to make the views evenly raked, looking down onto the elongated oval of the track, with three obelisks down the middle. The ground is still freshly cleared. Though it has not yet been compacted and made smooth for the chariots, it is close to completion.

"We think it may be usable this autumn, before the winter comes," says Rabirius.

The amphitheatre, when we come to it, is beautiful. It is set into the hillside, with five hundred marble-lined seats and the glittering lake and green hills as a natural backdrop. There is a frieze rising above the seating area at the back, depicting tributes to the Flavian dynasty's achievements, including references to Titus' generosity in aiding refugees from Pompeii and Herculaneum and theatrical images of gladiators, dancers, venatores and animals. Marcus' eyes rest briefly on the image of Pompeii before he looks away. Down the balustrades are decorative sculptures of actors' masks and dolphins and there is a space for the musicians and singers to stand so that their music and songs or speech can be heard well across the space. The velarium here is dyed imperial purple and has been beautifully painted with black silhouettes of animals; elephants, lions, giraffes, their unusual shapes lending themselves well to the silhouette-work.

"Very nice," says Marcus, looking around the arena space, which is ample for our planned performances.

"You would like to see the performance barracks, of course," Rabirius says.

Hidden behind a grove of trees close by, so as not to spoil the views, are two long low buildings, one for the animals, locked safely into their cages and pens, one for humans, which includes sleeping and cooking and eating quarters, simple but functional. Rabirius leaves us there, wandering back towards the stadium. Our crew is waiting, everything has been set up in our absence, ready for tomorrow's spectacle.

We have decided that the show should take place at night, complete with shining stars in the dark sky, since we have a location where it will be safe for the audience to return to their beds without risking Rome's dangerous streets.

"Only regular wolves round here at night, eh," says the comedian. "No she-wolves looking for their next customer."

We eat a simple meal of barley porridge, the standard food cooked for gladiators. It's a boring diet compared to Cassia's food, she knows how to turn the simplest ingredients into something delicious. Then it is time to sleep, rows of us laid out on sleeping mats. There is little need for blankets at this time of year, even if the hills are cooler than the city, we sleep in our clothes.

When the day breaks we start to prepare. Some people swim in the lake, I use a bowl of water to wash myself and comb my hair. I hang up my best tunic and headwrap to make them less wrinkled for the evening and wear the tunic I wore yesterday to do my rounds.

The animals look well. Most are being kept hungry, so they are keener to do battle, others like the horses and cattle are well fed to ensure they are docile. I check them off my sheet, watch the acrobat doing her exercises for the day and the gladiators likewise.

We send ten of the slaves off to erect the acrobatic structure at the amphitheatre and dispatch more slaves to scatter sand on the arena floor. The costumes are shaken out and hung up, the armour given a final polish. We eat a hasty lunch of bread and cheese, then erect a large screen of woven branches decorated with grass and flowers. This will be our hypogeum, the space from where we can direct the Games. The darkness will be our friend, we will fade into the night unless we come close to the edge of the arena.

The light is fading and torches are being lit all around the arena. I check that the floor is well-sanded, then that the ropes for the acrobat's structure have been hidden below the sand, to be revealed when we give the signal.

Slaves are laying out cushions so that Domitian and his guests need not chill their behinds. Aromatic incense is burning, to scent the air and keep away biting insects.

Marcus and I return to the barracks to dress and the animals are brought over in their wheeled cages.

We gather the team, everyone dressed in their costumes or armour. The animal handlers stand by the cages and soon we hear the murmur of many people and see flickering torches heading our way.

"Our audience," says Marcus. "May Jupiter watch over us and bless these Games."

Along the avenue comes a procession of a few hundred people, at their head Domitian and Domitia, flanked by guards and torch bearers, behind them their guests, more guards and torch bearers. They start to take their places. I spot several consuls, senators, and other important men, along with their wives, whose clothes make my best clothes look like those of a slave girl. Their jewellery glitters. Tonight is a chance to show off, to prove they are the elite of Rome, invited specially here to Domitian's own villa. Many of them have or are building their own villas in the area, keen to be seen as neighbours, as people who have the same taste and style as the Emperor. They will mention this evening when they return to Rome, of course, will drop it into conversations that are entirely unrelated and then raise an eyebrow when their friends have to confess they were not there, hurry to reassure them that of course, it does not mean *anything* not to have been invited, it means nothing at all… it was just an event between friends, nothing special at all. Oh yes, of course, there was *some* entertainment, the team from the Flavian Amphitheatre put on a little something, Carpophorus came out of retirement… and they will bask in their elevated status.

Amongst the crowd, I spot Stephanus, seated slightly behind and to the right of Domitian. As always he is well-blended into the background, drawing no attention to himself. But my stomach rolls over at the sight of the man sitting three seats away. Funis' father, the man who had his own son murdered because he was ashamed of him.

"What is that man's name?" I whisper to the comedian. It's the job of comedians to know all the famous faces of Rome, so that they can satirise them or outright mock them.

"Manius Acilius Glabrio. Consul."

My teeth grit together. This man is a consul? A man with no honour, no decency? Next to him is a richly dressed woman, who is adjusting her necklace and brooches, preening to ensure she appears at her very best.

"His wife Priscilla," says the comedian. "They had one son, but no other children."

I look away. Only one legitimate son, perhaps, but there was another and now he is gone.

Our musicians are playing a well-known tune, the singers sing as the audience gradually settles themselves under Marcus' watchful eye. At last he nods and the chorus steps forwards, the music softens so that they can be heard, the audience grows quiet.

"There was once a mortal woman named Arachne," they begin. "She was a most excellent spinner and weaver, but alas, she was also boastful and in her arrogance she claimed that she could out-weave the goddess of weaving herself, Minerva."

The acrobat portraying Arachne dances about the stage, while all around her spin whirling dancers draped with embroidered and woven cloths in bright colours, supposedly her creations.

I glance at Domitian, who is happily nodding to himself. Minerva being the goddess to whom he is most devoted, he will know this story well and appreciate the importance of respecting the deity which the story emphasises.

"So often and so loudly did she boast that Minerva herself heard her, and she was angered. She appeared before Arachne and challenged her to a weaving contest. Rather than fall to her knees and beg for forgiveness, as would have been wise, foolish Arachne agreed and the date was set for one month hence."

Minerva descends into the arena, clad in a white tunic and golden diadem and shoes to indicate her status. She points towards Arachne and her dancers, who shift across to the other side of the stage.

The story continues with each woman undertaking an intricate dance, showing that Minerva wove the images of each Olympian in all their glory and the outcome of Minerva fighting Neptune for control of Athens. But when she is done and it is the mortal's turn, Arachne takes each Olympian and shows them lust-ridden rather than glorious, each transforming into an animal in order to satiate their desires.

Minerva, furious, holds out her arms and from the arena's

sand, pulled by many hands, appears a tight-woven spider's web that dwarfs the spectators and performers alike, rising high above us all, hidden hands winching it and securing the ropes into place across the five platforms.

"So enraged was Minerva with Arachne's arrogance and disrespect for the gods that she cursed her, transforming her human shape into that of a spider: forever able to weave exquisite webs, forever despised and silenced."

Shedding her bright dress, Arachne displays a tightly shaped and multi-legged black costume, climbs up through the webbing, dangling above our heads from first one foot and then the other before pulling herself up and walking across the ropes in an acrobatic display while Minerva, arms crossed, watches her with satisfaction as the chorus completes the story.

Domitian dismisses the Arachne-spider with a smiling gesture and she swings from rope to rope until she disappears from view through one of the seating areas. He crowns the Minerva dancer with golden laurels, bowing his head to her as though in tribute to the real goddess.

"That went well," says Marcus with satisfaction. "He seems in a good mood. On with Hercules."

In order to end on the spectacular scene of Carpophorous battling with a lion, we have reversed the order of the labours. The slaves extinguish all the torches so that the audience is plunged into darkness and the chorus speaks, first laying out the birth of Hercules and his angering of Juno, before he begins his tasks, in penance to the goddess.

"Hercules was called upon to visit Hades, the land of the dead, and to fight Cerberus, a deadly three-headed dog."

Carpophorus enters and is greeted with a huge round of applause and much cheering. Holding a burning torch, he peers into the darkness, from which a baying comes, before three gladiators creep towards him, all dressed in black, only their shining metal, dog-head shaped helmets visible to us. The effect is frightening, some of the ladies in the audience squeal, though whether at the mythical beast or Carpophorus' rippling muscles and bare chest, it's hard to tell.

The fight is savage, fast, the chorus bays and howls as Carpophorus dispatches the beast, each gladiator throwing down his helmet as Hercules slices off each head, fading back into the darkness.

Labeo's giant stands in for Atlas in the next task, Hercules taking the weight of the world from his shoulders while Atlas brings back the golden apples of Zeus, then tricking the giant into taking back the heavy burden. Carpophorus takes his time distributing the basket of gilded apples to various ladies in the crowd, leaving the last and best for Domitian's wife Domitia, who accepts, smiling.

He battles monsters for a herd of cattle, before a tribe of Amazons attack him, their Queen Hippolyta offering up her magic belt after succumbing to his sword and charms, a scene watched with interest by men and women alike, for our Amazons are bare-breasted and the clinch between Carpophorus-Hercules and the gladiatrix-Hippolyta is passionate.

Hercules' journey continues, taming four glorious horses and fixing them to his chariot for a victory parade round the arena, before we release a vast black bull, enough to terrify any bestiarius, but a bull is nothing to Carpophorus, who leaps from the chariot and kills the beast with only his sword, all alone in the arena, to deafening applause.

We release over one hundred ibis for the Stymphalian birds, and our Hercules, with the aid of additional hidden archers, shoots them down in droves, their white bodies falling out of the darkness.

This leaves us with an arena full of birds and bloodied sand, so it is the turn of a mock-Hercules to take the stage, our comedian, who pretends to be Carpophorus being Hercules cleaning the stables of Augeas, with a lot of showing off his muscles, admiring his reflection in a well-polished shovel and winking at the ladies, which has the audience in fits of laughter.

"It's going well," says Marcus. The tension is leaving him, he has put on a good spectacle and we are one task closer to leaving Domitian's employ and Rome. I nod, although I can't rest easy until the lion scene has come and gone without event.

The arena clean and fresh sand strewn, it's time for the Erymanthian boar. A huge wild boar is released and despatched with aplomb by Carpophorus. I have to admire his bravery, it's harrowing to watch a single man face such large and aggressive creatures all alone.

Now Hercules must kill a deer sacred to Diana. The deer, its hooves and horns painted gold, bounds into the arena and Carpophorus pretends to kill it with the aid of some of the illusionist's tricks and fake blood, before falling to his knees as Diana descends. Learning of his quest, she forgives him and brings the "dead" deer back to life, allowing Carpophorus-Hercules to carry it over his shoulders in triumph at completing another task.

The eleventh task sees Hercules seeking to defeat the nine-headed water snake, the Hydra. Here Carpophorus battles nine gladiators dressed as snakes, but with the addition of nine real snakes, cobras we have had brought from Egypt to kill as well. For each gladiator he battles he must also kill a snake and the cobras are truly frightening, raising up their hooded heads to hiss at Carpophorus as he approaches each one, striking at him as he strikes at them, the audience screaming and cheering him on. We have kept the largest and most aggressive one for last and I clutch at Marcus' arm when it strikes at Carpophorus while he has half-turned away. But he catches the movement in time, whirls to protect himself and the cobra's head lies in the sand, tongue still flickering in its death throes. Domitian is on his feet, Domitia is screaming, the whole audience rises with them and Carpophorus takes a bow.

"He can't top that," yells someone.

But the audience is aware of what is missing from the twelve famous tasks, they know that we have yet to show them a lion, Hercules' most famous task. They chant Carpophorus' name and stamp their feet, excited to watch the final task take place.

The musicians start a low soft melody while the chorus tells of the Nemean Lion, a savage beast whom Hercules met in battle armed just with a club. And back into the arena strides Carpophorus, naked to the waist, carrying only a heavy club. He spends time posturing around the arena so that the audience can admire his muscles and powerful physique, while the musicians build the tension.

Marcus is about to lift his hand to release the lion from its cage, when Domitian stands and holds up his own hand.

The chorus and musicians come to an uncertain, stuttering stop, trying to look at both Marcus and Domitian at the same time, a difficult task. The audience is silent, craning their necks to get a good view of Domitian, wondering what is going on.

"I salute Carpophorus, a mighty bestiarius and one who has pleased us greatly this evening," says Domitian, throwing a laurel wreath towards Carpophorus. There's a ready round of applause. Carpophorus, confused, picks up the wreath and bows his head in gratitude but glances over his shoulder to get further instructions from Marcus, who gives a small shrug and shake of his head, awaiting clarity from Domitian. The audience is also looking towards the emperor, wondering what is going on. The benevolent gesture is expected, but not before the big moment of the show. Why would it not be given after the fight with the lion?

"However, I think he should leave the arena and allow another man to take his place and complete the story of Hercules."

The crowd murmurs, uncertain of where this is going. Marcus shakes his head, a deep frown on his face. For one terrifying moment I think Domitian will ask Marcus to step into the arena, as punishment for daring to want to leave imperial service. I clutch at his arm and he looks at me, confused.

"Step forward, Manius Acilius Glabrio," says Domitian.

There's utter silence. I can hear Marcus breathing, my own heart pounding. The Consul – Funis' father – does not move.

"Come, come," says Domitian. "Don't be shy, Glabrio. You are a strong man. A lion can be nothing to you, surely?"

The lion we have brought here is a magnificent beast that would stand above any man's waist, its teeth and claws are hungry for the food it has been denied for days, I can hear it behind me, pacing in its cage, ready to fight anyone, given a chance.

"Glabrio!" Domitian is no longer smiling, no longer coaxing. It is a command. The consul's face changes as he realises this is no joke, that he is about to be thrown into the arena in front of his peers, his wife, his emperor. He will have to fight a real lion. He has seen our animals, they have all been strong and powerful beasts, not weak or sick to make life easy for our Hercules. Only an experienced bestiarius like Carpophorus could have taken them on. An ordinary man has no chance against a lion.

Glabrio stands and his wife Priscilla gives a low moan, clutches at his hand, but he pulls away from her. I watch as he makes his way down the amphitheatre, step by slow step, each person whom he brushes against leaning to one side in fear of being tainted by his very touch. His arms seem well muscled, he is not portly like many of the senators. But as he reaches Carpophorus the comparison between them is absurd.

Glabrio holds out his hand, which is shaking, and Carpophorus puts his club into it, eyes flicking to Domitian for permission. Domitian inclines his head, then takes his seat again, crossing his legs and leaning back as though about to do nothing more serious than command a dancer to perform.

"May I know why I am thus called on, Imperator?" asks Glabrio. His voice remains steady, and for a brief moment I admire his courage.

"For conspiring against the empire," says Domitian pleasantly.

"May I refute the accusation?"

"No," says Domitian, still calm. "I call on our Manager of the Games to release the lion of Nemea. Carpophorus, you are dismissed."

Carpophorus, now without a weapon, steps backwards until he reaches us.

"I didn't know what else to do," he hisses to Marcus.

"You did the right thing," whispers back Marcus. "Now keep out of the way. No, wait. Get a sword and get the other men to stand by. This could go very wrong."

Behind me, Carpophorus and the other gladiators gather, their swords unsheathed. Having a lion in the arena is perilous in such a small amphitheatre, it takes an experienced bestiarius to keep its attention on himself and not let it charge towards the audience. This arena has fewer safety features than the Flavian Amphitheatre, where it is very hard for a dangerous animal to get into the audience.

Priscilla has hurried down the steps after her husband, now she throws herself on the arena floor in front of Domitian. "I beg for your mercy, Imperator," she cries out.

"I *am* merciful," points out Domitian as though she is unreasonable in accusing him of any lack of feeling. "I'm allowing your husband to fight for his life. I could just have had him executed for treason."

She stares up at him aghast, tears running down her face, but he waves her away.

"You're blocking my view," he says. "And I think you are in a position of danger, being in the arena when they're about to let loose a lion. I would return to your seat."

She looks over her shoulder at her husband, who nods, face tight with tension. She staggers to her feet and stumbles back to her seat, face white and shocked in the torchlight.

Glabrio removes his toga, gathers the heavy parcel of fabric in his left hand and flings it away from him, keeping the club in his right hand. The last time I saw him I pressed my bloodied hands against his toga, staining it with the blood of his murdered son Funis, wanting to proclaim his guilt. He deserves what is coming. He does deserve it. But still I feel sick at the idea of what we are about to witness. Behind me, there is a growl from the caged lion.

I step out from behind the screen, to the side, where I stand in the darkness and look towards Stephanus. He should not be able to see me in the dark, but perhaps he catches the movement, because his eyes turn towards me. His face does not change expression, but he gives a slow nod and I know, as though he had spoken the words aloud, that this is the justice I requested for Funis' death; a terrible revenge that has now been set in motion, which I cannot stop even if I wanted to.

Domitian nods approval at Glabrio's removal of his toga. He stands in his tunic, club in hand, expression fixed.

"Our hero is ready," Domitian announces. He waves a hand at the chorus. "Continue with the story."

The musicians begin the music prepared for this moment, a dramatic piece which will build to a crescendo as the fight goes on.

The chorus begin to speak, their voices hesitant at first. "The Lion of Nemea was covered in a golden fur, which could not be penetrated by any arrow, no, nor by any sword. And so Hercules took with him only a club and the local villagers prayed for him, believing that he would soon be killed, as so many brave men had been before him."

I turn to the side, where I can see Marcus. He hesitates, but in this moment he has no choice. He gives an abrupt nod and the handler pulls back the bolt of the lion's cage. Two slaves pull on ropes and the cage door flies open.

There is a moment's pause. Glabrio has turned towards the sound of the bolt and all of us hold our breath – and then the lion charges out of the cage and onto the arena floor, where it crouches down, its eyes focused on Glabrio. Its growl shakes the floor and Priscilla screams, but the lion is not distracted by her, all its attention is on Glabrio, who is standing his ground, the club held out to one side.

The lion leaps. It extends to its full length, claws outstretched, jaws open, its pointed teeth exposed. Glabrio brings his club swinging round and up above him, hitting it squarely on the side of the head even as one of its paws slashes across his chest, the tunic ripped away, blood trickling down towards his legs as the lion, furious with pain at the unexpected blow, whirls round and attacks again, slashing at Glabrio's legs as it roars. But the club falls twice more in quick succession and now the lion is hurt, one eye bleeding, its jaw thrown out of alignment. It roars again and swipes but Glabrio closes in on it, the club hitting the wounded animal again and again, crushing its skull until it lies, broken and bleeding on the sand, legs twitching. Glabrio is covered in blood and panting, he falls to his knees, dropping the club by his side, crumpling into a heap on the sand.

The night is silent, broken only by Priscilla's sobs, still in her seat, too afraid to go to her bleeding husband.

Domitian uncrosses his legs and leans forwards, staring at Glabrio. Behind him, Stephanus leans forwards and whispers something to which Domitian nods, then stands.

"Who knew our consul was a bestiarius, after all?"

Silence.

"Rise, Glabrio."

Glabrio stumbles to his feet. He's bleeding and his legs shake under him.

"Bravely done, I suppose," says Domitian. "Although, and this may seem unkind, given your display of courage, but I believe a consul should not also be a bestiarius. It brings Rome's empire into disrepute, and we can't be having that. So, you will resign your post and go into exile. I assume you have some place in the country in which you can go and live a quiet life?"

Glabrio, swaying on his feet, drops his head to his chest.

"Excellent," says Domitian. "Then I think we fully understand one another and it is time for all of us to withdraw for the night. A warm nightcap will be served back at the villa before we retire to the bedrooms. And of course, I was forgetting: a round of applause for a wonderful evening of Games. We thank the team of the Flavian Amphitheatre and all their performers." He begins clapping his hands and the audience, stunned and terrified at what they have witnessed, hurry to copy him. Glabrio, alone in the arena, the dead lion at his feet, stands still and silent as Domitian graciously offers his hand to Domitia and leads her away, the audience filing out after them in abject silence, the arena growing darker as many of the torch-bearers depart with them. Only Priscilla remains, she stumbles down the steps and throws her arms about Glabrio, who slumps against her, his blood staining her silks. They set off in the dark, he staggering, she trying to support him, following far behind the distant bobbing torches. The amphitheatre is empty, the lion lies in a pool of its own blood and Glabrio's.

Marcus pushes aside the screen and steps into the arena, followed by the lion handler, who kneels to check the beast is dead, then nods. The gladiators and gladiatrices, swords in hand, step forwards, slowly put away their weapons as Marcus checks there is no-one else left, only our own team.

"I'd advise everyone who witnessed this to keep quiet and not gossip about it," he says at last and there are silent nods. "Whatever went on to lead up to that moment, we cannot be sure if Domitian will do more of the same or if he may regret his actions. Either way, it would be best if gossip did not spread from us about this affair. We cannot know whether Glabrio will be recalled from exile and continue to be a powerful man in Rome or not." He takes a deep breath and blows it out again. "Enough. We are all tired, it has been a long evening. We will sleep, and tomorrow we will pack up and leave as soon as it is dawn. With any luck most of us will be back in Rome by nightfall. We can use the horses to speed up our progress and the cattle can be loaded into some of the pens of the animals who are dead, it will be faster than walking them all back. I want all of you out of here as soon as possible."

There is no further talk, everyone finds their beds and sleeps and the next morning all our items and the animals are rapidly packed up, our carts leaving the villa's grounds before the first birds sing, the sun not yet risen. None of us look back.

We say very little on the way home. The hours trundle by as we leave countryside behind us and return to the outskirts of Rome, Marcus and I eat some bread and cheese as we travel, without stopping to rest. Behind us the other carts are also quiet, I cannot hear chatter. Late in the afternoon we finally come back to Rome's walls, allowing the different carts to go their own ways once we are through the gate; most back to our warehouses by the docks, others to their own gladiatorial schools. When we get home Karbo takes the horses and cart for us. We wave away excited questions with promises to tell all about the villa and performing for Domitian tomorrow, and escape upstairs to bed.

Lying in the dark, Marcus lets out a shuddering breath. "I'm afraid," he confesses, voice low. "Losing his temper over us trying to leave his service, throwing people who speak ill of him to the lions, how is Rome to survive if he gets worse?"

I clasp his hand. "Glabrio might have been Stephanus' idea."

"What? Why?"

I tell him about Glabrio being Funis' father, how Stephanus seemed to have a plan for him, that I didn't know what it was until it was underway. Marcus is quiet for a while.

"It's possible that's what happened," he says at last. "Domitian was already pointing the finger at people whom he suspected of not being loyal enough to him and it sounds as though Stephanus just added Glabrio to the list. But Domitian is still acting strangely."

I am still shaken by what happened when we wake in the morning. We give a brief account of the villa, amphitheatre and show to those who ask, but we do not go into detail about what happened at the end. We leave it to others to gossip about the Emperor of Rome and his mental state, we do not wish to find ourselves in trouble because of people hearing what happened and the tale being traced back to us.

I am unsure how I feel about Stephanus. Is he trustworthy, or as strange as the Emperor? What he did, and I have no doubt that it was he who at least suggested it to Domitian, was an act of madness, yet there is a tiny part of me that feels justice was done as he promised me, and cannot help but be glad that Funis was avenged, that his father, so scathing of his son being a beast hunter for the Flavian Amphitheatre, should know what it is to fight with the beasts of the arena, no better than a bestiarius, no better than his son in the end.

Marcus no longer trusts Domitian to take care of our crew when we are gone. He arranges pay rises for as many people as he can manage within the team, he orders further repairs and comforts to be added to the slave barracks, so that their living quarters will be better quality, he arranges for the oldest slaves to be freed and asks for new ones to be brought in, the public purse can stand it.

"We need a meal for guests," he tells me. "Something special?"

He has never asked for such a thing.

"Who are the guests?" I ask.

"Julia, Fabius and Fabia."

I laugh. "They're our friends," I say. "We eat bread and cheese with them. Is there a special occasion?"

"Yes. But it's a secret."

"You can't have secrets from me, I'm your wife," I protest.

"It is a happy secret," he says. "Make a special meal? We'll eat on the rooftop under the pergola."

I cheat by using both Cassia, who fries a batch of her saltfish fritters, and the bakery, where I get oil-rich bread strewn with herbs and olives. To this I add a large salad flavoured with mint and thyme with cubes of fresh cheese, a basket of plums and cherries and little cakes made with soft cheese, honey and poppyseeds. I enlist Karbo to help me carry up a table and some chairs, as well as wine and jugs of water. We set everything up under the pergola, so that we are shaded from the rays of the sun but can enjoy the long warm evening.

"There," I say, putting down a vase of flowers. "A table fit for a feast."

"Why is it a special occasion?" asks Karbo.

"We'll have to wait till Marcus deigns to tell us."

Julia comes upstairs and spends some time with the nightingales, then takes a seat at the table. She looks pale for the height of summer.

"Are you well, Julia?"

"Oh, a little tired," she says. "The delivery carts coming into Rome wake me far too early most days, I sleep lightly."

Fabius arrives. "A beautiful table, Althea," he says. "And I smell good food."

"What is this special occasion?" I ask. "Or are you sworn to secrecy?"

He smiles and puts a finger to his lips. "All in good time."

"Your eyes are twinkling," I say. "I am beginning to think there is mischief afoot."

"Let us say it is a happy occasion," he says.

"That's what Marcus said," I say.

"Here I am," says Fabia, appearing round the corner of our roof hut. She is wearing a blue tunic with slashed shoulders held in place with little brooches and a green woven belt.

"You're so elegant," I tell her, stooping to embrace her little frame.

"Father said it was an important day," she says, then lowers her voice so only I can hear her. "Are we about to get good news?" she asks, nodding in the direction of my belly.

I giggle. "No!"

"I don't know what all this is about then," she says. "But I am hungry, tell me you have lots of food. I only grabbed a bread roll this morning and never got round to lunch."

"Lots," I assure her. "Come and sit down. You should get your assistant to ensure you get proper meals."

She laughs. "She follows me about telling me I need food, then I wave her off to go and eat her own meal while I make notes on my patients."

We settle around the table and begin the meal. I pour wine for everyone and pass dishes back and forth, keeping an eye on Marcus, waiting for him to reveal the purpose of the event.

"I have an announcement," says Fabius.

We all wait.

"I am retiring as physician to the amphitheatre."

I gape at him. "You can't!" I say. "The Games are in full season! And why would you, I thought you liked the work?"

"I do," he says smiling. "But my hands work against me."

"Your hands?"

He lifts them and I see what I have not before, that his long fingers are shaking slightly, a tiny tremor. "Not steady enough for surgery," he says.

"I'm sorry," I say.

"So was I," he admits. "It was a hard truth to accept. I have seen it before in other men, and though it begins gently enough, the shakiness grows over time and most tasks become hard in the end."

"That's why you were grumpy," I say.

"It is," he says. "I confided in Julia and she advised me to tell Marcus, I did not want to lose a good gladiator from some slip of the fingers because of my pride."

Marcus pours more wine for everyone. "I told him it was still early days. That he was more than able to finish this season and whoever comes after us can have the task of finding themselves a new physician. But I had a better idea."

Next to me, Fabia slowly lowers her cup of wine. I can feel her little body tense up, her eyes are downcast, fixed on the food in front of her, which she has stopped eating.

"You've chosen a new physician?" I ask, my heart beating faster. I hope that Marcus means Fabia, but he may have in mind some other person. If he does, Fabia, ambitious to be a great physician, will be crushed. I hardly dare look Marcus in the eyes, but when I do he winks at me, a smile twitching in the corner of his mouth. I hold my breath.

"Yes," he says. "I have found an excellent replacement. A physician of great stature here in Rome, with experience in the field and excellent skills. Fabius agrees with me, he has examined their work personally and recommended them for the role." He pauses, though my eyes are pleading with him to hurry and say the name I am hoping for.

"The only trouble is that of course, being so well qualified, they are already taken," says Marcus and Fabia takes in a little gasp of air, a half-sob.

I shake my head at him. "Don't."

He laughs out loud, a big warm laugh, and reaches out his hand across the table to Fabia. "Fabia Papirius, will you take on the role of physician to the Flavian Amphitheatre?"

Fabia raises her face to reveal both a wide smile and trickling tears, which she wipes away with one hand while taking Marcus' hand with the other and nodding fervently.

"Ah, Fabia," says her father, his own eyes glistening. "You could not have thought I would have recommended anyone else."

Marcus lets go of Fabia's hand and comes round to the other side of the table, his tall frame stooping over to embrace her. "You're the best there is," he says. "If I can't have your father there for old times' sake, you're the only physician I'd pick for the amphitheatre. And I wanted to choose you and have you established before some idiot comes along to take my place who doesn't know anything and picks someone useless."

Fabia finally finds her voice. "I won't let you down," she gulps.

"You'll show us all up, more like," says Marcus. "Embrace your father, he's been desperate to tell you these past few months but I told him we had to get everything in place and that I wanted to celebrate with you when we told you. We've already settled everything with Labeo, he wasn't pleased to be losing you but there's a young physician showing some promise and your father will mentor him for the rest of the season to get him up to scratch, so we can take you right away. Your apprentice and assistant will also join you, of course."

We all take turns hugging Fabia and toast her repeatedly through the afternoon until we are all quite tipsy and need an early night.

"Blessings on you, Fabia," says Julia before she leaves, placing her hand on Fabia's curls. "You are a credit to your profession. May Aesculapius and Minerva give you skill and wisdom." She coughs as she leaves.

"You said your cough would be better by the warmer months," I say.

She waves her hand, already starting down the stairs. "It faded. This one is different. It will be gone soon, I have a tonic from Fabius."

"Meet me tomorrow at the imperial palace," Marcus tells Fabia. "You'll have to sign a contract."

"What if Domitian doesn't want me?" asks Fabia, suddenly sober at the thought.

"He's caused me enough trouble this past year," says Marcus. "It's my turn to make decisions that suit me and that includes having a female physician for the Flavian Amphitheatre."

The next morning, while Marcus takes Fabia to sign legal contracts, I send word for all her equipment and supplies to be brought from Labeo's to the amphitheatre and we re-arrange the medical bay to suit her height, one of our carpenters creating a wooden platform which runs the length of the bay so that she can reach everything she needs to, changing the shelving so that her supplies are lower down and she does not have to rely on anyone else to get what she needs. As physician to the amphitheatre, not only will she have her existing apprentice and assistant but three more assistants as well, but Fabia likes to be independent and when she arrives in the late morning and sees our work her smile is warm. She is glowing with pride at having realised her long-held ambition.

"Thank you for choosing Fabia," I say to Marcus, slipping an arm about his waist as we leave her to settle in. "Some men wouldn't have chosen her, wouldn't have wanted a woman. Or a dwarf."

He shrugs. "She's her father's equal," he says. "I wasn't being polite. What she did for Alyssa…"

I lean my head against him. "Thank you anyway," I say.

"We must care for our own amongst all this madness," he says.

There are two weeks to go till the naumachia and it is time to fill the lake. We open up the aqueduct and water begins to flow. At first it appears somewhat pathetic, mostly draining away again.

"What if it doesn't work?" I ask Marcus, nervous. "What if we end up with a puddle and some mud?"

"Leave it a few days," he says, unflustered. "Then we'll see."

I want to visit daily, but Marcus shakes his head and keeps us away from the basin for four days. When we return, to my surprise the basin is two-thirds full. It is a murky muddy colour, however, not very attractive.

"The mud will settle," says Marcus. "You'll see. You always get mud after heavy rains and this is no different."

By the end of the week the basin is full and the water is beginning to clear. Marcus has a trireme and a quadrireme come through the canal and test rowing around the lake. It goes well, the canal is tight but not impossible and once on the lake they show remarkable speed and manoeuvrability.

"I didn't know they'd be so fast," I say.

"They won't be when there's lots of them," says Marcus. "That's why we'll do the parade first, it'll allow for some speed when we just have fifteen of them."

The water flow is carefully adjusted to allow the basin to stay topped up and the waters continue to clear. The naumachia is upon us.

THE STORM

O N THE EVE OF THE naumachia, I stand with Marcus on the edge of the newly made lake. No matter how annoying Domitian's extra tasks have been for us, nor how strange his behaviour, I can't help feeling pride at the sight before us. The deep blue July sky is reflected in the sparkling blue waters of the vast lake we have created from a patch of scruffy land, now surrounded by a smart high wall interspersed with sturdy gates enclosing neat wooden stands of seating. The pavement beneath our feet is pristine. A wooden bridge reaches out across the water to the central island, which is covered in grass and a multitude of flowers. There are even dragonflies skimming by, having scented the water and come to visit this new body of water. A crane stands on the northern shore, disappointed that the promising waters do not, after all, contain fish.

"Very impressive," I admit. "Do you think it will go well tomorrow?" I check the list on my tablet.

Marcus closes it and pushes my hand away. "Stop fretting," he says, smiling. "You've done everything that needed doing. The physicians and undertakers will be here first thing tomorrow to set up. The audience will arrive late morning, Domitian in the middle of the day. It'll be sunny. The biggest problem we'll have is people complaining there isn't a velarium and I don't care if they do. It's our last task. After this, there's only one month to go and we'll be closing the Games."

I wake at dawn, but Marcus has already gone. I hurry to pull on my tunic and shoes, then step out onto the roof terrace, shivering. Most mornings are warm enough, even in the dark, as there isn't time for the city to cool down before the sun's rays hit it again. But this morning there is a cold breeze, the sky is darker than it should be at this time. It's usually pale grey before the sun rises; this is a heavier colour, as though I have woken an hour earlier than usual. I shake my head and rub my arms, return to the roof hut to fetch my palla and wrap it about me. No doubt I will have to set it aside later, as the day's heat builds. I feed the birds, but the doves do not want to leave their shelter today, they huddle together and peck desultorily at the corn I offer. As I walk down the stairs I catch sight of Maria through her open door.

"It's going to rain," she calls to me, without any kind of greeting.

I walk to her door, where she's still fastening her belt.

"Rain?" I say, doubtful. "In July?"

She shakes her head. "I can feel it," she says, pointing downwards. "In my bones. My legs especially."

"But we never get rain in July," I say.

"I can feel it," says Maria, picking up her basket and following me down the stairs.

"I could do without it," I say. "It's the naumachia today."

"Be careful no-one capsizes," says Maria, about to turn right towards the bakery as I turn left to Cassia's popina.

"It won't be that bad," I say. "These are big ships. Mostly triremes and quadriremes. They're sea-going ships, not some little rowing boat for pleasure. They can take up to two hundred men on board. If anything, they're underloaded."

"Good luck," she calls over her shoulder. "May Jupiter be kind to you."

Cassia has a plate of sliced fruits ready for my breakfast and a cup of well-watered wine. Most days, the fruit is a refreshing start to a hot day, but today I find myself wishing I was eating pancakes or a freshly baked, still-warm fruit bun from the bakery.

"What's with the weather?" I ask.

Cassia shrugs, busy pouring wine with one hand, waving a rattle vaguely in Emilia's direction. "No doubt it'll warm up once the sun rises."

I amuse myself making faces for Emilia for a few moments, say goodbye to them both and head over the river towards the lake. The grove of trees rustle in the breeze, a loud swishing noise as I walk through them.

Marcus is already there. The sky has lightened as the dawn breaks, but is still a sullen grey, not the pale blue it ought to be.

"Are we going to have rain?" I ask Marcus when I reach him.

He puts an arm about my shoulders, pulls me into his chest for a quick kiss. "Hope not," he says. "It should warm up. Are you cold?" He wraps my palla more tightly about me. "There. Aren't you glad you're a married woman? Else you'd have to run home for a cloak. Here come the undertakers."

Given the number of fatalities we are expecting, the undertakers are necessary, there will need to be careful sorting, as the criminals and prisoners of war can be buried in a mass grave, but should there be any deaths of freeborn Romans or any gladiators belonging to specific schools, they must be returned to their families or schools for proper burial. The audience will mostly approach from the east, so the undertakers have located their carts and teams to the west, discreetly hidden behind the high stone wall close to one of the gates, which will enable them easy access once the crowds have left.

The undertakers ready, we welcome the physicians: Fabius and Fabia with their assistants, as well as Fabia's replacement at Labeo's, an experienced man. It is very probable there will be multiple injuries today, three thousand five hundred people fighting with real weapons are unlikely to escape unscathed, even if most of their efforts will be focused on the unlucky five hundred who will die today. We set up medical bays inside the northern gate, in a space we left in the seating, surrounded by screens.

"What happened to the sunshine?" Fabia asks, shivering. "Yesterday I was sweating all day and now…"

I shrug. "I know. We have to hope the wind moves the clouds along and the sun breaks through. Or at least that it doesn't rain."

I go with Marcus to check on the ships, which are lined up in the canal with more anchored behind in the Tiber, waiting for their signal to enter the lake. The lead ship is commanded by Servius, his men distributed as fighters between five ships.

"Looking forward to leading out the fleet?" Marcus asks, leaping on board.

Servius is shifting from foot to foot, nervous. "Yes, sir."

"You don't have to reassure us," I say, from the canal path. "It's natural to feel anxious."

"It is a great honour," he says, swallowing.

"You'll do just fine," says Marcus, patting his shoulder. "The music will start, I'll give the signal, three times round the lake with the other ships following you. It gives everyone a chance to admire the speed and the ships and get excited about the fighting to come when they see you all on deck in armour. May Neptune watch over you all today," he adds, jumping down from the deck back onto the canal path.

"Yes, sir," says Servius, straightening his shoulders and I smile at his nervous pride.

It will soon be time for the gathering crowds to be allowed in. We have numbered the gates one to eight, starting on the north gate and going round towards the east and south. Five of the gates are for the crowds, three to the west for the undertakers. People's tokens include the gate number they should come to. Each gate has four soldiers on it, to manage any rowdiness and to ensure everyone has tokens. Compared to the amphitheatre, which is a smaller space but has far more tiers of seating, we have fewer numbers here, but thirty thousand people still require a lot of managing.

"Is that rain?" I ask, feeling a few spits of wetness on my face.

"Better not be," says Marcus. "Here come the musicians and singers."

The musicians and singers are a larger team than we normally have, as they need to be evenly distributed around the lake's edge. Some are also located on Domitian's island, to ensure the Emperor can hear everything perfectly.

At last the gates are opened and the crowds file in, joking and excited, though there are plenty of passing comments about the weather. After the hot and sunny month we've had, why does today have to be cold and grey?

The stands fill up and already there are vendors of everything, from merchandise including toy ships for children to food and drink, wandering from stand to stand, calling out their wares.

We get advance warning that Domitian is on his way. I walk

round the lake, making final checks with physicians, undertakers, guards, nodding one more time to Servius as I pass the canal. Everything is in place, everything seems promising. If only the weather were better.

The wind is getting stronger. It's changed from a boisterous breeze to a real wind, tree branches waving, the surface of the water choppy and dark, reflecting the sky overhead which is a grim grey. The audience moves too, married women wrapping their pallas tight about them or draping them over babies and their smallest children, who huddle close to their parents, men and slaves shifting in their seats, wishing they had brought cloaks, but who brings cloaks anywhere in July?

"Domitian's here," says Marcus, as trumpets sound out from the east gate.

We watch as Domitian, accompanied by guests and guards, makes his way across the bridge to his own special island where he takes up his seat on the wooden platform. From his body language, he seems happy, nodding left and right to his guests when they speak to him and waving graciously to the crowd applauding him.

But there's wetness on my face again, it is beginning to rain, tiny droplets falling from the grey skies. The wind is cold and growing stronger. People shiver and as the gates begin to close, signalling that the show is about to start soon, one family gets up and leaves, having obviously decided that even a naumachia is not worth staying for in this weather. The gate closes behind them and overhead there's a rumble of thunder.

"We can't go ahead like this," I say to Marcus, fear rising up in me. "There's going to be a storm."

He's staring out over the lake, his jaw tight. "Are you going to tell Domitian he can't have his naumachia?"

"Someone has to. He might listen to a woman, take pity."

Marcus shakes his head. "He's not Titus. He's stubborn. When he wants something, he doesn't listen to anyone saying it can't be done and he can't have his own way. You saw him when he lost his temper. I thought he might kill me that day."

"But we can postpone it," I say. "It doesn't mean it's not going to happen at all, we just move it to another day."

"Just?"

"It's a lot of work," I say. "But if the storm breaks over us, we could lose ships. We could lose men. The audience will be soaked for hours. If it rains hard, the visibility will be awful anyway. It won't be a celebratory event, it'll be miserable."

"I should speak to him."

"Let me try," I say. "If a man talks to him he might feel he must be bold. If a woman asks, perhaps he will show kindness."

"Try. But don't get on the wrong side of him. If he's going to be stubborn, just agree and come back here."

I push through the crowds on the busy pavement and get to the bridge, guarded by the Praetorian Guards. The red token I show them indicates that I am a member of the team organising the event and I receive a reluctant nod, hurry across the wooden bridge and onto the island, glancing up at the darkening sky. Is this the blackness that the sorceress foretold? When I'm at Domitian's seating platform I spot the Aedile, who is theoretically in charge of all imperial Games.

"Ah," he says, recognising me. "Um, err… Althea?"

"Yes," I say. I lower my voice. "Aedile, if the storm breaks overhead, there could be dangerous consequences for the performers, the props, even the audience. The Emperor himself could be at risk. Can you convince him to change the date of the performance?"

He is horrified. "Um… the Emperor is not likely to…"

"I know he won't like it. But it would be better for everyone if we move the date."

The Aedile shifts from one foot to the other, his eyes flickering as though searching for an escape route. My patience runs out at his timidity.

"Never mind," I say. "I'll approach him myself."

The Aedile is vastly relieved. "Certainly," he says. "Certainly, if you think it…"

But I don't hear whatever else he was about to say, I'm already moving closer to the imperial seating area, a few steps away from Domitian, whose focus is on the lake. The nearest guard inspects me and lifts his chin in a gesture to approach.

"Imperator?"

Domitian snaps his head round as though startled. "What?"

"I am Althea Sc –"

"I know who you are."

"The weather is getting worse. The storm may break overhead."

"And?"

"We wonder if it might be… wise to reschedule the naumachia, Imperator."

"Reschedule?"

"We can set it all up for another day," I say, grabbing at my palla which is threatening to blow away in the rising wind. "It would be no trouble at all," I lie, with an attempt at a smile, as though re-organising thousands of men and dozens of ships, a vast audience and Domitian's own diary are all of no consequence. "You have only to name the day, we will take care of everything."

"I *have* named the day," says Domitian, and his voice is cold. "I named today."

"But Imperator –"

"You have a palla, do you not?" he says, gesturing at it.

"Yes, Imperator."

He makes an impatient gesture and a slave rushes forwards with a thick woollen cloak, which Domitian wraps about himself. "There," he says.

"Imperator?"

"We are both warm and protected," he says. "So proceed."

"The audience –"

"Can wear their cloaks and pallas. They will be fine."

"They may not all have brought…" I begin, but I am losing this battle, clutching at straws.

"Then they are foolish."

"The storm may endanger the performers," I try one last time.

He gives a snort of laughter. "Hardened gladiators, sailors and soldiers? I think not. They've seen far worse. Continue."

There is nothing I can say. I bow my head and step backwards.

"Wait."

Is he going to reconsider?

"No one is to go."

"Imperator?"

"Members of the audience are forbidden to leave."

"There are children –"

"Then they will be entertained. Inform the guards at the exits to bolt the gates. The guards may use force if necessary to keep people here. No-one is to depart until I do."

This is unheard of. The audience at the amphitheatre is always free to come and go at will. When it rains many audience members leave, which is why most of the Games are held in the spring and summer to avoid poor weather. To force people to stay when a storm is about to break right over their heads is the act of a tyrant.

"Imperator," I murmur, stepping away as quickly as I can, hurrying down the steps from his box. I do not want him to think of anything else to demand. I thought I might make the situation better, even if it meant more work for us, but it is now worse. Much worse.

I return to Marcus and relay the conversation.

He stares, shocked. "Guards on the exits? The gates bolted?"

"Yes."

"There are children here."

"I said that."

Marcus closes his eyes for a moment. Then he opens them again, looks up at the sky. "The storm is going to break over us," he says. "How many children do you think are here?"

I peer around, trying to guess. "One thousand five hundred? Two thousand?" The seating areas are all horribly exposed to the elements.

"There's one small area there," he says, pointing to the other side of the lake. "The trees might break the wind a bit. Can you move the youngest children there, and anyone who is infirm? I will instruct the guards to bolt the gates. Tell people in the crowd that the Emperor has insisted we go ahead and no-one is to leave, to protect themselves as best they can if they have cloaks, pallas, whatever. We will be cold and wet for several hours." He turns his head both ways, absorbing the vast area of seating. "Take as many of our team as you can get hold of to help you spread the word quickly," he adds. "The parade needs to start."

He raises his hand as I move away and the musicians strike up a military theme. I can see Servius' ship move forwards.

I spend the next hour making my way from section to section, trying to explain without sounding critical of Domitian and moving those who are willing. Karbo and thirty other members of our team are doing the same. Behind us, as we face the audience, the fifteen chosen ships circle the lake accompanied by music and singing, interspersed with rumbling thunder which is getting closer. By the time we are finished, the rain is falling steadily and the audience are sullen-faced, huddling as best they can from the rain and wind.

I go back to where Marcus is standing, passing bolted gates with guards standing in front of them, hands on the hilts of their swords. Marcus' face is grim.

"I've done what I can," I say, cringing as a crack of lightning cuts the grey sky to the north of us and the thunder comes almost immediately after it.

"We have to start the battle sequence," he says. "Five sets of two boats. Boarding and fighting."

My shoulders slump as he raises his arm, signalling for five additional ships to join the others and group into pairs. I watch as the ships change directions. They are all commanded by experienced sailors and rowed by professional oarsmen, but still, they are struggling, the wind is against them and the water is choppy, splashing onto the pavements, wetting the feet of those in the bottom audience tier. The ships lower their sails so that their commanders can better control their movement using only the rowers, even though this looks less interesting, less parade-like.

"Should we turn off the aqueduct?" I ask.

Marcus shakes his head. "We need the depth for the ships," he says. "Can't risk them running aground."

The first battle begins, the men and women of each boat trying to force a boarding, bringing their ships close together and attacking those close at hand. I can't see Domitian's face, he is too far and the rain is heavy, but he is leaning forward as though interested. The crowd is not, they sit huddled together, even stranger to stranger, their faces showing nothing but mute misery. There ought to be cheering and booing as the audience takes sides, lending a festive and exciting air to the event, but there is no sound from them. The musicians and singers keep going, the rain falls and the lightning flashes overhead, the thunder rolls above us.

"Can we cut it short?" I shout to Marcus, trying to be heard above the shouts and clashes of fighting.

He shakes his head. "Domitian is aware there's another round to come," he yells back.

I swallow. The final melee consists of thirty-five ships in an all-out battle. Even in calm weather it would have been a squeeze. With a storm breaking overhead, I am not sure how they will manoeuvre at all.

"It's too dangerous," I protest.

"I'll try to cut this part short so we can get on to the final part," he says and I nod. There's little else we can do at this stage.

Fabia arrives at my side. "They're going to be sick." Her face is serious. "This will lead to fevers. There are children and the infirm here. And even those who are healthy…" She shakes her head, angry. "What is he thinking? *Does* he think?"

I shrug, keep my voice low, bend down close to her. "When he wants something, he wants it. And he allows nothing to get in his way. He becomes deaf and blind."

Fabia tightens her lips. "I wonder if he'll open his eyes and ears when people start falling ill."

I am fairly sure about two hundred criminals and prisoners of war have been killed and fallen overboard when Marcus gives the signal, earlier than planned, for the final melee to begin. The ships already on the lake move so there is enough space and the final fifteen ships emerge onto the water.

Marcus is right, with all the vessels in place they can barely move, the whole of the lake is effectively one large ship. None of their sails are up, so they look more like a series of wooden rafts with thousands of oars sticking out everywhere, most of which have to be retracted as there isn't room for them between the ships. A few dozen are smashed to splinters before their commanders decide that there is no point having the oars out as no-one is going anywhere.

The storm has been raging for at least half an hour and I keep hoping it will lose its power, but if anything it is getting worse. The wind and thunder drown out the musicians and singers. It looks as though they are only pretending to sing and play, mouths open and hands moving, no sound emerging. Perhaps Domitian, provided with his own musical ensemble, can still hear them, no-one else can. What I can hear are children crying with cold and fear at the lightning and thunder.

There are groups of men and women at various gates arguing with the guards, demanding that the gates be opened so that they can leave, gesturing towards weeping children. One guard after another draws their sword and the defeated people return to their seats, heads lowered.

I run down to the bridge and stumble back to the island, the wind all but forcing me off the wooden planks. The guards do not even try to stop me, perhaps they hope Domitian will finally give in.

I kneel before him. "Imperator," I call out, raising my voice to be heard. "I beg you on my knees to stop this naumachia. It is too dangerous. Please. In the name of Minerva, goddess of wisdom, I beg for your wisdom in calling a halt to the melee."

Domitian gazes down at me, his face blank. "Minerva is also the goddess of war," he says. "A goddess of war would not call a halt to a battle. Continue."

There is a crack of lighting overhead and an immediate boom of thunder, then another sound, a whoosh, a thud. A woman near me screams and I turn to see one of the ships has burst into flames, hit by the lightning. The ships around it, wary of the flames, try to move away, but this is not possible. The crew on the stricken ship are trying to get off, the men and women on the deck desperate to find a nearby ship they can leap onto. The rowing team on the burning ship are below deck and they are struggling to get out, one hundred and eighty men pushing and jostling in panic.

I turn back to Domitian. Surely, he will change his mind, but he only gazes down at me, making no effort to wipe away the rain falling down his face. "I said, continue," he says. "Did you not hear me?"

I get up and run back across the bridge, which takes me closer to the burning ship. Marcus is on the shoreline nearby, climbing on board one of the ships so that he can give orders, direct the vessels to the canal so that some of them can leave and clear space to safely rescue the crew of the damaged ship. But the ships cannot move.

The burning ship rocks and tilts precariously, then goes too far. The battering ram on its prow, no longer carefully guided away from the ships alongside, slams into one, water immediately rushing in through the gaping hole.

"It's going to sink!" shouts Marcus.

He moves from the first ship to a second, trying to get closer to the two stricken ships, one in flames, the other one sinking fast, so that he can shout orders. The occupants of both are leaping off, onto other ships if they can, into the water if they cannot. But the wind is against them, two ships without commanders, their battering rams threatening to cause more damage to the ships wedged too close to them and worse, the ships round them unable to get out of the way to enable the desperate swimmers space to reach the shore. People in the water try to swim but are crushed between ships or pulled under as they move, their screams reaching me even where I stand.

Commanders and their officers shout orders, but there is too much going on. Marcus manages to get one ship out of the lake and into the canal, moves onto another, trying to achieve the same thing. But this makes some of the ships try to get closer to the canal and a second ship is ploughed into and there are more screams as water rushes in.

The audience are shouting and screaming too, some men rush forwards to try and help, but there is nothing they can do. The three ships in trouble are wedged into the eastern part of the lake, with ships all around them. The second ship to take on water is worse than the first, arms desperately wave from the lower deck where the rowers sit as water gushes into the splintered side. They are trapped by water and jagged broken wood with no way to escape.

Someone grabs my arm and I swing round to find Karbo, panting next to me. "He's leaving!"

I turn towards the bridge and there is Domitian, striding away from the island, hurriedly followed by his entourage and guests, all of them trying to keep their balance in the tearing wind.

"Unlock the gates!" I yell.

Karbo nods and darts away, heading south while I run north.

I run to each gate, telling the guards to unbolt them at once, that Domitian is leaving. The gates swing open and immediately fill with people trying to leave, cramming through the spaces as quickly as they can, while I fight against the oncoming throng to reach the next gate. Now that the Emperor is gone, the crowd might turn angry, but they are too exhausted and cold to do so, too afraid of what is happening behind them on the lake. They swarm out of the now-open exits, shivering and silent except for the children who are crying. The men's faces are rigid with unspoken anger, the women stare as they pass as though seeking explanation for what has happened. I cannot meet their eyes. It's not my fault, but I feel as though it is. If I had pleaded more successfully with Domitian, if I had managed to sway him… the thousands of soaked bodies who pass my post are a silent reproach. They make their way back through the grove of trees, many of which have crashed to the ground, bringing their too-close fellows down with them. I watch Marcus manage to get a further five ships out and into the canal, finally freeing up some space on the lake. But the two mauled ships have gone under, only their masts stick out of the black water. The burning ship still floats, blackened and smoking.

The last people have gone, only our team and the performers are left. I stand at the water's edge as the rain pours down, scanning the scene before me. The musicians and singers trail along the island bridge back to the shoreline, shoulders slumped. On the ships, men and women lean perilously over the decks, trying to reach into the water to pull up injured comrades, pushing and pulling to get sections of ships that have rammed together unstuck so that they will be able to steer back out to the canal and away from this horror. All along the shoreline I can see dead bodies. And Marcus.

I run to him.

He is kneeling on the shore, legs in the water, Servius' dead body in his arms. When I reach him he looks up and his face is stricken, tears trickling down. I kneel next to him in the mud, take Servius' body into my own arms. Marcus sits back on his heels.

"It's my fault," he sobs.

"It's Domitian's fault and no one else's," I say.

"I should have overridden him."

"Then you'd be dead." I look down at Servius' white face, all life drained from his skin, stroke his eyes shut.

"I presented him to Domitian. I made him known to him. He would never have commanded one of the ships if I hadn't done that."

I shake my head. "We needed thousands of men. We would have used everyone we could lay our hands on. Two hundred idle sailors, you think we wouldn't have used them?"

He won't be comforted. "What will his mother say? He kept saying she would be so proud of him. He was a boy and I put him in harm's way, I wanted him to rise and instead I have killed him. I will have to send word to his mother that her son is dead. At sea? By the hand of vicious pirates? No, in a lake we dug in the middle of Rome, for the pleasure of an emperor who has lost his mind."

I wave over two of the surviving sailors from Servius' crew, staggering along the shore, their faces shocked. They come to me and I tell them to carry Servius to the undertakers by the west gate and ensure they know his name. They lift him away. I take

Marcus' muddy hands in mine and wipe away his tears, leaving his cheek streaked with dirt.

"We would have been killed if we'd stood against him," I tell him.

"We might have saved hundreds of good men."

I hold him in my arms, the two of us kneeling on the cold shore.

The rain continues to fall, an endless grey misery in which we are trapped for what feels like eternity. We work until it is too dark to see, Marcus first guiding the ships out of the lake and back to the canal which will allow them to escape this cursed place and return, via the Tiber river, to their ports. They must reach safe harbour before darkness comes and their presence in the lake makes all other work impossible. Some ships still have their own commander, a few have lost theirs and their second-in-command officers step up to take their place, anxious at taking a promotion they never wanted to happen in this way. I send Karbo home against his will, telling him to let the rest of the insula know what happened, to get into dry clothes and go to Cassia's to be fed, then to bed. Meanwhile we gather up each lifeless body along the shoreline, log their name if known and deliver them to the waiting undertakers, all the while knowing the murky waters hide more of their fallen comrades. Those whose faces we do not recognise are laid out on the pavement to wait till tomorrow. At one point Fabia sits down and her assistant Sadiki kneels by her, takes her little body in his arms. I would go to her but I have no energy left to comfort anyone, it is all I can do not to sink down and weep myself.

"It's too dark to do more," says Marcus. His voice is hoarse from shouting instructions over the water. "I'm going to open the drainage system so the water will drain out overnight. Tomorrow we can come back for the bodies that have sunk to the bottom."

The rain has slowed to a fine drizzle. We round everyone up and send them back to their homes and barracks, the slaves down to the warehouse with a message to give them extra rations. Marcus and I are the last to leave. We walk hand in hand, though our hands have no heat left in them. Back at the insula, Maria has greeted each returning member of our community with dry clothes and hot water to wash with, and Cassia has a pot of stew ready. Adah has made hot honeyed wine more suited to the winter months, but we are grateful for it. Fabia, Fabius, Marcus and I eat in abject silence, then wish one another good night in low voices, while Quintus hurries away with all our wet muddy clothes to his family's fullery. The rain has finally stopped, the wind has dropped, now the evening is just cold.

I can barely climb the stairs, my legs tremble with each step and when I reach the hut I fall onto the bed, where Maria has laid out the winter blankets we have not used for months. I huddle gratefully under them and move close to Marcus when he joins me, the two of us clinging to one another. Tears trickle down my face until at last, exhausted, I slide into sleep.

I wake again and again in the night, images of Domitian's angry face before me, Servius' body in Marcus' arms, Marcus weeping, the silent miserable crowd. Every time I jolt awake thinking I am waking from a nightmare and then realise that it is true, that tomorrow I will have to face even worse.

The next morning dawns cruelly bright, sunny and still, with no sign at all of the previous day's storm except for broken branches and fallen trees across Rome. I send word to Strabo that he must manage the Games by himself for two weeks and we head back to the lake where the three hundred slaves of our team designated to the naumachia have gathered for the day's work. They are silent, their faces stricken at the events of yesterday and what is still to come. Also in attendance are Labeo, Paternus and the commanding officers of various ships and regiments, come to identify the dead.

Marcus unlocks the gate and we stand in silence, surveying the scene. The pavement around the bodies we laid out yesterday is covered in mud and leaves, the glittering water has drained away leaving a vast expanse of mud, littered with the wreckage of the two ships and hundreds more bodies. Only Domitian's island sits prettily atop the carnage, green and pleasant, still populated by the hardier flowers. I stare at it for a few moments, then direct the team. The undertakers will be returning soon.

The work is back-breaking and heart-breaking in equal measure. We must wade into the thick mud and drag back bodies, wash their faces and try to identify them, I keep a tally of their names if we can identify them, otherwise of their uniforms and any features that may help us name them later, so that their families will know they fell. The undertakers return hour after hour with carts ready for us to load the dead.

When the bodies have finally been removed, we start work on the broken ships, more carts arriving at the gates to be filled with shattered wood, taken away as the basin slowly empties.

It takes us four days of work to fully clear the site. When it is done, we usher everyone out and Marcus bolts the last gate shut behind us, his face pale, eyes red-rimmed. We spend another five days attending every funeral we can manage between us, from gladiators to sailors, choking in plumes of smoke as they rise upwards. Marcus writes a letter to Servius' mother, praising her son's bravery and respectfulness, his willingness to learn new skills, how the Emperor knew him by name and requested that he lead the parade. He tells her that she should be proud.

For three weeks after the naumachia people all over Rome are ill. From colds and coughs to fevers, the storm and Domitian's stubborn power can be felt across the city. A few people, already weak, die and there are mutterings against an Emperor so despotic that he insists on going ahead with an event for his own amusement, no matter the cost to his people.

Marcus, exhausted by his grief and guilt over what happened, gets a high fever. I sit by his side for many hours, taking turns with Karbo to hold cool cloths to his head. He recovers but is pale and sad. An imperial scroll is delivered.

"We're summoned to Domitian," I tell Marcus.

"I never want to see him again."

"I'll go alone," I say.

"I don't want you near him, either. He's a madman with no heart."

"We don't have a choice," I say.

"I'll go."

"No," I say. "You're not fit to go. "I'll go."

"If he… if he does anything, Althea, you leave."

Leaving may not be an option if Domitian is in one of his moods but at least I am sure that Stephanus will be with him, who seems able to manage at least some of his strange moods and I'm not about to worry Marcus any more than I have to.

For once I am shown in with no delay. Domitian is looking out of a window. I'm glad to see Stephanus is in his usual place in a discreet corner of the room.

"It is most regrettable that the storm during the naumachia led to many people being taken ill," Domitian says, turning as soon as I am inside the door. His face is sad. "I wish to offer a public banquet to let the populace know that I care for their wellbeing."

I stare at him, trying to change my expression to look less surprised. "Imperator?"

"There will be a private event for the senators and their families and suchlike," he says airily. "You need not concern yourself with that. But there should also be a public banquet, for the plebians. People can come and be fed, you will arrange for that. Set up long tables in the Forum, with shifts so that all who wish to be fed can come. Good warming food, meat from the amphitheatre, to be used in stews. Bread, barley porridge, cheese. Wine, of course. The imperial purse will take care of whatever is necessary." He nods, satisfied at his generosity.

I can't believe what I'm hearing. "And this banquet is your initiative following…"

"Following the storm at the naumachia," says Domitian. "It is given by myself to let the people know that their Emperor feels sad for them for having had such a terrible experience."

I don't dare speak, nor show any emotion. "As you command, Imperator," I say.

"I will escort you out," offers Stephanus.

He walks with me beyond the atrium, out into the busy Forum, where I stop and turn to him. I keep my voice low, but it shakes with the feelings rising up in me, I cannot help myself.

"What happened back there? Has he forgotten how the disaster came to happen? He speaks as though it wasn't his decision to keep us all there!"

Stephanus nods. "The Emperor has his passions and he finds it difficult, in the moment, to see beyond them. But when he has achieved what he wishes to achieve he sometimes reflects on what has occurred and feels…"

"Remorse?"

Stephanus gives a small shake of his head. "It is as though he cannot comprehend that his previous actions were the cause of the damage. He sees only the damage and feels that he can mend it, without perhaps making the link between his previous actions and those he is making now."

"He doesn't *remember* that he forced everyone to stay while a thunderstorm broke over us and hundreds of people died? That thousands were taken ill?"

"The passion of that moment has faded and so he sees the damage without perhaps seeing entirely what led to it, how he could have behaved differently. As though it were not possible for him to have behaved differently, in that moment."

I sigh. "I don't pretend to understand," I say. "It was like talking to someone who couldn't hear me and now it's like talking to someone who doesn't remember what they did."

"Perhaps a good way of thinking of it," says Stephanus. "I must leave you."

"Wait," I say.

He turns back politely. "Yes?"

"Glabrio and the lion…"

"Yes?"

"Did you arrange that?"

"The Emperor had a number of names of those whose behaviour was considered treasonous. The consul's was one of them."

"Did you add him to the list because of what happened last year?"

"The list was the Emperor's."

"And after he defeated the lion and was exiled?"

"It is my understanding that he died soon afterwards."

I raise my eyebrows. "Did you arrange that?"

Stephanus blinks. "His being alive was not in Rome's best interests."

"Really?"

Stephanus steps closer to me, his face calm. "I will repeat to you what I said when Funis died, Althea Aquillius," he says. "I believe in justice."

I gaze into his eyes and reluctantly bow my head in acknowledgement. "I would have liked the world to know what he did. That he had his own son murdered."

"That, I am afraid, is not always possible."

"Did *he* know why he was dispatched?"

"He knew."

And he's gone, walking briskly away, swallowed into the crowd, just one toga amongst many, yet with the power to change destinies.

At home, I open my chest of possessions and pull out a tiny cloth bag, tip the bronze bracelet it holds out into my hand. A bull's head at one end, opposite it the mid-vault body of a bull-leaper, the gift Funis gave me before his untimely death. I look it over, touch the flying body. However it happened, his death has been avenged. Perhaps now his shade will be at peace.

With everything that has gone on it is more than a week before I realise that I haven't seen Julia in the last few days.

"She's taken to her bed," says Maria, when I ask.

"Why?"

"Her cough got worse. She said she was in pain at night, that her back hurt and she couldn't breathe well, even coming up the stairs."

I could kick myself for not having noticed her deterioration. There's been too much going on, but I should have seen that her cough was still bad. When I visit her I'm shocked. She's lost weight in the past month or two, and she was always a slim woman, she had no bulk to spare. Her face appears gaunt, but she tries to wave away my concerns.

"I've had some headaches in the past few weeks, I thought resting would be good," she says, turning her face away to cough.

"I'm sending Fabius and Fabia to you and you're to do whatever they say," I tell her sternly.

But Fabius and Fabia look grave when they've seen her.

"I am not sure she will get well," says Fabius gently.

"What?"

"I've seen this before. We can only keep her comfortable."

"That's not possible," I mutter, shocked.

Fabia puts her hand in mine. "We must be prepared for her to leave us," she says.

A DYING BREATH

IN THE OPPRESSIVE HEAT OF August we take up a vigil in Julia's room, one of us always with her. When it is my turn at night, I keep only one lamp burning so that I can see, the room dim around us. I sleep when I am very tired, but mostly I sit and watch over her, listen to her breathe in and out. Fabius offered opium, burning the sweet-smelling seeds to produce a smoke to be inhaled using a reed, as a way to reduce any pain she might suffer, but she refused. As the days pass, her breathing becomes erratic, several times in a shift I will lean forward, afraid that this is the last moment, that she has taken her last breath, before her chest heaves and she gasps, then continues to breathe, slow in and out, a wheeze at the beginning of each intake, a rattle towards the end of each out breath. I find myself crumpling my tunic with my hands before trying to relax, unclutching the fabric, deliberately placing my hands in my lap, where my fingers intertwine again, pulling, rubbing, as though my thoughts were made flesh.

I cannot imagine the insula without Julia. She has always been here, this insula is built around her presence, even when she is absent. The very street it sits on, Virgin's Street, is named for her, bestowed by an awed local community who found themselves with a retired Vestal in their midst, the daughter of a great family living here in the Ninth Region, a nothing-place, apparently intending to live out her life here. Owner of a crumbling insula, she made it welcoming to all, the rooms taken by those who could only afford a low rent, those in need of care and companionship. She took in Marcus, when he was wounded and didn't know what to do with his life, Cassius and his wife when they were poor and trying to scratch a living by setting up a little popina, then Cassius alone when his wife died and left him with little Cassia to take care of. Maria, widowed young. Adah, old and without a family. Celer, battling drink and no longer able to drive chariots in the races. Balbus and Floriana, childless owners of the toy shop.

And others who came and went over the years. I had not realised how many there had been, but word has gone out across Rome and beyond that Julia is dying, and every day strangers arrive at the insula, hesitating in the gateway to the courtyard, looking about for her. It is usually Maria or Karbo who spots them and asks if they are here for Julia. They are directed up to her apartment, where whoever is on shift will invite them inside. They always come with gifts. Fragrant roses, sweet peaches and soft ripe figs, beeswax candles that fill her room with the smell of honey, fans to keep her cool. When they enter they stand helpless at the sight of her still body, fear that they have come too late to say everything they wanted to say, to give her gifts that are not enough for the gratitude they want to express. They stand or kneel by her, reach out trembling fingers to touch her hand. They speak out loud to her, or whisper. Their eyes fill with tears as they thank her for looking after them at times of hardship in their life.

"When my husband died…"

"My wife…"

"When we lost everything and had nowhere to go…"
"That night in winter when you took us in…"
"Thank you…"
"You helped us…"
"I will never forget…"
"May the gods bless you…"
"Thanks be to Vesta for giving us her handmaiden…"
And her name, whispered over and over again in the dimly lit room, *"Julia, Julia, Julia…"*

They hesitate before leaving, knowing they will not see her again, pause in the doorway, look at her with pleading eyes, desperate for a sign from her, a smile, a word, even for her eyelids to flutter. But she does not move, only breathes in and out, as though it takes everything she has, every last bit of life force, just to do this one thing. They stumble out into the light of day, arms empty of gifts, their faces streaked with tears. Some take time to visit the inhabitants who have been here longest. They chat to the baker's family, they eat a meal at Cassia's, a few of the men spend an evening drinking with Celer before they head home, heavy-hearted at losing a woman who meant so much to them.

"She helped so many people," I say to Maria after a night's shift. My eyes are gritty from lack of sleep and from crying. Hearing all the love and gratitude bestowed upon Julia, as well as the many tales of hardship she helped alleviate, is too much to bear.

"So many owe her a debt of gratitude," says Maria.

I turn at the end of the wooden walkway, conscious suddenly, even in my half-asleep state, that I've never asked Maria how she came to be here. "How did you – ?" I start.

She stares down, into the courtyard, into her past. "My parents died young. I was taken in by an aunt and uncle who were stingy, didn't want me for anything but as a house slave. They married me off as quick as they could to a man who wanted a wife he could control absolutely. He would get jealous over nothing, though Juno knows I never gave him cause. Even going to the market or the bakery to buy food, he'd follow me, ask why I smiled at one of the vendors, why I'd worn such and such a tunic, why I'd left my palla at home, was I trying to pretend I wasn't married? I tried to shop more quickly, closer to home, but nothing would please him."

"Did you at least have friends to visit?"

"I had three friends from my childhood but he discouraged me from going to the baths with them, wouldn't have them visit me and refused to let me visit them. He beat me if he thought I'd disobeyed him, and my uncle and aunt didn't care, they said a man had every right to beat a disobedient wife and that I should try harder to please him and be a good wife. But it didn't matter how hard I tried, it was never good enough. One day he saw some other woman he liked better and divorced me. From one day to another, without warning."

"Good riddance," I say. Her story is sadder than I expected, I had known she was a young widow but had thought she would at least have fond memories of the past.

"That's what I thought. But my uncle and aunt wouldn't have me back in their house. My friends had moved or forgotten me. I had no one and my new freedom was not as I expected. I shook when I had to go to market, I never went to the baths. Leaving the house grew harder and harder. I spent my days huddled at home, eking out food so that I would not have to go out again. His beatings, his jealousies, they were locked inside me, I couldn't let them go." She sighs. "In the end I had no money, I would have had to rent myself out as an indentured servant, little better than a common slave, but who would want a servant that refused to leave the house on errands? The landlord threw me out and I crept from street to street till I saw an open courtyard gate and huddled inside, just to let the trembling still for a few moments. When I heard a voice I tried to run but it was Julia, she caught hold of my arm and asked me what I was doing, what my name was, why I was in her courtyard."

I think of Karbo, how he, too, crept into the courtyard to be safe from the outside world. How Maria saw him and caught him. At the time I thought she objected to street children using the courtyard as their own, now I think she saw in him her own fears and needs, caught him out of kindness, knowing he needed more than a safe space for the night.

She gives a small laugh. "I was afraid of Julia but she took me to the popina and Cassia's mother fed me. When Julia saw how I was afraid of the world outside, yet calm inside the walls of the insula, she told me to stay. I told her I had no money and she shook her head and said it didn't matter. And I have been here ever since. All these years later and still I tremble when I leave the insula."

"I'm sorry," I say. It doesn't seem enough.

"Long time ago," she says, as though speaking of something she has left behind, but there is a tightness in her body that belies her dismissal.

Why have I never noticed before that I hardly ever see Maria leave the insula? Occasionally she will venture as far as our local market, but not even as a regular daily or weekly occurrence, as most people do. She eats at Cassia's or has food sent up to her, shops at the bakery. I often saw Julia bring back two baskets from the market rather than just her own and now I realise why. Maria has fruit delivered to her and makes fine preserves and drinks that Julia or other friends will take to the market and sell for her so she has a little money, but I never thought to ask why she did not run her own market stall. I think of how she sits on the balcony, watching over the insula, knowing everything about everyone, all our comings and goings. I used to find her bright colours, loud voice and nosiness amusing, but now I see her bravado is tinged with sadness. This is a woman who can barely leave the insula without fear, who has made this block and courtyard her whole world. I blink a couple of times, still exhausted from a night spent watching over Julia, then hug her without words. Her solid bulk feels fragile in my arms.

I go back along the walkway, up the stairs and fall into my bed as Marcus awakes, one arm outstretched to receive me into his embrace. He kisses me, slips out of the bed, pulling on his tunic and turning to ensure I am covered up, though the day's heat will soon make his care unnecessary.

Julia hasn't spoken for more than a week, yet still she breathes, in and out. I dribble water into her mouth and her throat moves to receive it, but not enough. Her skin is drawn, her lips dry. I moisten them with oil, wipe her face with a wet cloth, fan her.

When she speaks I jump.

"Cassia." Her voice is so raspy it barely sounds like her.

"Julia?"

"Cassia."

I run to the door. "Karbo!" I call down into the courtyard. "Tell Cassia to come. Right now!"

In a few moments Cassia is hovering in the doorway, out of breath, worried. "Althea?"

"She asked for you," I say, still shocked that Julia has spoken at all.

Cassia walks over to Julia, strokes her sunken cheeks, lightly touches her hand. "Julia?"

She doesn't open her eyes, but she speaks at once, as though she's been waiting only for Cassia, all this time. "Soon you must go to the Temple of Vesta and tell my sisters I am gone."

Cassia looks up at me, startled. "Yes, Julia," she murmurs.

"My will is lodged with them."

Cassia nods. Anyone with an important will leaves it in the care of the Vestal Virgins.

"You are named owner of this insula after my death."

Cassia stares. It takes her a moment to find her tongue. "Julia – I –"

"You have done what I have tried to do. Kept a hearth for the people of Rome. You have done it without being told, it came from your own heart."

"My mother –"

"You did not have to follow her example. Nor mine. You did it because you wanted to."

Cassia stands very still. Her bottom lip is trembling, I can see her try to form words, but they will not come out of her mouth.

"I hope you will continue to offer a refuge to those who have no home, as I have tried to do."

"Yes Julia." It comes out a whisper. "I don't know how to thank –"

Julia's head moves to one side and then the other. "I have seen your good heart from when you were a little girl. May the gods bless you, Cassia."

She falls silent again, exhausted, and though we hover over her, she says nothing more.

"Her time is coming," says Cassia.

We gather in her rooms, Marcus and I, Karbo, Cassia and Quintus with Emilia, Cassius, Celer, Maria, Adah, Fabia and Fabius when they can be spared from work, Balbus and Floriana, other people from the insula and the bakery. Her rooms are full, but very quiet, all of us watching her, unwilling for her to leave us, determined for her not to be alone when she does. We wait all of a day and all of a night and towards the middle of the second day her eyelids flutter.

"Julia?" says Marcus, taking her hand in his. "We are here, Julia. We are all by your side."

"Althea?" she says, her voice tiny in the quietness.

"I'm here," I say, taking her other hand. "I am here, Julia."

"A good man and a good woman," she says, and every word is an effort.

"Rest," says Marcus and she falls silent.

He is right of course, but my shoulders shake in silent sobs. I know, feel certain, this is the last thing she will ever say to me and the idea that Julia should call me a good woman is unbearable, as though a deity has pronounced me worthy and blessed me. Perhaps before, when I sat by her dying bedside for hours on end, I had imagined some grand speech by Julia with her last breaths, that she might say priestess-like blessings over us or speak some sort of prophecy, even though she has never claimed any such ability. But these simple words, the tiny press of her hand, they are worth more than any priestly blessing.

Her breathing goes on and on that afternoon and into night, yet none of us leave her side. We sit in silence, occasionally someone will pour new drinks, watered wine or the plum juice that is Maria's specialty. Quintus and Celer leave and come back with food. The baker's family come and go, one member always with us, the others hurrying to work and then back again as soon as they can. The cobbler closes his shop early and comes to sit with us. The children fall asleep, Karbo's head heavy on my shoulder, Emilia curled up in a ball on a folded blanket. Adah, sitting at my side, occasionally pats my hand or slowly strokes down the length of my back, a comforting silent presence.

And then, in the quiet room, there is silence. Without warning. Without a gasping, a rattle, a struggle. Nothing. Only a breath out, which none of us even noticed among the others, and no breath back in. Nothing. I hear the silence and look up, frown, watch Julia's chest for the gasp that must come. Nothing. I raise my eyes to Cassia, whose own eyes are wide, to Maria, who turns to Fabia, who rises and comes closer, touches Julia's throat, holds her wrist, looks at me and nods. Maria rises to her feet and kisses Julia's lips, to seal her body from her departed spirit. It should be done by Julia's closest relative, but all of us defer to Maria's long friendship with her, in the absence of any relatives.

Sobs break out, lamentations are made, we women scratch at our faces and call out her name. Prayers are whispered. Karbo wakes, sleepy-eyed and when he sees that she is gone he turns his face into my shoulder and cries.

"She was old," I whisper to him, trying to offer some comfort. Really Julia was not that old, she could have lived for many more years, but to Karbo no doubt she seemed so.

"She left the gate open," he says through his tears. My own tears spill at this other, unspoken kindness of Julia's over the many years, that the gate of the insula was never barred shut, even at night, instead left ajar so that homeless children could find somewhere safe to sleep at night, the pile of sleeping mats always stacked in a corner somewhere in our courtyard. I squeeze Karbo to me, grateful that this quiet gesture of hers brought him to me when he was younger and needed a family. I wonder how many people have slept in our courtyard over the years, dragged a clean sleeping mat over the cobbles and found a night of respite, the strength to go on the next day. Julia's quiet kindnesses were multiplied over the years by Cassia, who always has a bowl of soup for anyone who asks, by the baker's family who bring yesterday's bread out each morning and leave it in a basket by the gate of our insula, by Marcus bringing home meat from the arena for Cassia to dole out amongst our inhabitants, a welcome addition to many people's diets of vegetable porridge and bread. I stroke Karbo's wet face and nod to Cassia who gently leads him back to her own apartment to sleep, drowsy Emilia slumped over her shoulder.

Marcus is standing over Julia, his back to me.

"We need to wash her," I say gently.

He turns to me and his face is wet with tears. I put my arms about him and he pulls away from me, wiping his face with the back of his arm.

"I'll fetch the undertakers," he says, voice husky. "Can you manage to lift her?"

I nod. Men should not touch the deceased's body, so it will fall to Maria and I to lift Julia to the ground, Fabia being too short to manage the task.

Marcus leaves, headed for the headquarters of Rome's undertakers on the Esquiline Hill. We see them daily at the amphitheatre, one of them is always on duty at the Games, more when we warn them in advance there are likely to be multiple deaths. Today they are being called for a different task.

"Here," Fabia says, indicating a space on the floor, where she has laid out a blanket. Maria and I move close to Julia and gently scoop our arms under her, Maria by her head and I by her legs. She weighs very little for a tall woman, as though it was her departed spirit that gave her weight. We manage to lower her to the floor without any jolting movements, then the three of us kneel over her and undress her. I'm awkward, removing her clothes without her permission seems wrong. I try to look away but this makes the task harder, so I watch and follow Fabia, who is not awkward but instead both careful and brisk, passing each of us cloths and bowls of warm water that she must have prepared earlier, while we sat through our last drowsy watch. We wipe every part of Julia's body with care and I am grateful to Fabia for warming the water, it would seem unkind to wash her with cold water.

"Oil," says Fabia, pouring some from a little bottle into our hands. "She made it herself. It is right for us to use it," she adds.

I put my hands together and inhale. Jasmine and roses waft over me. Gently I place my hands on Julia's still-warm body and let the fragrance envelop her.

When Cassia returns from the Temple of Vesta she is in shock. Not only does Julia's will name her owner of the insula but her heir in all matters. There was enough money to upkeep the insula for many years to come as well as for Julia's funerary rites and the instruction that she be cremated.

Most common people would be buried as quickly as possible, dead bodies being offensive to the gods and polluting to those touching them, but Julia's status as a former Vestal Virgin and her origins amongst a great family, however much they have chosen to forget her very existence, means her treatment is closer to that of an elite family's departed. Some of them might lie in their home's atrium for up to a week, but this is a hot month and so Julia will lie for three days in the cool rooms on the ground floor, usually kept for storage but now hastily cleaned out and swept, decorated with cypress branches at the door and over our insula's gate to warn anyone of possible ritual pollution. Her body is placed on a funeral couch, in a reclining position, feet pointed towards the door, a coin placed in her mouth to pay her way to the ferryman Charon to take her across the river Styx and arrive safely in the underworld. But I shake my head at the offer to use cosmetics. I do not want her pale cheeks painted pink, it would look nothing like the woman I knew.

Many people visit over the three days, standing just within the door, whispering prayers and chanting her name. Meanwhile, without even agreeing on this course of action, the whole insula stops its daily routines, as though all of us were her family, bound to cease all normal activities for nine days, only eating and sleeping and watching over Julia, attending her funeral, and recovering afterwards. The shops close their shutters, even Cassia's popina is closed to outsiders, as we are all polluted. We cannot wash ourselves. We turn inwards on ourselves, use Cassia's large popina kitchen to cook meals that will serve all of us, eat in the courtyard in shifts, simple foods that can be quickly made and that are suited to the heat; flat breads and dips, large salads, olives and cheese. Each day outside our gate we find offerings from the local neighbours: bread from another bakery, baskets of fruit and jars of olives. We take them in, grateful for our neighbours' loving care, their tribute to the Vestal Virgin who came to live amongst them, forsaking her own wealthy family and Vesta's temple, choosing this run-down neighbourhood, these small streets and crumbling houses in which to build herself a home. We tell stories about Julia; the first time each of us met her, the times she helped us, the way she would look at you or say something important. We laugh as well, mostly at ourselves for being in awe of her Vestal past before finding her to be warm-hearted and caring. We hug one another.

We have to send messages to Strabo that he should manage the Games, for we have three shows promised during our mourning period and we cannot go to the amphitheatre. We send amended plans which allow for fewer senior staff on site and trust to the gods and Strabo to manage. He sends back messages each day telling us that all is well, setting our minds at rest so that we can focus only on Julia.

We rise well before dawn on the fourth day, the red-dressed undertakers already busy moving Julia's body onto the funeral bier, musicians waiting outside the gate to accompany us to the funeral pyre, to be held on the road outside of Rome. It is not seemly to walk in funerary procession in daylight, so the undertakers hand out torches to several of us, before gesturing the six men forward who will carry the bier. Marcus, Quintus, the baker and two of his grown sons, Celer. Cassius and Karbo, too old and too young, walk behind, as though lending what strength they have to the men carrying her.

We set off in the flickering darkness, through Virgin's Street and down Sand Street, across the slow-moving summer river and beyond, walking through empty streets to the mournful, eerie sounds of flutes and drums. Here and there we come across carts making their deliveries before dawn. The drivers pull aside when they hear us coming and see our burden, bow their heads as we pass but also, by their sides, discreetly gesture against evil spirits, against the pollution of death.

The road outside Rome's gates is lined with graves as far ahead as we can see in the faint light that is beginning to break the sky. Guided by the undertakers we arrive at the designated spot for Julia's funeral pyre, which stands ready for her. The undertakers lift her white-wrapped body from the bier onto the pyre.

A portable altar has been set up, its coals already white-hot, nearby is a tethered pig, softly grunting to itself.

"Her heir?" asks the priest.

Cassia steps forward. Her hands shake as she takes the sacred mola salsa mixture of salt and flour, and sprinkles it over the pig. "An offering to Ceres, warden of the door between the living and the dead," she says. "May you allow our beloved Julia to pass through with ease."

The hammer comes down fast, the pig barely sighs before it is laid on its back and gutted. The priest's assistant hands over an earthenware bowl of the steaming guts to be examined. They are swiftly determined to be acceptable and thrown into the coals to feed the goddess, where they hiss and spit, sending up a thick stink of roast pig and faeces, hard to bear so early in the morning and on an empty stomach. The pig is quickly butchered, most of it will come home with us for the funeral meal, a portion goes to the priest along with their payment, another portion will be burnt with Julia. We will eat later on, it would not do to eat at the same time as Julia's portion is burnt. To share a meal with the dead is an offer to share their world, which none of us are ready for.

It is time to light the flame and we gather around the pyre. Cassia is hesitating to light the fire beneath the white shrouded body. I take her hand and squeeze it and she averts her face from the pyre as is correct, about to lower the torch she is carrying onto the wood. But there is a murmur behind us and we turn to see the crowd parting, heads bowed.

Two large closed litters have appeared, each carried by six slaves. The drapes pull back to reveal a group of women dressed all in white, their hair bound into intricate plaits laced through with red ribbons. The Vestal Virgins. Five of them emerge, one left behind as ever, to guard the sacred flame. The oldest leads the way to the pyre, carrying a burning brazier. The other four follow her in solemn procession, the youngest only a wide-eyed child of seven, chosen to take the place of Cornelia, the Virgo Maxima entombed alive last year. She follows the others, each step particularly careful, anxious to perform correctly in front of all these onlookers.

We step back to let them approach and they slowly circle the pyre, Julia's body making up the sixth white-clad figure, part of a complete set of Vestals for the last time in her life. The new Virgo Maxima kneels and uses her brazier to light the pyre, Rome's most sacred flame brought to this dusty road outside Rome's walls to send a Vestal who served her time on her way to another world, far beyond the city that was her home. The crowd is quiet while the Virgo Maxima lifts her palms and prays, then moves obediently out of the way as the five women turn and return to their litters, the drapes closing behind them as they are carried away, back to Vesta's Temple, the crowd closing behind them as though they had never been here, a vision, born from our imagination.

But the fire has been lit, it stands testimony to their appearance. The first licks of flame here and there give way to a dull roar as the pyre takes hold properly and we stand in silence as the silent figure within slowly disappears, taking Julia away from us and replacing her with nothing but our community, the people standing all around her, touching hands or shoulders, wiping tears or murmuring low comforts.

Later that week the undertaker visits us personally, at home, a rare honour. He carries with him an urn, which he holds with reverence. He finds me making cuttings of Julia's herbs, putting them into tiny pots that I can take with me to the farm, where I can grow them in my own garden and think of her when I see them.

"Never done a Vestal," he comments, handing it over. He stares around, curious. "This where she lived?"

"Yes," I say, turning the black urn in my hands, wondering how all of Julia's spirit and presence can possibly be contained in this clay pot, such a small plain receptacle for a woman who tended Rome's most sacred hearth and who caused heads to bow wherever she went, long after she finished serving Vesta. The very first time I saw her, walking down the staircase of the insula, I was struck by how still she was even when she moved, her gaze falling on me and how I would have known without being told that this was a woman who had spent most of her life as a priestess. My eyes prick with tears at the thought that she welcomed me to Rome but will not be able to bless me when I leave.

"What was she like?" asks the undertaker.

"She kept a hearth burning for the people of Rome long after she finished tending Vesta's flame," I say.

"Right," says the man, obviously unable to imagine what I'm talking about.

"Thank you for this," I say, in a voice that suggests he leave. He does so, still looking curiously about him, as though expecting to see something fascinating, not a simple insula like any other in Rome.

I take the urn to Cassia and she, too, turns it in her hands as though bemused by it, by the absence of Julia. Later that day we walk together back to the road outside the walls, to where a waist-high stone-built edifice awaits the urn. Cassia sprinkles wine over the open urn, closes it again and places it carefully on the interior ledge, next to another.

"Back with her husband," I say.

Cassia nods, wipes her tears. "I'm not good enough to do what she did," she says, voice low.

"She didn't ask you to do what she did," I say. "She asked you to do what you already do and gave you the insula so that you could do more of the same."

She gives a watery grimace-smile. "I hope it is good enough."

"It is more than enough," I say. "She saw your good heart, Cassia."

Julia's epitaph has been carved into the stone, under her husband's which praises him for being "a man who gave his protection and love to the handmaiden of Vesta". To which we have added, "who now lies beside him, having cared for Rome's sacred hearth beyond her term of office. May their shades walk together always hand in hand."

THE BATTLE OF CRANES
AND DWARFS

I WAKE FAR TOO EARLY BUT I can tell from his breathing that Marcus has done the same.

"What time is it?" I whisper.

He chuckles. "No idea. I couldn't sleep. I'm too excited. Do you realise that after today we will be free? This is the last day of the Games. Next season will be run by someone else and we will be at our farm."

"We can't even go to Cassia's yet, she won't be open," I say. "And the streets are too dark to go to the amphitheatre. What are we going to do for the next hour or two?"

"Oh, I have ideas for that, don't you worry," says Marcus, drawing me closer.

Even after we have dressed and fed the birds we are early, we arrive at Cassia's as she's pulling up the shutters.

"The fire's barely started," she says, laughing at us. "You two are overly keen to get today over and done with, aren't you? You'll have to wait."

Marcus is all jollity, chasing Emilia about the popina and devouring a large breakfast of bread, cheese, wine, fruits and even a fig tart which he shares with Emilia while cracking jokes with our fellow customers.

"I spoke with a neighbouring farmer when I went to the farm last autumn," he says. "There is a stock market in Puteoli in about a month's time, we will attend to buy the animals we need: chickens, doves, pigs, sheep. I gave our neighbour money to buy two oxen this autumn and keep them for the farm, there'll be no time to wait for the market to start the ploughing season. Strabo is a hard worker, but there will need to be slaves, too. There will be a lot to do."

"I can't wait," I say. "Although you will have to be patient with me, I know nothing of farming."

"You knew nothing of the Games," he reminds me. "And you became the domina of the amphitheatre. There was nothing you didn't work out how to manage. Farming will be nothing to you, people will think you were born and bred to it. You will do well."

His cheerfulness is infectious and I giggle at silly puns Marcus and Quintus trade between them and give Emilia a ride on my shoulders, before we walk hand in hand to the amphitheatre. Marcus greets Strabo with a hearty embrace and gathers together our entire team to announce, to cheers, that after today's show there will be wine and cakes for all at the barracks. Strabo is also full of good cheer, giving instructions with a smile. Only Fabia is downcast.

"I'll miss you," she says.

"It's not goodbye today." I sit on her platform so that I'm the right height and wrap my arm around her. "We'll still be here for a few weeks, lots of time to spend together."

"But then you'll be off and what will I do without you?"

I hug her. "I'll miss you. But you'll come and see us? And we'll come back to Rome to see you all."

She nods morosely and carries on setting up for the day. "They're going to start building two more gladiatorial schools. The Ludus Dacius for gladiators who come from Dacian prisoner of war stock and the Ludus Gallicus for Gallic gladiators."

"You'll be so busy you'll forget we're not here," I say.

Marcus has decided the last day of the Games for this season should be an evening show, the better to showcase Ignis' work.

We have spent the past three days preparing the velarium. We removed the canvas awnings and packed them away for next season; they will not be used for the final day. Then we carefully lowered the whole structure back down, so that the metal circle rested on the arena floor. Ignis spent a whole day with our slaves, mixing vile-smelling combinations of pitch and spreading it along the ropes before allowing it to dry. The sailors re-winched it up into position, the circle and its two hundred and forty ropes like a sun with rays hanging above the amphitheatre.

The amphitheatre is packed to bursting for the final show of the season. I'm fairly sure we're stretching our seventy-thousand-seat capacity beyond its maximum capability.

Domitian arrives with the usual fanfare of trumpets and we stand in the corridor to welcome him, eyes lowered. I don't trust him, don't want to interact with him in any way. Today has to go smoothly and then we will be free.

I smell Domitia pass, hear the swish of silks and the thud of marching feet, wait for the second swishing noise, the silk curtains of the imperial box closing behind the imperial party. My head still lowered, I hold out my hand to Marcus and he squeezes it.

"Almost done," he whispers and hurries off to his seat, from where he will give signals for each stage of the show. I go down the steps into the darkness of the hypogeum and to a grid through which I can see into the arena and catch a glimpse of Marcus.

It's already twilight and so we quickly begin with the venatores. We had planned to repeat the story of Hercules and the Stymphalian birds and although Marcus was reluctant to repeat anything linked to that horrific night at Domitian's villa, the theme was appropriate. We release five hundred ibis and a venatore playing Hercules, along with our hidden archers, shoots them down, their fluttering bodies falling in heaps on the arena floor, only a lucky few managing to escape the amphitheatre and disappearing into the night sky.

While we still have some light the jugglers provide light relief accompanied by the musicians, allowing the audience time to purchase food and drink from the wandering vendors, or to visit the toilets.

The stars come out and now we have the criminal executions for the evening, featuring a cruel task: the sixteen criminals we are to dispatch must try to cross from one side of our arena to the other. It seems a simple thing, but perched on a painted rock we have two harpies, the bird-women of myth, personifications of destroying winds. One is played by gladiatrix and trainer for Labeo's school, Alyssa, who despite her bronze hand is still one of the best shots with a bow and arrows that I have ever seen. Beside her is a young gladiatrix whom she has trained up and who has gained a reputation as a fearsome archer. They wear magnificent feather headdresses and feathered armour, their faces boldly painted to accentuate their features.

Our criminals set out across the arena. There are fake rocks here and there, which they try to cower behind, but one after another falls in agony, pierced by arrows. Some die immediately, two have to be dispatched by Charon's deadly hammer, Strabo in his last appearance of the season.

At the end of the sequence Alyssa is chosen by Domitian to approach the imperial box and receive a wooden sword, symbol of her freedom, which she holds aloft in her bronze hand, tears of joy running down her face.

"That's another one who won't actually retire," says Strabo, watching beside me. "She loves the training yard too much. But she'll be safe from the arena and will live to train the other women."

"Thanks to Fabia," I say.

Domitian stands and begins to hurl wooden balls into the audience, aided by our staff across the whole of the amphitheatre. Each ball names a gift for the person who catches it. Today's gifts are all related to birds, from a dozen eggs to birds both alive and dead, fit for eating or singing. Some are even moulded in gold or silver. The balls are snatched up by their lucky winners and exclaimed or gloated over.

It's fully dark. Torches are lit around the edge of the arena so that we can tell the story of the Cranes and the Dwarfs from start to finish. The chorus take their places and the musicians strike up.

"Amongst the Dwarfs there was once born a girl named Oenoe, who was by nature most beautiful but also too proud."

Labeo has found us a dwarf gladiatrix, who has been elegantly attired with jewellery and extra tresses. She enters with the other dwarf gladiators, parading around the arena.

"And when Oenoe married a man and bore her first child named Mopsus, she did not give thanks to Juno for blessing her as a wife and mother, but accepted as her right the many gifts and honours which her people bestowed on her in celebration.

And Juno was angered, and ordained that Oenoe should be made into a crane, and forever lose her child."

A flock of crane dancers enter, their white wings wafting. They surround the unlucky Oenoe and transform her into one of themselves, with a white tunic and wings, her swaddled baby passed back to the dwarf gladiators.

"Lonely for her child, Oenoe the crane flew again and again to the village with her fellow cranes. But the Dwarfs, not knowing her, and fearing that the birds were attacking them, took up their weapons and fought off the birds, killing and wounding many. And from that day to this, the Cranes come yearly to the dwellings of the Dwarfs and attack them, and the Dwarfs live in fear and hatred of them."

The crane-dancers are replaced with crane-gladiatrices and the battle commences in earnest, some bouts focusing on two gladiators against each other, some in groups. The fighters are well matched and the crowd enjoys the rarity of watching dwarfs fighting women in hand-to-hand combat, something we rarely showcase.

Finally the battles are done, the winners garlanded, the losers mortified. The audience is pleased, they whoop and cheer, stamp their feet and Domitian stands to take their applause, his usually expressionless face lit up with pleasure.

"Now," says Marcus and all the torches are extinguished. The crowd murmurs in confusion, surely the show is complete? How are they to find their way out?

But in the darkness Alyssa appears again, standing in the dark arena with only a burning arrow notched to her bow, which she lifts, the audience falling silent, watching.

Like a shooting star, the arrow arcs through the air and touches the metal circle hanging above. It instantly bursts into flames, then splinters outwards, each flame rapidly traversing the ropes, each rope burning a different colour: red, orange, yellow, green, blue, violet, the pattern repeated forty times around the amphitheatre, a glittering sparkling crown which has the crowd gasping in awe as the flames spread outwards, filling the whole of the visible sky with shimmering, flickering colours.

"Magical," I say to Ignis, who is watching by my side. "You have created something wonderful."

He nods, satisfied.

The torches are re-lit, not so many that the crowd cannot still admire the sparkling crown of fire above them, but enough so that they can see to leave. Domitian first, as usual, then the crowds start to leave.

"You are an extraordinary maker of flames," I tell Ignis.

He smiles and walks away, disappearing into our hypogeum's maze-like rooms.

I hurry to our planning area, near the stairs that Marcus will use to join me but I find him already there; he must have all but run back.

"We're done," he says. His shoulders are slumped, but his face is lit up with happiness. "We're done, Althea. Come here." He enfolds me in his arms and I rest my cheek against his chest. We have finished our final task, we are free of this place and its demands on us.

"We're done," I repeat into the folds of his toga. "Thank the gods. We can leave."

"Thank the gods," echoes Marcus. "May Janus watch over us as we start our new life."

There's the tramping of feet and we both turn, Marcus' arm still around my shoulders, to find ourselves face to face with the

Aedile. As usual he is surrounded by an entourage, who cram into the limited space, some of them still on the lowest steps.

"Magnificent show," says the Aedile. "Truly spectacular."

"Thank you," says Marcus. "It has been an honour to serve Rome," he adds. "I am grateful for the opportunity I was given and the trust placed in me to serve two emperors in this way. Though I am glad my time has ended now." He smiles. "The honour can go to another man and I will be glad to retire to my farm and live a quiet life."

"Of course," says the Aedile. "And you have more than earned that life. Absolutely." He gestures to his entourage of bodyguards, scribes and hangers-on and they head off through the corridor leading towards the stairs that will take them all out of the amphitheatre, though he remains behind.

Marcus is distracted by Strabo, who is carrying a heavy chest. "It can go in one of the pens, Paternus will send a man to collect it tomorrow," he calls out. "Crane costume helmets," he adds to me by way of explanation. "No doubt they can use them for some other show in the future. Or have them re-fashioned into something else. Expensive pieces."

The Aedile is still hovering.

"Yes?" asks Marcus, over his shoulder. He's less deferential in his manner, he feels free of the service he has performed these past years. The Aedile has no further hold on him.

"The Emperor," begins the Aedile, "has, umm, requested, that you undertake one last task for him."

"No," says Marcus immediately, turning to face the Aedile. "No. I have done everything that was asked of me and more. The season is over and I am free. I will be leaving Rome very soon."

"Ah, yes, ummm…" says the Aedile. He rearranges a fold of his toga, clutching at it for comfort. "He, that is to say…"

"Domitian," says Marcus. "That's his name."

The Aedile swallows, glances over his shoulder. "Yes, of course," he agrees, but still he lowers his voice. "Domitian wishes you to create a private banquet for him. In ten days' time."

Marcus shakes his head. "I already did a private event," he insists. "It was supposed to be a one off. And look how that went," he can't help adding.

"It is a most particular event, and… *he*… would most particularly like you to arrange it."

"Why?"

"He wishes it to be… theatrical. In its… ah… *execution*."

Marcus stiffens. "Execution?"

"An expression."

Marcus stares at him in silence.

The Aedile's shoulders slump. He speaks in a hurried whisper, his words spilling out rather than with his usual endless hesitation. "There is to be a spectacular private banquet in ten days' time. No expense spared. Theatrical. Extraordinary. Invitations will be sent to very high-ranking senators only. He has demanded in no uncertain terms that you must arrange this event for him. That you are not to leave Rome without completing this final task." He finishes, panting, sweat beading on his forehead.

Marcus' voice is so low I can barely hear him. "Are these men going to return home to their families, after this banquet?"

The Aedile's face is pale, his voice a tiny whisper. "I don't know."

"And if I refuse to undertake this… task… will *I* return home to my wife?"

The Aedile's body stays rigidly still, but his head moves side to side, a tiny movement, barely invisible.

Marcus straightens, his shoulders back, chin up, voice clear.

"It will be my pleasure to do as the Emperor commands," he says. "I will report to you for my further orders and instructions, Aedile."

The Aedile steps backwards, nodding violently. "I will see you in my office tomorrow, Scaurus," he says, too loudly and then he turns and scurries away. I can hear his shoes on the stairs as he half-trips in his hurry to get out of the darkness.

I look up at Marcus, can only see his profile as he stares after the Aedile, his jaw set hard, his eyes cold.

"Marcus…" I begin, tentatively putting my hand on his arm. I'm not sure what I'm going to say. It's clear he cannot refuse, to do so would bring real danger upon us, but my stomach is heavy with dread at what he's getting himself into. An event that must be theatrical and spectacular, which must be *executed* to perfection? For high-ranking men who may or may not return home safely? How can this end well?

Marcus moves his arm abruptly, dislodging my hand. "I'll do what has to be done," he says. "You, however, will have no part of it."

"But I can –" I begin.

"No," he says and his voice is hard, as though he were talking to a stranger. "You will not be involved in this in any way, Althea. You will continue to plan for our departure from Rome. You will not ask me questions about what I am asked to do, you will not attend any location where I am told to stage this… event. You will pretend you never heard the conversation we have just had. And in ten days' time it will be over and we will ready ourselves to leave for the farm. Do you understand me?"

I nod.

"Good." He turns to face me, his voice softening. "I will not have you caught up in something like this."

"Do you think…?" I begin but he shakes his head.

"You know nothing about this event," he says. "Promise me, Althea."

I hesitate but put my hand in his. "Karbo will be wanting his supper," I say. "We need to get back to the insula."

His hand grips mine more tightly than usual all the way back to the insula, his pace too fast, so that I have to ask him twice to walk more slowly, which he does at once, before speeding up again.

Cassia has put on a good meal for us in the courtyard to mark the last night of the season. Adah is helping her set up a table of food for all to share.

"We'll have a real banquet before you leave," she says. "But tonight should be celebrated."

"May the gods bless you, Cassia," says Marcus, giving her a quick hug. "I could eat a whole sheep."

"Good thing I made plenty," she says. "Here, make yourself useful and carry this platter out to the table."

Most of the insula comes by over the next two hours to sit and eat and drink with us. We toast to Julia's memory and the end of our time at the Games. Cassia keeps the food coming, simple familiar comforts like warm flatbreads to dip in olive oil and garum, salted roast chickpeas, cheese, her tasty barley porridge scented with dill and cumin, platters of new season grapes, pears and apples. Marcus laughs and jokes with our friends, but occasionally his face turns thoughtful, as though his mind is elsewhere, before visibly making an effort to smile at our neighbours or raise his cup for a toast that has been proposed.

When the evening has grown late, we climb the stairs to our hut and in the dark Marcus holds me to him too tightly, as though I might be taken from him.

GOD AND MASTER

WHEN I WAKE LATE THE next morning the sun is fully risen. Marcus is gone and so is his toga, so he must have gone to the Aedile to be briefed on whatever Domitian has ordered for his private dinner in ten days' time. I hope when he returns that I will be able to coax him into telling me what it is all about. Perhaps it really will turn out to be nothing of importance, just more of Domitian's strange stubbornness.

I feed the birds, then make my way to Cassia's for breakfast. It always feels odd when a season has ended and there's no need to rise early, to hurry to the amphitheatre. I will never have to do that again. I am done at last. My shoulders relax, my chin lifts and I arrive at Cassia's with a smile on my face.

"Tay-ah," says Emilia when she sees me, waddling over to me.

"Hello, little one," I say, picking her up. "I see you've eaten your breakfast." I wipe her face, which is smeared with porridge.

"I've got some freshly baked apple rolls," says Cassia, hurrying past with a wine jug.

Emilia wriggles to get down again. "Tay-ah," she repeats, tugging me over to her corner, where she has a half-eaten bowl of barley porridge topped with date syrup.

"Oh, you haven't actually finished," I say. "Big mouth?" I offer her a spoon of the porridge.

She shakes her head vehemently, picking up her small doll, lovingly carved by Quintus, and holding it out to be fed.

"Your porridge is too good for a doll," I say. "I may have to eat it myself." I lift the spoon to my nose and smell it. "Mmm, delicious," I say, but my stomach turns. I drop the spoon and run out into Sand Street, where I vomit copiously across the cobblestones.

"Are you ill?" asks Cassia, her face worried, leaning over the counter towards me.

I shake my head. "I smelt the porridge and it made my stomach turn. It smells horrible, sour."

Cassia starts laughing.

"What?" I ask indignantly. "If there's something wrong with it, Emilia shouldn't be eating it."

"Nothing wrong with the porridge," says Cassia, pouring wine for a customer and winking at another. "What would *you* say was wrong with Althea, Maria?" she adds, spotting her heading to the bakery with a basket over her arm. "Took one smell of my good barley porridge with date syrup and threw up into the street."

"Dea Bona bless you," says Maria. "I knew by your nose."

"Knew what?" I ask.

"A baby on the way," says Maria. "What a blessing. Juno has smiled on your marriage."

I stare after her and turn back to Cassia. "It can't be!"

"Why ever not?"

I stand in the street, one hand pressed to my stomach. "Truly?"

Cassia beams. "I am so happy for you," she says. "Now get

out of the street before someone runs you over," she adds. "Come here and flip pancakes for me while I throw a bucket of water to clean up that," she adds, gesturing towards the fetid puddle at my feet.

"I'm sorry," I say.

"You donkey," she says, hugging me as she passes over pancake duties.

"How did Maria know?"

Cassia giggles. "Half the women round here find an excuse to come into our courtyard when they're not sure, noses in the air so Maria can tell them if there's a baby on the way. Doesn't look any different to me," she adds, as I squint at my nose trying to see what's changed. She takes a bucket and disappears into the courtyard to get water from our fountain, returns to sluice the street clean before taking back the pancake-making. "Apple roll?"

I take a small tentative nibble but the soft warm apple smell has me retching.

"Stale bread and water for you, I'm afraid," says Cassia. "Or pickles, if you're that way inclined."

I wrinkle my nose.

"Stale bread it is."

She passes me a piece of yesterday's bread, which I manage to chew and swallow without incident. "Is that all I'm going to be able to eat for months?"

Cassia laughs. "Just a month or so."

"Much use I'll be on the farm if I'm vomiting everywhere."

"It's a hard life being a woman," says Cassia. "Juno and Bona Dea be kindly to you."

When Marcus returns I want to rush to him and share our

happy news, but he is grim faced from his meeting and it makes me fearful. He shakes his head at my tentative questions and goes to take off his toga, before eating the food I have ready in silence, ignoring both my troubled face and the nightingales who are singing for all they are worth. That night when we are alone together, I think that if he unburdens himself to me I can comfort him, he will be more cheerful and I can tell him about being with child, there is something forbidding about him being so serious, I do not want to offer up the secret joy I am holding inside.

"I worry about you," I say. "Is there nothing you can tell me that I could help with? It surely can't be any worse than some of the things we've faced over our years together. Worse than Glabrio?"

Marcus' voice is quiet in the darkness. "He's making people call him God and Master," he says.

"*God* and Master?" I repeat.

"Yes."

We're both quiet for a few moments. It's common for an emperor to be declared a god after his death, but not while he's still alive. It echoes the sort of thing Nero did and a shiver goes down my spine. "Is he dangerous, do you think?"

"Possibly," says Marcus and his admitting it frightens me. Before, he has always brushed such questions away, tried to allay my fears. But to declare yourself a god… I tremble and Marcus' arms tighten about me.

"It will be an affectation, that's all," he says quickly returning to his habit of offering comforting words. "Don't worry about it. There are only a few more days left, that's all. It's nothing we need to worry about."

"But this… event he has asked you to arrange…"

"It is nothing for you to worry about," says Marcus. "It will be over soon."

"But –"

"But nothing," says Marcus. "Sleep."

But neither of us sleeps for more than an hour that night, both lying in the silent darkness, unable to stop our fearful thoughts.

I wake to see Marcus tiptoeing from the room.

"Marcus."

"Shh, go back to sleep," he says, bending to kiss me. "I'll be gone all day. Rest."

"I need to tell you something."

"Can it wait?"

"No." When I tell him he will be happy and whatever Domitian has asked of him will pale into insignificance.

He perches on the edge of the bed. "Tell me."

I am suddenly shy. "I… we…" I take a deep breath. "I am pregnant."

He stares at me. "What?"

"We are going to have a baby," I say.

He crushes me to him, so fiercely that I can hardly breathe, his face buried in my neck. When he pulls back his eyes are full of tears but he is not smiling at all, only looking at me with worry.

"I'm well," I say. "Except for not being able to eat Cassia's good food." I grin, hoping he will laugh, but he only strokes my face, his expression still serious.

"Marcus," I say. "Please tell me this… banquet you are arranging for Domitian. You *are* safe?"

He nods at once. "Of course, of course I am safe," he says too quickly. "All is well. You need have no fears, none at all."

"Marcus –"

He lays a finger on my lips and manages a smile at last. "We will be so happy," he says, his voice shaking. "So happy," he repeats, as though to himself, then stands, dropping a final kiss on my head. "I must go."

I sit on the bed when he has gone. Marcus' reaction was not what I was expecting. I had thought there would be laughter and kisses, embraces and chatter between us, names, visions of our future. Happiness. This strange fierce reaction, his tears, they must be connected to what Domitian has asked of him, the joy of a coming child not enough to overcome the task ahead of him. I don't know what form it will take, but I'm convinced that Marcus is in danger and our future – the future of our child – uncertain.

I try to put on a brave face that day. Fabia comes to check on my wellbeing and pronounces herself satisfied.

"I have some news of my own," she confesses when she is done.

"What is it?"

"I will be married next June."

I gape at her. "Sadiki finally asked you?"

She's blushing, I've never seen Fabia so girlish, her usual scholarly demeanour swept away. "Yes. Father is delighted."

"And…" I don't want to crush her happiness, but it matters to her to still be a physician. "Your work?"

She's all smiles. "Sadiki knows I will always want to be a physician and he does not mind. We will work together until he is no longer an apprentice and then he may become a physician in his own right, perhaps for Paternus, as his own physician is getting older. And I told Maria and she is already wanting to care for our children." She giggles and I embrace her.

"I am so happy," I tell her. "You've made me happy enough to be hungry, even. Come to the bakery with me."

At the bakery I discover I can indeed eat without the nausea of the previous day, so I make the most of the reprieve. We fill ourselves with fruit rolls and little cheese breads, laughing at everything and nothing until Fabia says she promised Sadiki they would go to the baths together.

I return to the courtyard from the bakery and find Celer sitting in the pale autumn sunshine. He seems better than when I first met him. In those early days he would have been drunk by breakfast, one cup too many rolling him from one late evening into a befuddled morning. Now, he drinks less frequently of an evening and has a relatively clear head come the morning.

"Can I tempt you with a blackberry pastry?" I say.

He accepts and I sit with him, eating another one. How can one be so hungry one moment and vomiting the next, I wonder.

"I hear there is a baby on the way," says Celer. "Bona Dea bless you."

I smile and touch my belly. "Thank you. It hardly seems real yet."

"It'll be running around in no time," he says. "If you thought Karbo was a handful you've not had a really little one yet. You'll have your hands full."

"I don't want anything bad to happen to Karbo," I tell Celer, anxiety rising up in me.

"I'll be watching out for him, I give you my word by Neptune," says Celer.

"You can't keep him safe on the track, that is in the hands of the gods," I say. "But don't let him…"

"Drink too much? Gamble? Womanise? Get in with the wrong crowd?"

"All those things," I say firmly.

"I understand better than anyone what excessive drinking can do," says Celer. "And I've seen what happens with the rest as well. I care about the boy too much to let him go down those paths, Althea, I'll watch over him like he was my own. I feel as if he is, sometimes," he adds.

"You're an uncle to him," I say. "And you'll have to be a father to him when Marcus is far away. I know you'll do what you can to keep him safe."

He nods. "I drink less when he's around," he says. "He gives me reason to stay sober."

I pat his shoulder. "Thank you, Celer. I'll sleep easier knowing he has you around. And now I need your help."

"Anything."

"We need to buy a second cart and two mules. We have one cart in the storage rooms and we'll take the two horses from the stables, but we'll have a lot to take with us. Strabo will drive one cart and Marcus the other. We'll keep the horses for riding and use the mules for farm work."

"Leave it with me," says Celer, getting to his feet. "I'll get you a good price for the mules and a sturdy cart."

I watch him go, my mouth set in a determined line. I'm not sure what Marcus is doing, but I will not stand by and watch our future be ruined by Domitian's whims. I will not wait for Marcus to have everything ready for our departure to the farm, I will do it myself and as soon as this final task is over, we will leave. I find myself whispering a prayer to Janus, god of new beginnings, to help me. I find myself caught between the past, where Marcus is struggling to satisfy Domitian, and the future, the baby and the farm offering a happier time ahead of us, if we can only escape Rome and reach Puteoli safely.

By the end of the day Celer has already delivered on his word, a second cart has been brought into the courtyard and put in a corner out of the way. It was pulled by two young mules, good-natured and calm. I feed them apples before Celer takes them to be stabled alongside our two horses for the few weeks we will still be here. Adah comes to stand by me, strokes their noses and makes soft sounds to them, before picking up an amphora of water to carry to her room on the roof.

"That's too heavy for you," I say. "You should have called me or Karbo. When I'm gone, promise me you'll ask him for help. He's a strong boy. He'll look after you."

She follows me up the stairs, her feet slow. "Time was I could carry two, all on my own."

"Those days are gone," I tell her. "Ask for help. Promise me."

I turn to look at her and she gives a half nod.

"Can I ask *you* for help?" I say.

"What is it you need, child?"

"Come with us to the farm," I say. "I'm going to be all alone there, Marcus will be out with the animals and the land. I'll be in a new home with a hundred tasks I'm unfamiliar with and a baby on the way. I would like someone with me."

"I know nothing of chickens and farms," she says.

"You know about bees," I say. "There are old beehives there, I saw them years ago, all broken and falling apart. We will have to set up new ones. You could look after the bees and the doves while I learn to care for pigs and chickens and tend a vegetable garden. I'd enjoy the company."

Adah looks away. "I'm too old for change."

"Nonsense," I say. "You don't have any family left here in Rome. We've known each other all these years. Come with Marcus and me. Marcus will have Strabo to be his right-hand man, but I'll be needing a grandmother for this baby. The four of us have hardly any family left to us but between us we can start a new one."

She shakes her head but her eyes are sad.

"Think about it," I say, leaving the amphora by her door, and she shuffles silently back into her room. I watch the door close. Am I promising her something that will never happen? No. I have to believe we are still going to the farm, no matter what Marcus is working on. I have to keep reaching out to the future, making it possible one step at a time, I cannot stand still and allow all our plans to be taken from us.

When I tell Karbo a baby is on the way he is all smiles, then solicitously asks how I am feeling, which touches me, my once little son now looking after me. We sit together in the pale autumn sunlight and for once I let him talk about his future as a charioteer and keep a smile on my face, do not wince or mutter dire warnings, instead I tell him how brave he is, how gifted with the horses. The decision is made now, and I need him to feel my pride as well as my fears, even if they rush back to me from time to time.

Marcus comes home late but gratefully accepts a bowl of vegetable porridge, a cup of wine and an onion bread. He asks how I am feeling, pats my still flat belly with affection, but does not say anything about his day. I watch him eat, desperate to ask more.

"Are there many people invited to the banquet?" I ask, trying to sound as though I am just passing the time of day.

His shoulders tighten immediately. "We agreed you would not ask questions."

"I was only wondering."

He shakes his head, carries on eating in silence, refuses to meet my gaze until we go upstairs to bed.

"You spoke in your sleep last night," he says in the dark.

"What did I say?"

"'Karbo.'"

"I said his name?"

"And gave a little sob," says Marcus, pulling me close to him. "Are you fretting about our boy?"

"He will be all alone," I say, my voice wavering though I try to control it.

"He absolutely will not be all alone," says Marcus. "I would not allow him to stay if I thought that. He will live here, surrounded by people who are family to him and have been for years. Maria will look after him, Cassia will feed him, he has his own roof hut here and a driving place at the stables. Celer watches over him and his friends seem like good boys."

I let out my breath. Hearing Marcus speak about the future is comforting, even if it is Karbo's racing career. "I know. Just… he is very young. Even if he has done his Liberalia."

"Plenty of people make their way in the world alone at his age," says Marcus. "He will be well cared for. The most dangerous part of his life is the racing and I'm not sure we could have changed that even if we stayed. I could have forbidden him from being a driver, but he would find a way to do it anyway, you know he would."

When I wake the next morning I set to work on Karbo's roof

hut. Even though it was only rebuilt recently, I drag everything out of it and clean it thoroughly, patch-painting the odd dirty bit of wall without disturbing the paintings of the chariot drivers.

"You can't touch them," says Karbo in the doorway. "They're my lucky charms. They're the reason I'm going to be a charioteer."

"Never mind them," I say. "Get those cobwebs off the rafters while I take these blankets to be washed and we'll beat your mattress."

"Are you nestbuilding for me?" he asks.

"Yes," I say. "I want to think of you warm and safe in your bed here."

He grins. "You're a fussy mother hen."

"Yes I am," I agree. "It's my right and my duty as your mother."

He drapes one long arm about me and gives me a gentle head-butt with a small sound attached to it which might be a kiss. "You're a kind mother," he mutters.

I hug him but he pulls away too quickly for my liking. "Got cobwebs to clean," he says. "Can't be hanging around cuddling you all day."

I watch him, marvel at his height as he pokes at the cobwebs with a broom, before getting back to my painting. The room smells fresher already, a young man does not always have the most pleasant smell about him after a day's hard work. "You're to wash every morning and go to the baths regularly," I instruct him and get an eyeroll for my trouble.

I bring out the heavy woollen blankets from storage and have them washed at Quintus' family fullers, re-paint the exterior of the hut adding a fresh red trim to the base of the wall, even though it would have done for another few years. The work has already taken me three days. Marcus, coming home early for once, smiles when he sees my project and does not comment. The next day, he drops a bundle of cloth in my lap.

"What is it?"

"Cloth for new tunics for him. And I've ordered him new winter boots at the cobblers and left money for next year too. Maria is stitching him a cloak with a thicker cloth I bought, the height he is now that cloak you made him last year will be too short by spring, might as well sew him a man's size and be done with it."

The cloth is good wool in two colours, a blue and a green, the colours Marcus himself favours. "Thank you."

"We have done all we can to keep him fed and clothed, housed and looked after. He has good friends and this insula is a family to him, even if we are not here."

I nod, trying not to let tears fall. "This lot will keep me busy," I say. "I better get started."

He strokes my hair, drops a kiss on the top of my head and I smile, reassured. It is only when he has gone that I realise that all his comforting words were about Karbo's future, not ours, and feel anxious again.

I spend three days sewing for all I am worth, with Adah at my side, who weaves two beautiful belts for Karbo to go with his new tunics. Finally, I stand with Karbo in his refurbished hut, clean and freshly painted, his chest filled with warm clothes and good strong boots for the winter. I lay herbs on top of them to keep a pleasant scent about him and he smiles at the sight of them.

"Fausta used to smell of rosemary and mint. She used to brush her hands along Julia's plants and rub them over her toga."

"She did," I say. The little boy he was, curled up weeping,

holding her toga pressed to his face so he could smell her when she had been taken away. It seems a sad recollection, but he is smiling. "She was fierce," he says with admiration. "She made me feel safe, like nothing could get me when she was around."

"I hope you feel the same now," I say.

"I didn't for a while," he admits. "When she died, I thought I was all alone again. But you were there. You and Marcus. And now –" He gestures about himself. "I have a home. I have parents, and even if you are moving away I am a man. I have a job, friends."

"Do you remember anything else from before?"

He shakes his head, but his face is still open. "Nothing worth remembering," he says. "I look to the future."

I can't help welling up. "You're wise for such a young boy," I say. "I'm proud of you."

"Less of the boy," he says lifting his chin and grinning. "But wise, I will admit to."

"I wish you were coming with us," I say. "But I will bring your brother or sister to see you race one day, so you'd better be good at it." *And stay alive*, I add in my head. *To all the gods, keep my boy alive.*

He's already standing taller at the very thought. "Yes," he says. "You can bring them when I am the Purple team's top driver and they can watch me earn a laurel wreath."

"I will do that," I promise. "One of many, I'm sure."

My efforts at keeping busy have used up eight days and the thought of Marcus' mysterious event being in only two days makes me anxious. I find myself searching for more things to do that will help our longed-for future plans come true. I find a seller of seeds and order everything I will need to begin a vegetable garden as well as several sacks of wheat and barley. Marcus and Strabo will need to begin ploughing as soon as we reach the farm in order to plant the crops in good time. I think of the tasks Marcus has mentioned in the past when we have talked about the farm and visit a tool shop to purchase the tools we will soon be in need of, from a plough to shovels, sickles and pruning knives. A farm that has been abandoned for many years will have many trees and vines to prune. No doubt we will need to purchase oxen for the ploughing and slaves to work the farm, but these will be better off being bought locally, city slaves would hardly be accustomed to farm work or have any useful knowledge related to farming. I ask for the heavier items to be delivered to us the next day, carry the smaller pieces back myself. When I come back to the roof I find Adah sitting in the sunshine, having finished tending to the bees. I sit next to her and turn my face to the sun, soaking in its warmth.

"Have you changed your mind, Adah?"

She gives a little smile. "Always persistent."

"Do you remember when we first met? You startled me, appearing out of the darkness, up here on the roof."

She touches my hand. "You asked if I was warm enough. A kind child."

I lean against her. "You always call me that. I'm a grown woman."

"I'm too old for you to be anything but a child to me."

"In that case you should come with me to the farm to care for me. You can't leave a child like me all alone in the world." I make a pitiful face and hear one of her rare chuckles.

"You always were good at persuading people."

I straighten up to look at her. "Is that a yes, Adah?"

She shakes her head. "No. You're right, you're a grown woman, you will find your own way in this new life without help from an old woman like me."

I sigh. "If you change your mind, tell me. Even if our cart is halfway down the street, we would turn back for you. I'll miss you. And your songs. And your honey."

She pats my hand. "I'll pack some for you to take. And candles. You'll need them."

"Won't be the same without you there."

"Marcus will take care of you. He's a good man, a good husband."

"He is the best husband," I say smiling. "Only I'd have liked another woman about the place. I'm leaving behind Cassia and Fabia and Maria. I've already lost Julia. And I have to leave you too. Marcus will have Strabo, but who will be my right hand?"

On the day of Domitian's banquet Marcus does not leave before I wake, as he has the other days. He spends time with me in our hut, gentle and loving, then comes with me to Cassia's for breakfast. Although I have been nauseous on many of the past few days, for once my stomach does not rebel and I wolf three pancakes drenched in date syrup, then gulp fresh grape juice, making up for lost meals.

"Thought you didn't care for sweet things?" I ask Marcus, who has, unusually, ordered the same pancakes as me

"I care for you and what you enjoy," he says, taking another bite. He sips some of the grape juice before grimacing. "That's far too sweet," he decides. "Wine, please, Cassia."

He spends time chatting to Quintus and plays with Emilia, nods when I tell him about the mules and extra cart.

"Most of what we need is ready," I say. "It only needs loading up and the horses and mules bringing for us to leave. When will we go, do you think?"

He turns his face away. "Soon."

I want to keep talking, but Marcus looks up at the sky and frowns. "Time for me to leave."

"Already?" I ask and I can't help holding his arm tighter, wanting him to stay with me.

"There are things to prepare for this evening," he says, and his voice has lost all its happiness.

"Tell me you will be safe tonight, Marcus," I whisper, and my voice shakes.

"You are safe here," he says and touches my belly. "This little one is safe. Karbo is safe. That is what matters."

"That's not what I asked," I say, suddenly cold in the sunshine. "Marcus —"

"I have to go," he says, pulling away from me.

Reluctantly, I let him go, but as soon as I do so, he turns back and hugs me fiercely, crushing me to him. When he lets me go his eyes are serious. "If anything —" he stops and then starts again. "Strabo is a good man, he'll look after you. Trust him."

"Marcus! What do you mean if anything happens — Strabo? — what are you *saying*?"

"Goodbye," he says and he's gone, striding out of the courtyard gate. I stand staring, then run after him but he's already crossed Sand Street and is disappearing into the jumble of tiny streets that will take him towards the Forum and the imperial palace. I want to follow him but a rumbling ox cart is passing in one direction and two smaller mule carts are headed in the opposite direction and by the time they've all moved out of my way I have no chance of catching up with him.

I spend the rest of the afternoon alone, pacing about the rooftop, uncertain of what to do, if there is even anything I can do. His behaviour, his last words to me, have frightened me more than I can admit to anyone.

I try to comfort myself by thinking of the first time our paths crossed when I was still a slave. The dinner party that Marcus and his team arranged for my rich merchant master could easily have turned into an orgy but Marcus' orders meant that any such notions by the guests were quickly directed elsewhere, protecting us household slaves from being used for their pleasure. I think of his calm and commanding presence over the years I have known him, how he turned difficult and frightening situations around and kept us safe. The sun sinks and I try to imagine what kind of a banquet he has been asked to create for Domitian. A triclinium at the imperial palace, mosaic floors and wall paintings, sculptures and stucco reliefs for decoration, lamps everywhere. Couches with bronze and ivory decorations, gold and silver tableware. The courses: the gustatio of small and tempting treats such as honeyed dormice to whet the appetite, a main course flaunting such extravagances as peacocks served with their feathers re-attached for decoration, sow's udder, giant eels. Sweet items to complete the meal, perhaps cream puddings, honey-soaked cakes, elegant pastries and gilded fruits, elaborately displayed on golden platters. To drink, well-watered fine wines, either heated or iced. Then some form of entertainment: dancing girls, musicians, perhaps gladiators putting on a show. These would all be commonplace at an elaborate meal fit for an emperor and his guests.

But what has Domitian asked for that has kept Marcus busy and fearfully silent for ten days, has made him say goodbye to me as though he might not return, committing me to Strabo's care as though I am about to be widowed?

The guests, who are they? The Aedile only said they were men of importance, senators or the like. Are they about to be punished in some horrific way, as Glabrio was? Poisoning by mushrooms, daggers hidden until it is too late? Something in the wine?

What has Marcus been asked to arrange?

THE DARKEST NIGHT

I CAN'T SLEEP.

I lie rigid on my back on my bed, staring into the darkness. How long has it been since Marcus left? How many hours? Once again, I imagine the likely event. Some sort of dinner. In the palace. In the old days, the first thought would be some sort of orgy, but Domitian is known for his strict rules against that sort of thing. So what? Games like the ones we held at Domitian's villa, with the aim of punishing someone, as he did with Glabrio? If so, why the secrecy? He hardly bothered to keep the last event a secret, why would he want to do so now? Unless it is even worse? And what would be worse? Attacking multiple people? Torture? I think back to the Aedile's answer when Marcus asked him outright whether the guests would be returning to their families, his fearful uncertainty.

I try to sleep again, roll onto my side and close my eyes. Marcus knows what he is doing. He has created plenty of spectacles in his time, including this kind of overly lavish dinner. If Domitian wishes to harm someone, like he did at the Alban villa, that is his business. Marcus need have nothing to do with it.

Unless.

Unless what he is about to do is so awful that there must be no witnesses.

My eyes fly open again and I stare into the dark as another thought comes to me, a cold weight in my stomach.

Darkness. I am surrounded by darkness, just as the sorceress said. Is this what she saw? Me in the dark, with danger coming closer? If something were to happen to Marcus…

I roll out of bed, stumbling in the darkness to find my shoes and belt. No time to light a lamp. Instead I feel my way out of the hut, where a full moon lights up the rooftop in cold pale shadows. Leaving the door open I reach back to grab my palla and wrap it about me, cross the roof to Karbo's hut, where I knock softly, then pull the door open and lean in.

"Karbo."

"Wha –"

"Wake up."

The shadows move. "What's going on?"

"I need you to get up."

"Why?"

"Just get dressed."

I reach for the lamp he keeps on his shelf, spend a few moments cursing under my breath as I try to light it, the little sparks from the flint and steel striking together failing to ignite the little scraps of linen strands kept for this purpose, before finally a small flame flickers. As the room brightens Karbo squints, half-falls over his shoes and turns to face me. "What's going on?"

"I am afraid for Marcus."

"Why? What's happened?"

"He had to undertake a final task for Domitian tonight at the imperial palace."

"I thought you did all three tasks."

"We did. This is an additional one. A secret event."

"What is it?"

I shake my head. "A dinner for Domitian and his invited guests. Marcus wouldn't tell me the details. But I have a bad feeling about it and I'm worried for his safety."

"I'll go and find him."

"No," I say. "I can't let you do that. I need you to wake Cassia and everyone else who can help and get us ready to leave Rome."

"You're going to leave now?"

"When I find Marcus and bring him back here, yes."

"But things won't be ready."

"They will if you get them ready for us," I say. "Most things are packed, but the two carts need loading. We'll need the horses and mules fetching from the stables and we need food to take with us. Cassia can take care of food and Celer can get the horses. Can I leave you in charge?"

"I don't think you should go alone," he says, his face worried. In the poor light he is a child again and I place my hand on his shoulder.

"I have to go alone," I say. "I can't draw attention to myself. I just want to find Marcus. I don't care what Domitian wants. If Marcus is in danger I need to get him out of there."

"But what if the event isn't finished, or Domitian —"

I pull him towards the door. "There's no time for guessing what's happening," I say. "It's time to act. I have waited too long on the whims of emperors. I won't lose my happiness because of one. I won't lose my husband and your father if he's in danger because of some scheming plan of Domitian's. We have given enough to this life. It's time to claim our own lives back."

"I'm scared," says Karbo, his voice a whisper.

"Don't be scared," I say. "Just do as I say. Get everything ready for Marcus and me to leave while I find him and bring him back here. I'll find a way to get Strabo to join us." I squeeze his hand, hurry down the stairs and across the courtyard as he makes his way to Cassia's apartment to wake her and Quintus.

The courtyard gate is ajar, as Julia always had it. I slip out and jump back, terrified, at the sight of a dark figure standing in the moonlight.

"The darkness has come," she says and I recognise the sorceress.

"I felt it."

"Leave now," she says.

"I will, but I have to find Marcus. He's undertaking a task for Domitian."

"Do you want me to come with you?"

"No."

"What can I do?"

"Pray. Or cast a spell. Or whatever you can do. Keep Marcus safe. Keep this insula safe so that no-one can find us till we leave."

"Run," she says, and walks back down Virgin's Street, into the darkness of the night.

I run. Through the dark streets, heart pounding from fear, legs shaking under me as shadows move or sounds come from behind me or to one side. Rome's streets are dangerous at night, I am risking my own safety and that of my baby. But I have to find Marcus.

The tangle of small streets leading to the Forum, so well-known to me, seem strange and different at night. I'm grateful there is a full moon, there would be no light at all to guide me otherwise. At last I reach the Forum.

But these vast open spaces are even more menacing. The giant temples and public buildings loom over me and yet contain their own shadows, perfect places for thieves or other evildoers to hide and watch a woman, all alone, making her way towards the imperial palace. I am panting, ragged breaths that sound too loud even to me, that I fear will draw attention to me from unseen eyes.

The burning torches and Praetorian Guard in full uniform outside the palace are a welcome sight as I draw closer. At least there is more light and if I were to scream now someone would come to my aid. Outside the front are more than a dozen dark litters, waiting for their wealthy owners to emerge and be carried home in style. Beside each one, a black-hooded figure with a blazing torch, presumably their servants, although they are standing oddly still, not milling about taking the opportunity to talk to one another and pass the time.

"Althea?"

I jump, but it's Strabo. I could cry with relief. I lean against him and he tentatively puts one awkward arm around me. "Is – is everything alright?"

"I need to get Marcus away from here," I say, still gasping from my run. "I'm afraid for him, Strabo."

He doesn't argue with me. "Me too. Have you seen?"

"Seen what?"

He doesn't answer, only takes me by the hand and leads me to one side of the palace's frontage, where a small gap leads to a narrow alleyway, probably a service entrance which slaves and servants would use, away from the grand palace frontage.

"Look," he says, under his breath.

From this angle, the hooded figures are even more unsettling, their skin seems to be black, but not like Karbo's deep brown, rather an odd glistening black. I squint, tilt my head.

"Painted," says Strabo.

"What?"

"Their skin's been painted."

Everything was black.

"Who are they?"

"The guests arrived and once they'd gone in, Marcus came out and dismissed their own servants and litters. Then these arrived."

Everything was black. You were dressed in black, all around you was black. Everything. The words of the sorceress. I glance at my palla, a rich blue in the flickering light, a darker colour in the night, my pale green tunic under it. *They're not black*, I think, as though this makes any difference to the fear gripping me. But these hooded men, their skin painted black... the odd sheen to their faces, their eyes showing white against the unnatural darkness, some of them now turning to look at us.

"Where is Marcus?" I ask under my breath.

Strabo points down the alleyway. "There's a door there," he says. "I saw him go in there. He told me to stay here, not to move until he emerged."

A safety measure. Marcus has seen fit to have burly Strabo waiting for him to accompany him back to the insula through Rome's treacherous streets. This only serves to unsettle me further. Marcus is not given to unnecessary fuss over his own personal safety.

"I need to find him," I tell Strabo.

He shakes his head. "He said not to go in there."

"I don't care what he said. When did the guests arrive?"

"Not long ago."

"It's very late to be starting a dinner. Strabo, I'm going in. Stay here as Marcus told you to."

He grabs my hand, his face anxious, but I pull away and he lets me go. I stop at the start of the alleyway, staring again at the strange glistening faces turned my way, before walking down the dark alley. It's a tight space, if I were to fully reach out my arms I could touch both walls. Below are neat cobbles, but there are no torches here to light my way. Halfway along, I find a door on my left, a plain wooden thing, nothing like the grand doors at the front of the palace.

I put my hand out, feeling for a handle, but the door begins to move. I take a deep breath and push.

The room I step into is a kind of backstage to an event, familiar from my years under the arena. There are burning lamps for light, additional ones unlit in case anyone should require them. Black cloaks hanging up in a corner, little pots on a shelf with paintbrushes beside them. Scrolls, half unrolled on a table. A pile of plates, as though a meal is about to be served. A knife. A discarded flute and pipes. A giant hammer such as the one Charon carries.

I move further into the room. Opposite the door by which I came in is another door, which must lead further into the palace, to wherever Marcus is. I put my hand on the door, hesitate, but the door moves under my hand, swings open and I gasp, staring up into the black mask of Charon worn under a hood, the figure looming over me.

I scream and the black-clad figure swoops on me, puts a hand over my mouth, holds me so tightly I can't move.

"Be quiet," and even in my terror I recognise Marcus' voice, slump against him in relief and he lets me go. He reaches up and lifts away the black mask, revealing his face underneath. His skin is painted black around his eyes and mouth.

"What are you doing here?" His voice is very low, his skin, where it is not painted black, is pale. I've never seen Marcus this scared and it terrifies me.

I take a step backwards. "I wanted to make sure you were safe."

"I told you to have no part in this! You need to leave."

"But —"

"But nothing. Leave. Leave *now*, Althea." His voice is cold. He is angry, as men often are when they are scared.

"Will you be safe?" I ask, stubborn.

"I don't know," he admits.

He is not even certain enough of his safety to blithely lie to me, pretend that yes of course, all is well, run along, he will be home soon. "I'm not leaving."

"You have to. I can't guarantee your safety."

"That's why I'm staying. Because you can't guarantee yours."

"Please don't make me drag you out of here by force, Althea," he says.

"I'm not making you do anything," I say. "But I'm not leaving."

We stand staring at each other. My heart is beating fast, I think of my baby within me, its mother leading it into danger. But what would my life be without Marcus?

"Tell me what's going on," I say.

"There isn't time."

"I need to know. It's a dinner?"

"Yes."

"Who's attending?"

"Important men. Those who have spoken behind his back.

Those who are known to dislike him. Enemies. They've been kept waiting for more than two hours. They have no idea what's going on."

"How many?"

"Seventeen. Plus him, of course. Two tables of nine."

"Is he – is he planning to poison them?"

Marcus swallows, there is fear in his eyes. "I don't know."

"What did he ask you to plan?"

"I'm running out of time, Althea. They're about to arrive."

I clutch at Marcus' arm. "Don't go in there. Whatever's been arranged. Don't go."

"I have to."

"Come with me. We can leave."

He shakes his head. "The doors have all been closed. There's only one way out now."

"But we could use the side door –"

He's fumbling with his mask, fastening it back onto his face with thin leather straps, pulling up his cloak again to cover his hair. "Stay in this room. I may be able to slip away. But not now. If I leave before it is over Domitian will notice."

"I want to be with you. I'm not letting you out of my sight."

"You have to."

I shake my head, still gripping his arm, looking at his eyes through the black mask.

He breathes out in a rush. "You're the most stubborn woman I've ever met. You can't go in there without a costume or you'll be found out." He pulls away, picks up a pile of black cloth and throws it at me.

"Put it on. And come here." He picks up one of the little pots and a brush as I pull on the cloak. "Head up."

He dips the brush into the pot, holds my chin and paints something wet and cold across my face.

"Open your mouth and close your eyes."

The cold wet paint is daubed onto my eyelids, my lips, even my ears, down my neck. When he's done he pulls the cloak tighter about me, uses brooches to pin it so that my clothing underneath is hidden. I try to imagine what I must look like, think of the glistening black faces in torchlight of the hooded figures by the entrance but there's no time, Marcus is kneeling at my feet. He removes my shoes and paints my feet black too.

"What have you arranged in there?" I ask, but he doesn't reply.

"You're done," he says at last. "Follow me. Don't speak. If I give you something to carry, carry it. Otherwise, stand still and be quiet."

"Marcus –"

"There's one moment when we could leave. When Domitian orders a final drink, a nightcap. We can't leave before then or he'll notice. Once that drink has been ordered, slaves will bring the drinks and the evening is over. We can leave at that moment, but we cannot leave before, we cannot draw attention to our absence. You must trust me."

"I trust you," I say, but my voice shakes.

"Follow," he says. "And remember, don't speak."

He's already striding across the room and I follow him. Before he opens the double doors he picks up the large hammer, turns his head and blows out the two lamps, plunging the room into darkness. He pulls at the door and we emerge into the triclinium.

The whole room is black. I almost stop walking, but self-preservation keeps my feet moving, following Marcus' billowing cloak as he enters the room. The ceiling is black.

The walls.

The floor.

Everything is black.

Flickering lamps around the room give light, but even the lamps are disconcerting, they are funerary lamps, like the one the sorceress saw in her vision, like those hung up in roadside tombs, lit by the descendants of the departed.

We are not alone. All around the room, standing against the black walls, are young boys of perhaps Karbo's age. Stripped entirely naked, they have been painted all over with thick black paint. Even their hair has been covered in it and slicked back. They stand in silence, like statues, only their eyes watch Marcus and me as we enter the room.

There are two black tables in the middle of the room, each furnished with three black couches, so that two groups of nine men can eat in comfort.

If it can be called comfort. The couches are plain wood, painted black, bereft of furnishings: no cushions, no drapes. They look like funeral biers. Any Roman would feel deeply uncomfortable at the idea of lying on one.

My stomach lurches. This is the blackness the sorceress saw. Me dressed in black, the black all around me. This was her vision and it is coming true. I had thought the blackness referred to the storm, thought the danger had passed, but I was wrong and now there is no escape. My hand shapes into the gesture against evil spirits. Domitian's guests are doomed. How can he have anything but death in mind for them?

Marcus gestures to me, directing me to a space of wall not taken up by the boys. I stand against it, wrapped in my black cloak, afraid. I have begged to be here, but I will surely be noticed, since I do not look like the others. And if I am not found out, I will be standing here, watching while a dinner takes place, during which, no doubt, the guests will be poisoned or have their throats cut. Why did I insist on coming in here? Why did I not do as Marcus told me and stay out of this altogether? I hesitate and Marcus' eyes are on me at once, a quick shake of the head. It is too late anyway. I can hear footsteps in the corridor and the doors are flung open as the sorceress' warning echoes in my head: *should you recognise the place I saw, leave it immediately, no matter the risk.*

"Welcome, honoured guests," Marcus says, his voice low and deep. "Welcome to this most distinguished gathering."

The guests in the doorway have stopped at the sight of the room. They are older men, balding or with grey or white hair. Usually they would wear togas, as befitting their senatorial or knightly status, but this is a banquet, and so they have arrived in their dining clothes, brightly coloured, loosely-belted synthesis: dining robes, which allow for comfort while lounging on couches eating. At a formal dinner, surrounded by elegant furnishings, they add to a bright and engaging scene, suited to a party. Here, standing in a black abyss, they look like a strange joke, like a gaggle of vain women inappropriately parading their finery at a funeral.

"Enter," says Marcus, to the still frozen group. "Take up your places."

If they could turn and run, they would, but there are guards behind them, blocking the door through which they came. These men were invited to a dinner with an emperor they dislike. Nevertheless, they expected to be safe, have not thought to be fearful, have arrived in their finest clothes. Stripped of their own slaves, who might have protected them, they have realised their mistake. Have remembered that the man they have reviled behind his back has the power of life and death over them, every day, and today he has decided to exert that power.

"Enter," says Marcus again and it is a command, they have no choice but to step into the black room and face their imminent death. Their eyes flicker round and meet the eyes of the silent, black-painted boys. My attire draws a few extra glances, but they return their gaze quickly to Marcus, his height and mask dreadful to them. They have all been to the Games, they have all sat and applauded as Charon has made his entrance, summoned by the chorus calling his name. Striding across the sand, his deadly hammer raised and then the sickening sound of a skull being crushed, another gladiator or criminal dispatched to the underworld. Now they wish they had not enjoyed that spectacle so much, they wonder if Domitian will applaud as their skulls are crushed in this black room, whether their families will ever know what happened to them.

"Take your places," says Marcus.

A dining couch should be relaxing to lie on. Guests at grand dinners hosted by my former masters all but threw themselves onto the couches, with a grunt of pleasure and a call of, "You there, bring me wine," to the nearest slave. These guests shuffle to their places, half-kneel, then lie, stiff as corpses, on the funeral biers. It takes a few slow moments. The men on the table where Domitian will take his place leave a vast gap for their host, while they crush together on the couches. Those on the second table are no doubt grateful to be further away from their host – or is that a bad thing? Are those close to the host there to watch the other table die? Their faces are full of barely suppressed panic as they take their places, stiff and awkward at the bare table in front of them. Usually the tables would already be lavishly laid with dishes of olives, dates, tasty snacks to munch on before the main courses arrive. These tables have only black olives in small black dishes, which no-one seems inclined to touch.

Marcus turns to me and holds out his hammer. I step forward, reach out one hand, take it, return to my place by the wall. The hammer is heavy, I lower it to my side, but the weight of it pulls on my arm.

Marcus claps his hands and the guests wince at the loud sound. Something is about to happen.

The door opens again. The guests are unsure of what to do. They are already lying down but in the doorway stands Domitian, their emperor, whom they should greet with some kind of obeisance, a dignified bow or even embrace, if they know him well. Some half-kneel in an attempt to get up but think better of it. All of them try to bow their heads which results in dipping their heads over the edge of the couches, baring their necks as though waiting for the slice of a sword. They jerk their heads back up, crane to watch Domitian take his place.

He is dressed in a finely woven synthesis robe, as is correct for a dinner, but in an unheard-of black, with a black woven belt, worn loose as though in anticipation of a good meal. His eyes are bright and all can see he is excited by what is to come. He glances approvingly round the room, nodding at Marcus' dark-clad Charon as at a good friend, giving his quick odd smile, teeth bared.

"Time for dinner, I think," he says, and takes his place. The men closest to him pull back so far that they are in danger of falling off the couch.

Marcus gives a tiny nod and the boys around the room come to life. They move away from the walls, whirling to the centre of the room, where they begin a dance without music, an eerie slow spinning about, arms undulating, as though shades of the dead have drifted here from the underworld and are celebrating something we know nothing of, perhaps an imminent increase in their number. The men watch, their faces full of fear. Only Domitian seems calm, entertained.

The dance is over but instead of returning to their places by the walls, the boys pass by the doorway, where an unseen person gives each of them a funerary lamp. The boys reverently place one lamp by each guest, before circling the room again and this time returning with black painted slabs shaped like miniature gravestones engraved with each diner's name. The slabs are placed on the table in front of the diners, as though they were dinner plates. The men recoil from the slabs, though Domitian strokes his engraved name as though admiring the craftsmanship. The boys take up places, one behind each diner. The guests look over their shoulders, searching the boys' hands to see if they are holding a weapon.

"I'm hungry," announces Domitian. "Serve the gustatio."

The doors swing open. The guests, rather than lounging peacefully, indolently waiting to be fed, twist to see what is coming, are not soothed by the entrance of yet more black-painted naked slaves carrying jugs of wine and black cups, one of which is set by each man, the wine mixed, water and ice added. Most diners at such a meal would direct the slave as to their liking: a little more ice, a little more wine. These cowed men remain silent as each slave prepares their drink, except Domitian, of course.

"Not so much ice," he instructs the slave. "Start again. It's a warm night for the time of year but it doesn't agree with my digestion to have too much ice. Don't you agree?" he adds, speaking to the man on his left, a ruddy-faced senator who has turned very pale.

"Absolutely, Imper – our Master and God," stutters the man.

Domitian nods, serious. "I prefer the winter, when we warm the wine," he says, as though speaking of something of great importance. "Poor digestion is not a thing to be taken lightly. I have suffered with it often and my physicians tell me we must be mindful of small matters of health if we do not wish to die before our time."

There are a few awkward nods.

The slaves retreat and then return, laying out spoons and forks carved from black onyx. They hoist up large black platters heaped up with something I cannot see until they lower them to serve the guests.

"The entrails of birds," announces Domitian. "From the Auguraculum. I had them brought here this very day."

The guests are served with heaps of carbonised remains of entrails that have been burnt, such as those offered to the dead at a funeral.

"Eat, eat," says Domitian, using his spoon to scoop up the blackened mess and chewing it with every appearance of enjoyment.

The guests pick up their spoons, poke at the stinking charred piles, tentatively scoop up minute amounts, put it in their mouth, try not to gag, struggle to swallow. To eat the food reserved for the gods or for the dead is a blasphemy and a danger. A blasphemy if it were stolen from the mouths of the gods. A danger from the mouths of the dead, who may feel you are one of them, summon you to the underworld to continue dining with them. These guests might scoff in daylight at the idea of the gods punishing them for some misdemeanour, but not now.

Not in the dark night they find themselves in, in this black room they cannot escape, with an emperor run mad.

"You must eat it all," says Domitian. "Else how can I serve the next course?"

They choke it down, the foul-tasting combination of faeces and soot, drink more wine than they should to manage to swallow, even though every sip they take might be poisoned. Somehow, the food is eaten.

"You may bring the next course," says Domitian graciously to the slaves.

The doors are opened, more black platters brought out, this time laden with towering piles of seafood. At the base, shining heaps of black-shelled mussels, atop of which vast black eels are coiled together, mouths propped open to show their razor-sharp teeth. Served alongside is a black bread. I am not sure how the cooks have achieved this, perhaps using squid ink. The diners' faces grow ever more distressed as they are served. Not so Domitian, who has begun to chat with great animation about gladiatorial combat and its origins.

"Of course today it is only for spectacle," he says. "The Flavian Amphitheatre has been my family's great legacy to Rome. The entertainment is magnificently orchestrated, wouldn't you say?"

The diners hurry to assent, mumbling about how wonderful the shows are, such generosity from the imperial purse, the vision of the Flavian dynasty in providing a wonder of the world, nothing like it anywhere in the empire.

"But they did not *begin* as spectacle," says Domitian. "The gladiatorial Games have a distinguished tradition of being performed as part of funeral rituals."

The diners fall silent. Domitian's continued references to

death are adding to the horror of the room. They try to continue eating, even though every mouthful of the black food must be an effort.

"What we now call *munera*, the Games," Domitian says. "From *munus*. A gift. A gift for the dead. A tribute to those fallen. Livy talks about their origin in his writing and of course they are well documented during the Punic Wars. Some people suppose they come from burial rites of the Etruscans, but no-one is quite sure, only that they have been linked with funerals from the very beginning. Deaths to honour death." He gives his bared-teeth smile and takes a large portion of eel onto his fork.

"Delicious," he pronounces, when he's finished chewing in the silent room. "Yes," he continues, "the Games have always been a tribute to the shades of those gone before us. A way to honour and remember them. I find the Games most exhilarating, the ceremony and rituals, the rules of combat. I am very particular that referees for the Games should be well-trained and uncorruptible. Rules must be adhered to. Otherwise you have nothing but chaos. People need to understand the rules and what happens if you break them." He gives a bark of laughter which makes several men jump. "Death, of course, if you're a gladiator!" He adjusts his position on the hard wooden bier. "Excellent food," he says. "More eel here."

A slave hurries to fill his plate. Domitian nods benevolently and proceeds to eat more of the eel, occasionally switching to the mussels, dropping the empty shells onto a plate next to him, the clatter of each shell keeping everyone's nerves at breaking point. At last he lifts a finger. "I will need to clean my hands after those excellent mussels."

Black finger bowls and napkins are distributed. Watching, I realise that this dinner is also a conspicuous show of wealth. True deep black is a hard colour to achieve through dyes, Domitian's event is not just frightening in its chosen theme, it is also a demonstration of the riches he can call on to implement whatever undertaking he wishes, the vast power at his fingertips.

"I have made a study of the Games over the years, they are a special interest of mine," says Domitian. "The number of gladiators who actually die during the Games these days is much lower than people think. Of course the promoters like to boast that there will be 'fights to the death' and suchlike, but really there are not that many. Most of the deaths in the arena, as you all know, are criminals, those who have committed misdeeds such as murder or treason."

Two of the senators put down their forks. Everyone seems to be having trouble chewing and swallowing.

"Their deaths provide a warning to others, as well as spectacle," continues Domitian. "I can see their purpose. And I do enjoy the spectacle. Some of them are very elaborate. Very well planned. Complex plots and staging, magnificent costumes and props. Wonderfully engaging to observe."

One of the knights has given up. He drains the dregs of his cup and waves for more wine, so drunk he is barely able to focus.

"Our evening here was arranged by none other than the organiser of the Games at the Flavian Amphitheatre," says Domitian. "I thought he would put on a memorable evening. And of course he already works for me, so there was very little added expense for his time and effort. I like to be mindful of the imperial purse." He beams at the guests and one or two try to smile back, lips stretched across teeth in unnatural grimaces.

"A treat, something suitable for the autumnal season," says Domitian.

The slaves bring out tiny dishes, one for each guest, each

with whole, perfect mushrooms, cooked but intact, so that their shapes can clearly be seen. There are yellow ones which grow in a cluster with long stalks which are safe to eat, but also some pure white ones, which could either be deadly, as there are two types of fungi which look identical.

"Delicious," says Domitian. "A favourite at imperial tables, I believe. Eat, eat," he adds encouragingly, holding a white mushroom by the stem and popping it into his mouth in one go.

Claudius. It can be the only thought in the room at this moment. Emperor Claudius died from eating poisonous mushrooms barely thirty years ago.

"*Eat*," says Domitian.

There is no choice. No possible way out of this. The men pick up the yellow mushrooms first, except for the drunk knight who has chosen to hurry his fate along and has already finished all the white mushrooms on his plate, dropping the yellow ones on the floor in his haste. He is lying back and staring at the ceiling, waiting for the cramps in his belly to start.

Slowly, slowly the mushrooms are chewed and swallowed under Domitian's beaming smile, each man wondering who has been given the deadly fungi. Will it be them? Another man? All of them?

"Delightful," says Domitian when everyone has finished. "Dessert," he adds, waving one hand. The slaves clear the tables, taking away the tiny empty mushroom dishes, the sharp-toothed mouths and skeletal bodies of the eels. "I do enjoy something sweet to finish a meal, even though I try to stay trim, for my health. My digestion is not always good. My poor departed brother Titus, now he was *too* fond of dessert." He laughs and the sound echoes horribly around the black room. "Too fond of the good life and it did not do him any good, in the end."

The guests cannot laugh along with him. They can only think of Titus' plump cheeks, his portly belly and the rumours – were they only rumours? – that his sudden death had something to do with his brother. All that talk of a fever and dying, just like that, with no warning? At the time the rumours faded as quickly as they rose but now, trapped in this room with Domitian and no way out but at his command, they arise again in the minds of all who are here tonight. The room stays quiet, no-one can manage even a small laugh.

"I like the rituals gladiators live by," continues Domitian. "When they are condemned to die, they are given whatever good food they ask for and often, so I hear, even a woman." He thinks about this for a moment. "I am afraid there are no women here tonight for such services." He tuts. "I do not condone such dissolute behaviour, so you will have to do without those delights of life. But food, that I *can* provide and here it is, dessert!"

Of course dessert is black, of course it is. The diners are resigned to their fate, the food is no longer a surprise. Heaps of black-skinned figs, blackberries and black grapes are served in beautifully arranged, intricate patterns on flat black platters, along with a black custard served in black cups with onyx-carved spoons to eat it with. The figs have been split open to reveal their twisting scarlet insides, a shocking burst of colour in this setting but the colour brings no relief. They look like blood, like entrails, which all of them are expecting to see at any moment.

Perhaps the colour is a signal to an unseen hand that holds a knife? Perhaps it will come now?

Or now?

Or now?

It is the waiting that is taking its toll. Some of the men must wish it were all over, they have given up all hope of getting out of here alive and can only hope their end will not be too painful. Poisoning would be worse than a quick knife, perhaps. Most of the men's faces show nothing except a stoic acceptance of the inevitable. They are certain of death. They await the stabbing pain of poison in their guts or the sharp slice of a blade, can only hope there is nothing worse planned after Domitian's endless talk of the Games. Several are sweating copiously, mopping at their faces as discreetly as they dare. Two or three down cup after cup of wine, perhaps hoping to slide painlessly into oblivion when their time comes. One, the furthest away from Domitian, has tears sliding down his face, which he does not dare to wipe away, for fear of drawing attention to himself. There's the sharp tang of urine in the air and I'm fairly sure one of the senators has wet themselves, his fine clothing soaked in fear. After a few moments I can hear the drip-drip-drip of the urine onto the floor, the elegant evening robe unable to absorb it.

"No women," repeats Domitian. "But some entertainment, that we should certainly have."

A group of musicians, dressed all in black, skins blackened, come into the room. They take up a stance and proceed to play the music that would accompany a funeral procession through the streets.

"Wonderful," says Domitian. "Such talent. And now for something in keeping with our earlier conversation."

Two black-painted gladiators enter the room and begin to circle one another, waiting for the opportunity to strike. They wear black leather and black-painted armour, reminding me of our Minotaur last season, a mythical horror made real. Usually, the guests would be cheering and jeering, throwing coins or calling out suggestions, laying bets with each other. The silence is eerie, the only sound the dripping of urine and the shuffle of the gladiators' feet as they circle round each other, then the sudden lunge of one and the hiss-whisper of the blade. The guests' eyes are fixed on the weapons the gladiators are holding. The moment of death has come. The room contains what the men have been expecting for all of this long terrible evening; two men trained to kill, bearing weapons. They may be putting on a spectacle but it would only take a few moments for them to kill everyone in this room, a quick whirling change of direction and focus, the blades falling on scrambling terrified bodies, necks exposed as the guests try to rise from the awkwardly-placed wooden biers, the emperor watching as his plan comes to fruition, the black room filling with blood splattered everywhere, the silence of the night rent with the screams of the dying.

The gladiators finish in a dramatic flourish, one man standing over the other with his sword at the other man's throat, who holds his hands up in submission. Domitian claps loudly, the guests closest to him jerking back in startled fear, one letting out a yelp of terror.

"Very good, very good," says Domitian. He tosses a laurel wreath towards the victor. "A fight well fought, we will not be shedding any innocent blood today, though. You may rise," he says to the defeated gladiator, who rises and then bows his head, before both men leave the room. "A wonderful display. So engaging, when one is so very close to the action, do you not think?" he adds to his nearest companion, a senator. "When there are deaths in the arena, you can actually smell the blood in the air, hear the dying breath of a man. The Games are an emotional experience."

"Yes, Imperator," manages the man in a half-whisper.

"Time for a nightcap," says Domitian.

It's the words I've been waiting for all evening, praying for. I don't even think, just step forward, nodding my head to Marcus as though this was all pre-arranged. I walk briskly from the room and into the service room. The relief I feel when the door behind me closes and I turn to find Marcus has followed me is so great I almost collapse. I rip off the cloak and grab my shoes.

"We're leaving. Now."

He doesn't argue. He drops his cloak on the floor and his mask on the table. I push against the small door, afraid it will creak, that at any moment we will hear a summons from Domitian in the room behind us. We slip out into the passageway and Marcus gently presses the door closed before we all but run back to the front of the palace. We slow as we reach the open space outside the palace, emerging at an overly-casual pace, as though it is perfectly normal to emerge from a side passage of the imperial palace, faces painted black, in the dead of night.

Marcus looks down the street, away from the waiting black-draped litters and the hooded figures, thankfully turned away from us, towards a growing flicker of light. "Here he is."

I can see Strabo's worried face illuminated by the torch he's carrying.

"Marcus," he says with relief. "I thought – never mind. The gods have kept you safe."

"Let's go," says Marcus, touching Strabo's shoulder. We move into deeper shadows, hidden behind a column where our torch's light will be diminished.

I look back over my shoulder at the litters and the hooded figures standing by them.

"Will they get home safely?"

"I don't know."

"Did you arrange… something?"

"No." He breathes out. "That doesn't mean something hasn't

been arranged though. Someone else might have been in charge of that part."

"As they go home?"

He shrugs. "Each of them in a litter, travelling across Rome in the dead of night with four unknown male slaves carrying them and a torch-bearer? With none of their own household servants or slaves to accompany them? No bodyguards? Anything could have been arranged."

"Shouldn't we tell –" starts Strabo.

"Who would you like to tell? Someone who ranks higher than Domitian? Who would step in to change something he has arranged, against his will?" He takes a tighter grip on my hand.

"We need to leave Rome," I tell them both.

"Now?"

"Now."

"But –"

I lower my voice. "If Domitian has arranged for all these men to die, do you think he will leave a witness? Do you think he wants the man who arranged this event to tell people what happened?"

"I didn't arrange for them to be killed!"

"You arranged for them to be here."

Rome's streets are truly dark at night. Strabo's torch is barely enough to see by and I stumble more than once on uneven paving. I keep a tight grip on Marcus' hand and it does not comfort me to see that both men have one hand on their belts, where knives are concealed in a fold of their tunics. Their fear echoes in me and more than once I glance over my shoulder for shadows turning into silhouettes.

"What did you plan for the end?" I ask at last, my voice low. I'm not sure I want to hear the answer.

"After the nightcap they're supposed to be taken home by the servants waiting outside."

This in itself may not sound like a frightening prospect after the evening they've just been through, but to a man of distinction, travelling Rome's dark streets at night with servants who are not his own, people who have no loyalty to him, is tantamount to expecting to be killed at any moment by enemies, thieves or any other horrors the night may hold. Their relief in being allowed to leave and their horror when they see they must leave in litters carried by Domitian's own people, not their own.

"And?"

Marcus shakes his head. "When they get home they will receive a visitor 'from the Augustus.' Gifts from Domitian."

My skin goes cold. "A visitor?" A summons, a knock at the door of their home just when they thought they were safe, the calling out to know who is there and to be told that the Augustus, the Emperor, has sent them a gift. They cannot refuse to open the door, they cannot turn away someone under Domitian's protection. Perhaps they will ask if the visitor can return in the morning, in the comforting light of day, and be told no, it must be now and they will open the door and...

"And?"

"It will be the boys who served them. Each one washed and dressed finely, a new slave for their household. Bearing gifts: the silverware they ate from."

"Silver? Everything was black."

"Painted black. The tombstones, the cups, the platters they were served from: all of it was silver painted black. The onyx forks and spoons will stay black, but they will receive those as well."

"And?"

"I don't know," Marcus confesses. "That is what I was told to arrange. Nothing more."

"No harm will come to them?"

"Not that I arranged."

That does not mean anything of course, Marcus was to arrange a spectacle, someone else could have been told to arrange other things.

"You think it was only for show? To frighten them?"

"Perhaps. A joke."

"A *joke*?"

"He's odd. He might have thought it funny to frighten them, a warning without harming them."

"Those men in there are terrified."

"But not dead. So far."

I hardly think a night of terror has done the men no harm, but I can only hope Marcus is right: that the night has indeed been Domitian's strange idea of a joke, a warning without physical harm done to the men who have spoken about him behind his back, whom he may suspect of plotting to undermine or overthrow him. If so, there could be no warning so frightening as this, a night of staring into the eyes of death, of lying on a funeral bier and eating the food of the dead, knowing that at any moment your host need only say the word to end your life.

I am not reassured. Just as Marcus has thought ahead and had Strabo come to protect him on his dangerous journey back to the insula, has Domitian not planned ahead to what Marcus may do? I think again of the Emperor's face, the narrow shape of it, the way his eyes flicker away from direct gaze and yet his utter focus on something of interest to him. His patience with our animals when he wants to approach them and his furious rages when something displeases him. He is not stupid, I'm sure of that. His mind seems full of ideas and visions for Rome that only he can see clearly. It frightens me that Marcus may have misjudged the timing of our escape, that Domitian may have a man or maybe even several in the shadows even now, following us and waiting for their moment, a quick sharp knife to the ribs. Or perhaps ahead of us, not behind us, waiting on a street corner close to Virgin's Street, knowing we must pass that way to get to the safety of the insula. Or has he gone one step further and sent his men to wait inside the insula, perhaps to harm those we have left there? My stomach turns and I walk faster, pulling on Marcus' hand, Strabo lengthening his stride to match our increased pace.

"What is it?" Marcus asks in a low voice.

"Nothing," I say. "Walk faster."

DAWN FLIGHT

The gate of the insula is closed. We stop and stare at each other. What can this mean? Julia always kept it ajar, even at night, so that anyone wandering the streets in need of safety could slip in and sleep safely in a corner of our courtyard. Marcus pushes it open and we jump back at the sight before us.

Lamps and people are everywhere, but everyone is working fast and silently, gathered around the two carts, one harnessed to our two horses, the other to the two mules. There is no chatter, only the odd whisper. When the gate squeaks everyone turns and there is a collective sigh of relief when they see us.

"You're safe," says Karbo, submitting to a tight embrace from Marcus.

"You did a wonderful job."

"Is there still danger?"

I can't lie to him but I don't want him to be afraid. "I hope not. But we think it's best to be gone by dawn."

"I harnessed the horses and mules."

"Thank you," I say. I'm trying to keep my voice steady, trying not to cry because I do not want to upset and frighten him. "You're so good with them."

Quintus approaches us. "How did it go?"

"We didn't stay to find out," says Marcus. "It seemed safer to leave."

"The dinner or Rome?"

"Rome," says Marcus. "Bar the gate," he adds. "I don't want anyone coming after us without warning." The muscles of his jaw are tight, there is still fear in his eyes.

We've never locked the gate before. At first we can't find the bar that would fit into the brackets, we find it in a corner, forgotten except as a children's toy. We push the gate shut, then drop the bar into the brackets, push it down as far as it will go.

I start checking the carts with Marcus. A lot has already been packed. Everything I had already bought for us, but also amphorae of wine and oil, sacks of grain, jars of preserves.

"This is most of your food stores," says Marcus to Cassia.

"You don't have time to shop right now," she says.

He nods and reaches for his money bag.

Cassia shakes her head. "A gift from Julia," she says firmly and Marcus gives her a quick hug, goes to help Strabo lift up the heavier tools waiting to be packed.

"Do you have to leave now?" asks Cassia.

I'm shivering even though the night air is warm enough. "Marcus is scared and he's not often scared. We were going to leave in a week or so anyway."

Cassia wraps her arms around herself as though she's cold too, then gives herself a shake and nods. "Right," she says. "You'll need food."

"We have enough," I say, but she's already heading to the popina's entrance, determined to do things her way.

I climb the stairs to the roof hut. I thought there wasn't a lot to do, I've always kept it tidy and we don't have many possessions. I've done most of our packing, Marcus will only need to carry our bed, wooden chest and blankets. But I have to pack our cloaks and my sandals, wrap the Lararium in a blanket to keep it safe on the journey. I pause when I lift it from the shelf, take out the little doll with the curly black hair that represents Fausta, set her aside.

Karbo has followed me up; he is hovering in the doorway. "Why did you take Fausta out?" he asks.

I pick her up, hold her out to him with both hands, a sacred object. "I want you to have her. She was like a mother to you."

"You're my mother,' he says and the way his voice trembles stings tears into my eyes.

"I am," I say, pulling him to me. "I always will be. But she was fierce, I want her watching over you on the racetrack when I'm on the farm."

He clings to me, face buried in my shoulder. "I'll stay alive," he says at last.

"That's all I ask," I say. "That and that you be happy."

We smile shakily at each other. He darts away to his own roof hut with the little doll, comes back to help me drag the heavy wooden chest to the top of the stairs to await Marcus and Quintus. We carry the bed rolls first, then return for the lamps and Lararium. The whole insula is awake, people everywhere dashing back and forth with items we may need, piling them up in the carts.

Everyone is trying to feed us. The baker's family load baskets of still scalding bread and pastries into the cart as though feeding a whole army. Quintus is wrapping a large pot of stew in a blanket to keep it warm and wedging it into the back of the cart so it will not spill. He goes back to the popina and returns with wine, water, a basket of late figs and grapes, a bowl of nuts and a platter of Cassia's famous saltfish fritters. Maria is putting little pots of her plum conserve and dried spiced figs into every available gap between our belongings, ignoring Marcus' efforts to load weightier items. Celer lifts in another amphora of wine. Karbo is following Marcus everywhere as he packs the cart, like the early days when he joined us and hero-worshipped him. I want to ask him again to come with us but asking now is unfair, he might say yes in the emotion of the moment and I know it is not what he really wants. But I still have to stop myself, have to swallow the words.

"You must eat something," says Cassia.

"I can't," I say. "My stomach's rolling badly enough as it is, I'll throw up."

"We'll keep Karbo safe," she reassures me, seeing me glance at him.

"What if Domitian –?"

"He'll be safe," she repeats. "I promise."

Emilia sets up a wail, clinging to Quintus' leg and holding out her other hand to Cassia and me.

"What will I do without you?" I say.

"You'll have to learn to cook, for starters," she says. I make a face at her and she laughs, although it sounds like a sob.

"Marcus is going to starve."

"Maybe *he'll* have to learn to cook."

"Will you visit us one day?"

She nods, black curls bouncing like the first time I saw her, smile stretched wide. "We will. About time I had a rest from the popina."

We stand silent for a moment, staring at each other, our eyes filling. "Be happy," I say at last.

She nods, the tears spilling down her face. "You too."

We embrace, crushing Emilia between us, who wriggles and

grabs a fistful of my hair and cries when we separate again. I kiss the child's round cheeks and stroke her ruffled hair and she buries her face in Cassia's shoulder, looking at me with reproachful eyes.

"She knows something's up," I say.

"She'll miss you," says Cassia.

I nod. "I'll miss all of you. The insula. Rome. Even the amphitheatre. I can't imagine life on a farm."

"Your hands will get dirty," says Cassia.

"Oh no, really? I hadn't thought of that. I may have to stay here after all."

Fabius is putting a selection of medical supplies in the cart and reminding Marcus about the dangers of ploughs, scythes and stubborn oxen.

Fabia hugs me. "Get in the cart. You're just putting it off."

"I have one thing left to do."

I stand on the rooftop and open the cages of the nightingales and doves. They are sleepy, befuddled. The dawn has not yet fully broken, the dim light makes the doves afraid of too much movement. I reach in and take each one in my hands, lift them out of the cages, place them here and there on the outer wall of the rooftop or on top of the cages. One or two peck at me, thinking me a predator come to grab them in their sleep. They refuse to fly, huddling together, feathers ruffled and uncertain, taking small steps to one side or the other, shuffling to and fro, peering at me. They feel the breeze on their wings, enticing them to fly, but they are still unsure. The nightingales have never known freedom, are unsure of what it might hold or what to do with it.

I watch them, waiting for the moment when they realise they are free, for them to take flight in a glorious moment of release as they search out their new lives, but they do no such thing, only make small uncertain sounds and peer doubtfully over the ledge to the city below.

"I was expecting a more impressive spectacle," I say, half-laughing. My voice sounds too loud in the cold air and the empty space around me. "I'm not sure you're a very good omen for my new life if you won't fly at all."

They stare at me, turning one eye and then the other, as though I am the spectacle.

"I'll leave you to it," I say, disappointed. I had hoped for them to take flight at once, to revel in their freedom, to fully experience the munificence of my actions, but it seems as though they cannot be persuaded. "Goodbye," I call as I hurry back down the stairs. I pause on the second floor, where Julia's apartment used to be, now the home of a new family who have just moved in. The father injured his leg and cannot work, the mother came to Cassia and asked if there was a cheap room they could rent. Julia would have been glad that her rooms were already being used by those in need.

A tug on my sleeve. I turn to find Adah standing by my side. Her wizened face is tilted up to me, her dark brown eyes wary. I wait for her to speak but she hesitates and when I glance further down I see that she is clutching two objects in her left hand; a small bag, bulging as though it has been crammed too full, and her silver candelabra, the one with many arms, her most precious possession.

"Are you – are you coming with us after all, Adah?" I ask.

She gives a shrug. "I will not be a burden to you," she mutters, failing to meet my eyes. "I can work. I can care for the bees. A farm should have bees," she adds as though I have argued against her on this point.

I crush her tiny, hunched body against me in a fierce hug. "I am glad," I say. "So glad, Adah."

She pulls away, shrugs again as though I am making a fuss over nothing. "I will come because you asked it, child," she says. "Only because you asked." But there's a smile on her face, a tentative happiness that fills up my heart.

I grin back at her, a huge, happy grin. "Marcus," I call over the side of the stairs. "Adah is coming with us."

He looks up over his shoulder from where he is packing the cart that Strabo will drive. "I have a warm blanket here for you to wrap yourself in, Adah," he calls back, as though her presence had never been in doubt. "And a sleeping mat for you to rest on. Come here so I can make you comfortable."

She shuffles down the stairs to him and I follow behind. He picks her up as though she were a child and settles her in the cart, the promised blanket wrapped about her as though it were a palla, her meagre possessions lying safely at her side.

"We need to go," he says. Celer and Quintus unbar the gate, look cautiously out, nod. The street is empty, our path is clear.

There is a flurry of hugs and promises, a moment when Marcus, Karbo and I hold tightly together and suddenly I am sitting at Marcus' side at the front of the cart, my palla in disarray about me, the wheels already rumbling out of the courtyard while the crowd follow us to the gateway and stand in a cluster, arms lifted, softly calling blessings. Jupiter for great ventures and Janus for new beginnings, Bona Dea for mothers and children, Juno for wives and hearths, Ceres and Saturn for farming and crops and our own names mixed in amongst them, spoken by those who love us.

I look back, past Strabo's cart following us along the broad length of Sand Street, to the dim flickering lanterns hanging outside Cassia's popina, and the insula above it, the shadowy group of people I can only just make out at the entrance to Virgin's Street, their arms still lifted to wave us farewell. I shape my mouth into an ugly hard grimace as tears fall down my cheeks, the welling up of grief at leaving so many people behind that I love and who love me, fear gripping my stomach at the unknown future ahead.

Marcus sees my tears falling, he takes my cold hand in his warm one and squeezes it, puts one arm about me and pulls me close.

"They will still be there when you need them," he says gently. "And they will all take care of each other, while we build a new life."

I nod and swallow back some of my tears.

"One last look," says Marcus.

I look back. A faint light is rising on the eastern horizon, illuminating the insula. From its rooftop, in the pale dawn sky, a flock of birds take flight across Rome.

I hope you have enjoyed the final book in the Colosseum series. If you have, I would really appreciate it if you would leave a rating or brief review, so that new readers can find *The Flight of Birds*. I read all reviews and am always grateful for your time in writing them and touched by your kind words.

As ever, I am sad when I write the last book in a series and have to say goodbye to the characters I have grown to care about, but I hope you will come with me as I journey on to another place and another time, in search of more stories to share with you.

Have you read the Forbidden City series? Pick up the first in the series FREE on your local Amazon website.

Lonely. Used as a pawn. One last bid for love.

18th century China. Imperial concubine Qing yearns for love and friendship. Neglected by the Emperor, passed over for more ambitious women, Qing lives a lonely existence. But when a new concubine comes to court, friendship blooms, bringing with it a taste of happiness.

For the first time in her life, Qing has a friend and perhaps even a chance at loving and being loved. But when the Empress' throne suddenly becomes available, Qing finds herself being used as a pawn by the highest ranked women of the court. Caught up in their power games, on one devastating night everything she holds dear is put at risk.

As the power players of the Forbidden City make their moves, can Qing find the courage to make one last bid for love? Can an insignificant pawn snatch victory from the jaws of defeat?

The Consorts is the captivating prequel novella to the Forbidden City historical fiction series. If you enjoy slow-burn romance, courtly intrigues and the intricately researched legends of real women, then you'll be swept away by Melissa Addey's enchanting novella.

Enter the exquisite and stifling world of China's Forbidden City. Download *The Consorts* for free today.

AUTHOR'S NOTE ON HISTORY

THIS IS THE FOURTH AND final book in a series that started as a simple question I asked myself: who were the people who made up the backstage team for the Colosseum? There is hardly any mention whatsoever of them and yet Games on such an immense scale could not possibly have been put on without a very large and permanent team in place. The Flight of Birds takes air as its theme, including the fitting of the velarium and the new top tier of seating in the amphitheatre, the Cranes vs Dwarfs battle mythology and the Roman use of birds as omens, which I then used to play with illusions and prophecies, not to mention the final flight of our lead characters from Rome. The other three books in this series focus on the same team through the themes of fire (*From the Ashes*), water (*Beneath the Waves*) and earth *(On Bloodied Ground)*.

One of the ideas I have continued with in this book is that Emperor Domitian might have been on the autistic spectrum. This was first suggested to me by my historical consultant Steven Cockings, who is himself autistic, and is based on the preliminary work of Jen Cresswell, *Domitian and Asperger's Syndrome – a retrospective diagnosis*, which draws attention to Domitian exhibiting certain characteristics linked to autism, including a preference for solitude, some difficulty engaging with people, obsessions (including a huge building programme and the gladiatorial Games/chariot racing), and a love of routine. As my son is autistic, and I found the historical evidence interesting and compelling, I have built in this concept and used examples of behaviour from people I know who are on the spectrum. Domitian seems to have been judged overly harshly by historians in comparison to other emperors and I thought perhaps he lacked some of the social skills required to endear himself to people generally or to explain and promote his actions and choices. I also thought that the more positive aspects of his reign (such as the vast public building programme he undertook and his cleaning up of the administrative system, wiping out excessive taxes, bribery and corruption) might have made people nervous because of Nero's similar building interests. Nero's madness would still have been very much in living memory and I thought that any odd behaviour, coupled to a similar building programme, would have made people around Domitian wary of history repeating itself and therefore quick to judge him. Whereas in *On Bloodied Ground* Domitian stays calm in his behaviour, if a little odd, in this book I allowed him to have a real meltdown moment in response to the idea that there would be key staff changes at the amphitheatre which might derail his building plans and other ideas for events, as change (especially in relation to their areas of special interest) can be very unsettling and upsetting for autistic people.

Domitian had an architect named Rabirius, who undertook most of the emperor's many building works. Very little is known about him, although he is mentioned with praise by the poet Martial. It is likely that he would also have designed Domitian's villa and its surrounding buildings like the amphitheatre.

The velarium was an extraordinary feat of engineering when you see the size of the Colosseum and imagine trying to fit an awning to it. It follows exactly the same principles as the 'Roman blinds' we have today on windows but laid horizontally. There are lots of interesting videos on YouTube with CGI reconstructions if you'd like to see it in action.

I have brought forward the event at Domitian's villa where Domitian had Manius Acilius Glabrio, a consul, thrown to a lion, which he somehow managed to kill before being exiled (and killed while in exile). This happened in 95AD and there is not much clarity about why he was executed. A few high-ranking people were executed around the same time on charges of conspiring against the empire, but we have no further details. I have borrowed the event to have Manius be Funis' father.

The naumachia happened as described: you can see its location at Augustus' Lake on the map at the start of this book. The Roman historian Suetonius says in *The Twelve Caesars*, *"Domitian had a volatile temper and could be quite arbitrary. In AD84 Domitian held a naumachia on the reservoir built by Augustus for his naval games. As the battle raged a sudden storm swept down on Rome. Two of the ships capsized, drowning their crews, while bitterly cold winds and heavy rain lashed the audience. Finally the storm passed, but the audience were drenched to the skin. It was said that for some weeks afterward all Rome was ill, and many people died from the fevers they had caught. Suddenly remorseful, Domitian laid on a free banquet."* This erratic behaviour would have made those around him worry about his state of mind.

I assumed I would need to invent some kind of spectacle for the Colosseum involving birds for my 'air' themed book with birds in the title, but then found a description of the Cranes vs Dwarfs battle put on in the amphitheatre, complete with birds being set loose and even a spectacular light show in the sky. Once again, the history of the Colosseum is more extraordinary than anything a fiction writer could come up with!

The terrifying black dinner really did happen, although probably later than 82AD. Suetonius describes it and it sounded to me like the sort of event Marcus might have been asked to stage manage, given his arranging of private lavish parties back in the very first book of the series. *"On another occasion (Domitian) entertained the foremost men among the senators and knights in the following fashion. He prepared a room that was pitch black on every side, ceiling, walls and floor, and had made ready bare couches of the same colour resting on the uncovered floor; then he invited in his guests alone at night without their attendants. And first he set beside each of them a slab shaped like a gravestone, bearing the guest's name and also a small lamp, such as hang in tombs. Next comely naked boys, likewise painted black, entered like phantoms, and after encircling the guests in an awe-inspiring dance took up their stations at their feet. After this all the things that are commonly offered at the sacrifices to departed spirits were likewise set before the guests, all of them black and in dishes of a similar colour. Consequently, every single one of the guests feared and trembled and was kept in constant expectation of having his throat cut the next moment, the more so as on the part of everybody but Domitian there was dead silence, as if they were already in the realms of the dead, and the emperor himself conversed only upon topics relating to death and slaughter. Finally he dismissed them; but he had first removed their slaves, who had stood in the vestibule, and now gave his guests in charge of other slaves, whom they did not know, to be conveyed either in carriages or litters, and by this procedure he filled them with far greater fear. And scarcely had each guest reached his home and was beginning to get his breath again, as one might say, when word was brought him that a messenger from the Augustus (Domitian) had come. While they were accordingly expecting to perish this time in any case, one person brought in the slab, which was of silver, and then others in turn brought in various articles, including the dishes that had been set before them at the dinner, which were constructed of very costly material; and last of all came that particular boy who had been each guest's familiar spirit, now washed and adorned. Thus, after having passed the entire night in terror, they received the gifts. "*

As the guests all got home safely and were given lavish gifts, the event seems to have been a warning or perhaps even a practical joke on the part of Domitian, but it would have been truly terrifying for the men involved, who would have expected to die at any moment.

When I was about four years old, my mother moved house, taking us from a block of flats on Sand Street (Via Arenula – arena means sand because of the sand thrown on the arena floor) in Rome to a farm in the Italian countryside with a grape vine that grew strawberry grapes.

GLOSSARY

Aedile   A senator in charge of commissioning the gladiatorial games.

Bestiarius   Gladiator specialising in fighting animals (plural bestiarii).

Bulla   Protective amulet worn by boys. Girls wore an equivalent pendant in the form of a crescent moon.

Cithara   Roman precursor to the guitar.

Cosmetes   Beautician (plural cosmetae).

Domina   Mistress.

Dominus   Master.

Fullery   A laundry which washed, dried and also dyed garments. Human urine (collected on street corners) was used as a cleaning and bleaching aid.

Garum   Fish sauce, a very popular condiment.

Gustatio   Hors d'ouvres (starters in a meal)

Imperial Palace	The place indicated on the map is an approximate location of Nero's Golden House (which Titus might have continued to use for official receptions) and also, later, the building started by Domitian at the beginning of his reign and completed in 92AD. There were additional locations, both official and residential, where the emperors would have been located in Rome.
Insula	Block of apartments/individual rooms, often built around a central courtyard.
Lararium	Household shrine.
Liberalia	Festival in which Roman boys became men.
Naumachia	Water-based spectacle often featuring re-enactments of sea-battles, held on lakes or in flooded man-made structures such as the Colosseum.
Nereids	Sea-nymphs (goddesses of the sea).
Ornatrix	Hairdresser.
Palantine	One of the hills of Rome, used by many as an expression to suggest the Emperor's residence.
Palla	A large rectangular outer garment of wool or linen, worn predominantly by married women, draped around the whole body, a fold of which could be placed over the head for protection and as a sign of propriety.

Popina	Streetside café (most poor Romans did not have cooking facilities, so street food outlets were very common and popular).
Tablet	A wooden 'book' of two or three 'pages', filled with wax, on which notes could be made using a metal pen called a stylus, then erased when no longer required. More formal, permanent writing could be done with ink and a reed/quill pen onto scrolls of papyrus.
Triclinium	Dining room.
Tullianum	One of the very few prisons in Rome, used for high status prisoners or those to be made an example of, as prison sentences were not used as punishment, only as brief holding places.
Velarium	Awning at a theatre or amphitheatre.
Venator	Performer who hunted animals for the morning hunt (technically not gladiators or bestiarii as it was hunting, not combat).

THANKS

THANK YOU TO JESSICA BELL for beautiful book covers and to Streetlight Graphics, who always have my back and make my life so easy.

Thank you to my beta readers for this book: Helen, Etain and Martin. Your comments and ideas are always insightful and help the stories grow. Thank you to my editor Debi Alper for continuing to improve my craft and giving me new perspectives on scenes.

Many scholars and historians were very helpful during my research. My thanks for all their fascinating work and most especially to my historical consultant for this series, Steven Cockings: you've been wonderful to work with, so generous with your historical expertise and hospitality.

Birds in the Ancient World by Jeremy Mynott was very useful to me in writing this novel, with its theme of air and birds.

All errors and fictional choices are of course mine.

Chosen for imperial service, some concubines rise to power. Others fall to madness.

The Forbidden City series. 18th century China. An extraordinary lost world of exquisite beauty, hard-won power and deeply emotional choices.

**Why did a Muslim emperor pick the son
of a Christian slave as his heir?**

The Moroccan Empire series. 11th century Morocco
and Spain. An epic journey of complex choices and
opposing faiths told by the voices of forgotten women.

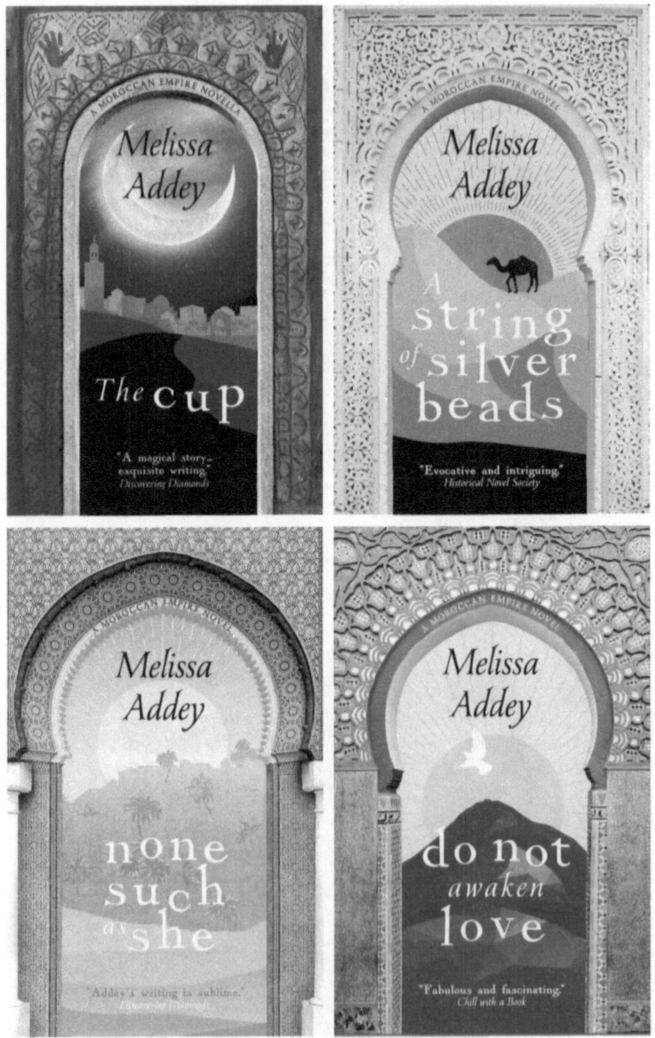

CURRENT AND FORTHCOMING BOOKS INCLUDE:

Historical Fiction

China

The Consorts (novella, free on Amazon)

The Fragrant Concubine

The Garden of Perfect Brightness

The Cold Palace

Morocco

The Cup (novella, free on my website)

A String of Silver Beads

None Such as She

Do Not Awaken Love

Rome

From the Ashes

Beneath the Waves

On Bloodied Ground

The Flight of Birds

Regency

Lady for a Season

Picture Books for Children

Kameko and the Monkey-King

Non-Fiction

The Storytelling Entrepreneur

Merchandise for Authors

The Happy Commuter

100 Things to Do while Breastfeeding

BIOGRAPHY

I WRITE HISTORICAL FICTION SERIES SET in different eras. So far, I've written about 1st century Rome following the backstage team of the Colosseum, 11th century Morocco as a Muslim empire arose across North Africa and Spain, and 18th century China in the Forbidden City. I'm now moving into the Regency era in England, so coming a little closer to home. I have a PhD in Creative Writing from the University of Surrey which looked at the 'play' between fact and fiction in historical fiction and I enjoy speaking at literary festivals. I campaign with the Alliance of Independent Authors for ethics and excellence in self-publishing. I live in London with my husband and two children.

For more information on me and my books, as well as a free novella, visit my website www.MelissaAddey.com